M000009290

The Red Door

Vonceil Tubbs

Copyright © 2018 Vonceil Tubbs

All rights reserved.

ISBN:
ISBN-13: 978-1-720-15985-8

DEDICATION

I used to think that I needed an abundance of money and a host of people around me to encourage my success. I began to realize that people will only encourage your success if it keeps *them* in *your* spotlight. I learned that money couldn't prepare me for this journey and people aren't capable of carrying me to my appointed season. I questioned my strength, my gift and my God. Until one day, I took notice of just how small a mustard seed is.

Everything I am, I owe to God. And all that I'll become will glorify him.

To my first love, the woman who without compromise loves me just the way I am. Thank you for being more than what's required and giving more than what's needed. I learned how to be strong because you were strong first and I learned how to stay in the fight because you never gave up. Thank you for being my sounding board, reading chapter after chapter and not holding back when you didn't like something. It's a privilege to call you friend, it's an honor and a blessing to call you mommy. I love you, Pudd.

Every blue moon, you'll come across someone who's capable of changing the way you think and even the way you love. Their spirit demands something deeper from you and it makes you uncomfortable because you have to admit that you don't even know who you are.

To my wife, my best friend, my cheerleader and my voice of reason, I'm so grateful for you. You have been the very thing that I've prayed for so many times. Thank you for believing in me when I didn't. Thank you for not fussing when I came to bed late because I couldn't break away from my craft. Thank you for giving it to me straight with no chaser. It made me step up my game. Thank you for taking a casual walk with me in the neighborhood. Who knew that a book would be conceived? It hasn't always been easy, but our scars have their own story to tell. I love you, Twink.

To the three life lessons that have structured my very being and taught me that it's not always about me and it's truly the little things that matter the most. Rajaad, Secret and Indiya, I love you.

Many, many, many thanks to Demetrius DeBerry better known as Sokartis for clothing my book. I provided the vision, you set it in motion and what a beautiful outcome. facebook.com/onyxtemplegrfx instagram.com/onyxtemplegrfx twitter.com/onyxtemplegrfx sokartis.deviantart.com

Last, but most definitely not least … to you; thank you for being intrigued enough to pick up my book and support my dreams. It's been a long time coming. I hope you engage in the journey of these characters just as much as I did when creating them. Grab a glass of wine and get ready!

Your support means the world to me. God bless.

The Red Door

It has been said, dreaming of a red door signifies harbored fury or concupiscence. If the red door is ajar, it represents the confrontation between yourself and troublesome emotions.

-Old wives tales

PROLOGUE

"I didn't answer because I was unable to and what gives you the right to question me about where I lay my head? You know better than that."

His voice was reprimanding and peremptory. The affair was only four months old and mirrored the demolition of a failed marriage. The sound of Christian Louboutin's Napoli Flat conversing with the freshly waxed hotel lobby floor provoked the next question.

"I'm sorry, daddy. Are you still in the building? I can hear you walking."

"You stalkin' me now?"

"Go back to the room, please. I'll be there in about fifteen minutes."

"I don't have fifteen minutes."

"Good bye."

The tension began when the conversation ended. He stood in front of the gold elevator doors contemplating a pretty white lie to gift wrap his ugly truth in. He paced for five minutes before going back to his deluxe suite where the sheets still held the scent of adultery from the night before. He took his suit jacket off and laid it across the divan, noticing on the floor just under the desk chair the loaded condom he thought he had lost. A timid knock came from the opposite side of the hotel room door. He invited his guest inside then hung the do not disturb sign on the door handle. He was pushed onto the bed. "Take your clothes off." He unbuttoned his shirt, exposing bulging muscles and a fresh bite mark on his left shoulder. The faint sound of a cell phone's ringtone fought its way through the navy-blue leather duffle bag that stood guard in front of the closet door.

"Move, I have to get that."

"Let it ring, I need you!"

"Shut up, don't say a fuckin' word!"

He answered the phone in a tone contradictory to his mood. He assured his wife that he would be on his way momentarily and would pick up the few items that were requested of him. He ended the call with, I love you too. "Your best bet is to be on my heels when I leave." He tucked his shirt inside his pants and put his suit jacket back on. He adjusted his penis then kissed his admirer on the lips. "Don't worry there'll be plenty of time to suck my dick tomorrow."

CHAPTER ONE

Fall always made The Brigance Hills look remote and abandoned. The trees were stripped of its leaves down to brittle sticks, and the grass would not recover its vibrant, lime green color for another three months or so. The Brigance Hills is a diamond tucked inside the rough of Renfro City. All the houses in Brigance were statuesque with manicured lawns, extravagant landscaping and hired help to maintain its properties. The ex-wives of movie makers, celebrity attorneys and best-selling authors resided within the comforts of this coveted and esteemed haven. It was a place where even the blind could go sight-seeing.

Perfect. Everything was too damned perfect in this stuck up, worlds away from the struggle, mine is bigger than yours, neighborhood.

A man resides with his wife in one of the most beautiful houses Sandra had ever seen. She often sat by the bedroom window in her rocking chair and stared at the house with the big bay windows and the big, pretty, red double doors wondering where that well-dressed man goes every morning. How does he make his money? Is he a good husband? A good person? Sandra's green tea had gotten cold, now she did not want it. She glanced over her shoulder at her beautiful past and her uncertain future and sighed. He was knocked out, snoring like overworked and underpaid laborers. His snoring would get him kicked out of her rundown studio apartment back in the day, but lately it helped her sleep through the night. Her husband is so good to her. After she miscarried their third child, there was nothing Sandra asked for that she did not get. Guilt took her on extended weekend trips to California and shopping sprees in Paris, affording her expensive jewelry, clothes and shoes. Jackson did not want to be a father. Although, he never admitted it to his wife, his actions spoke clearly; a baby would cramp his profligate lifestyle. After all the trying and disappointments, Sandra felt obligated to give up on becoming a mother. It was the one thing that she desired more than anything.

Sandra rested her teacup on the windowsill. Just as she reached for the arms on her rocking chair to lift herself up, Mr. well-dressed from across the street, rushed out of his house. She scooted to the edge of her seat and stalked him. Maybe the Mrs. had kept him up all night making love or maybe she picked a fight with him this morning making him run late for work, Sandra thought. Before he opened the door to his Raspberry, 1965 Jaguar E-Type, he gripped the thigh of his slacks then bent down to pick up the keys that slipped from his grasp. He stood like his penis was heavy. And just like that, Sandra wanted a little bit.

Jackson turned over on his back and sighed heavily as Sandra crawled onto the bed. Still asleep, his face looked as if he were bored with the dream he was having. She slowly pulled the covers back and woke him with warm breath baptizing what laid lifeless in between his thighs. Jackson liked to watch Sandra pleasure him, which is why she was confused when he pushed her away gently by the shoulders until he slipped from her puckered lips.

"What's wrong, baby?"

"I got shit to do. I need to get up, so I can get outta here. Thanks for waking me up."

"Jackson?"

Jackson got out of bed and stretched with his back turned to his wife. He grabbed the pair of jeans that were lying on the floor and put them on. "Jackson. Jackson, I know you hear me." He continued to ignore Sandra until he was fully dressed. Jackson finally looked at Sandra and offered her a closed lipped smile, she did not smile back. She asked him with her eyes if he loved her, he did not respond. Sandra pulled the strap of her gown on her shoulder then sat on the edge of the bed. "So, we aren't speaking? Did I miss something?" Jackson put a 'for sale' sign on a secondhand excuse and Sandra bought two. He went into the bathroom, brushed his teeth and washed his face then left the house, but not before kissing her on the forehead. Sandra dragged herself into the bathroom after watching Jackson pull out of their driveway. She ran the shower and frowned at his underwear that had been tossed in the corner. Really? Commando? She scoffed; he didn't even wash his ass before he left. The doorbell surprised Sandra. She was hoping Jackson had come back to fuck the shit out of her. She left the shower running and ran downstairs. Before she opened the door, she checked herself in the framed wall-length mirror that met her at the bottom of the staircase. A tall white lady in purple sweatpants and a wrinkled Mississippi State Alumni T-shirt was standing on her porch. Her nipples were erect, and her bra appeared to be unsnapped, she had either been exercising or running from Mr. Dartwell's Great Dane. Her skin was flushed, her red hair damp, and finger combed.

"Hi. I um, I live across the street and I was wondering if I could…" She paused as if she were waiting for Sandra to finish her sentence. Sandra waited in anticipation of what her neighbor's next words would be. "I don't mean to be a bother. Would it be ok if I ...?"

Red kept looking over her shoulder, causing Sandra to feel uncomfortable. She was standing there with no bra or panties on wondering if this woman could see through her nightgown and wondering why she did not bother checking the cameras before opening the door. The well-dressed man who always leaves at the same time every morning was now returning home. Before he got out of the car, his wife was back across the street. Now, that's pussy control, she smirked. Sandra leaned against the door jamb staring intensely until she realized, she was staring with the door wide open. She returned to the bedroom to stare from the window, instead.

What did the lady from across the street want? What did I have that she couldn't buy two of? Sandra wondered. That was the first encounter that Sandra had with any of their neighbors since she and Jackson moved to Brigance almost two years ago, except for Mr. Dartwell. Mr. Dartwell and Sandra met some time ago when Jackson's mail was mistakenly delivered to his house. The people of Brigance kept communication from a head nod to none at all. The weekends found all the school aged kids at Violin or Tennis practice and pets were confined to kennels in backyards with ten-foot privacy fences and Olympic sized pools. Sandra was starving for attention. The one friend that she had was hundreds of miles away, both emotionally and physically.

Sandra pouted, she ain't thinking about me and it's all my fault. But what was I supposed to do? I love Jackson and even though my sister from another Mister wouldn't lie to me, what reason would I have not to believe my future husband? Yes, Jackson is flirty and yes, he has access to any woman he wants, but he would never cross the line by propositioning my best friend.

Sandra had almost forgotten that the shower was running. She stood up and had a good stretch. She looked out of the window and noticed Mr. Well-dressed standing in his driveway, staring in the direction of their bedroom window. Her heart began to race. How long had he been standing there? She dropped to the floor and crawled to the window, bracing her hands on the windowsill pulling herself up slowly until she could see over her fingers, he was still there. He pulled his hands from his pants pockets and began walking towards their house. Sandra looked around trying to find a hiding place. She closed the bedroom door and sat with her back against it. She waited. There was a masculine knock at the front door, she dared not move. It took a few minutes, but she scooted to the nightstand and grabbed her cell phone. Sandra called Jackson; she took deep breaths trying not to sound panicked. Jackson answered on the third ring.

"Hey, the meeting was cancelled, Jacob called me before I could get to the office. I'm headed back to the house."

Sandra was instantly relieved. "Hurry, please."

Silence kept Sandra company while she waited on the next knock. It never came. The sweaty and out of breath wife at the door was one thing, but what the hell did her husband want? Sandra showered in cool water then tucked herself under the oversized comforter on Jackson's side of the bed. She had created a safety zone from the boogie man and if she moved, he may get her. It took Jackson over an hour to get home. The sound of footsteps approaching the bedroom caught her attention just before she dozed off for the second time. Jackson walked in and immediately began to undress, his body is a work of art, lean and brawn. He stood at the foot of the bed chiseled like he had been carved from stone with a taunting erection. Sandra crawled from under the covers to finish what she had started. Jackson pushed her back onto the bed, grabbed her legs and pulled her towards him until he was inside of her. His breath warmed the right side of Sandra's face sending a chill down her spine.

He whispered as he bit her on the neck, "I can feel you pulsating on my dick."

Jackson lifted Sandra until her legs were draped over his shoulders, her back pressed against the cold wall. She inhaled. He moved his tongue like a roller coaster, and she rode it until the moisture from between her thighs wet his chin and chest. She exhaled. Her body was a slave for this kind of attention from this man. His thrusts were unyielding, penetrating her insecurities and peaking her curiosities. Jackson likes to fuck, Sandra knew that about her husband, but they were making love the way they used to when all they had was each other. Sandra began to cry, confused. How could her own mind blind her from what was right in front of her face? Sweat dampened Jackson's hair, making it curl into loops; sweat dripped from his chest onto Sandra's breasts. His body requested her submission and she signed it over to him, expecting nothing in return. His strokes became faster and shorter. His breathing was heavy, absconding through clenched teeth. Jackson's release felt warm inside of her, she bit his left shoulder in anger and in ecstasy, breaking the skin. His body jerked from the sting. Jackson caught his breath and attempted to kiss Sandra on the lips, she declined by sliding from under him. She locked herself inside the bathroom and rested her forehead against the linen closet door, in search of understanding, she wanted to scream at the top of her lungs.

"*Jacob called before you got to the office*, bullshit!"

Jacob is Jackson's right hand; one would believe the same right hand that jacks him off. Jacob did not cancel meetings because he did not have the authority to call them. His circumstances became evident when Sandra listened to a voicemail intended for Jackson some time ago. Jacob was begging for a job because the one he had lost as a bartender apparently paid all his bills. Jackson imposed on Sandra's cogitation when he banged on the door.

"Babe open up. I gotta take a piss."

There were five other toilets throughout the house that Jackson could have peed in. Sandra positioned the new puzzle piece in its place fearful of what the big picture would look like. She would never accuse Jackson of cheating, but something was going on. Sandra opened the door and walked out in her bathrobe. She eyeballed his designer jeans that were thrown on the floor, wondering what was on the receipt that was sticking out his back pocket. She grabbed it quickly then slid her hands inside her robe pockets. She regained her composure when she heard the toilet flush.

Jackson slid his arms around Sandra's waist. "You ready for round two?"

Sandra adjusted her mask until her smile was in place, she released the receipt from her palm then took Jackson by the hand.

"Always ready to even the score."

CHAPTER TWO

The phone rang six times then retired to voicemail. The phone rang again, unanswered; the blue light began blinking indicating new voice messages.

Firm hands were braced palms up against the hotel wall while concentrating on his balancing act.

"Damn, that ass is tight, like virgin pussy." Jackson firmly slapped his lover on the butt with an opened hand. "You want this cum inside you, don't you?"

"Yes!"

"Say it, say cum inside me. Say it!"

"Cum inside me!"

Jackson came inside of a Kimono Maxx condom. The room was dimly lit, and the television was too loud. Jackson stepped on the black condom wrapper that was tossed aside and disregarded as he reached for the warm bottle of water that was knocked to the floor during his sexual charge.

"I don't come inside faggots."

Jackson took the condom off then finished his complimentary water. He lost his balance and stumbled to the floor when his lover jumped on him placing kisses all over his face, chest and neck. Emmanuelle playfully bit Jackson's nipples and massaged his abs that tightened when he grabbed Jackson by the balls; he playfully bit the head of Jackson's penis.

"I bet wifey wouldn't see it that way."

Jackson began packing, leaving accessible a pair of clean underwear and socks, his Brunello Cucinelli suit posed on the signature wooden hanger. Emmanuelle purred, "Let's stay a little while longer. It's not like we have tons to do today."

Jackson forced his wedding ring on and wiggled his fingers in his lover's face. "I always have tons to do."

"Are you cheating on me?"

"No, I'm cheating on my wife."

"You know what I mean, asshole."

"What I know is this conversation is becoming redundant."

"Damnit, Jackson! I can't keep doing this."

"Then stop."

"If I could, I would save lots of wasted money on these Brazilian Waxes, Mr. I like it smooth."

"How'd you like the show?"

Jackson sat on the corner table naked and bit into the cold half eaten double cheeseburger that room service had delivered over two hours ago.

"The camera loves you baby, you know that."

"I'm thinking of having a celebrity guest co-host a couple shows for the finals. I have a few prospects in mind."

"So, are you?"

"Am I what?"

"Cheating on me?"

Jackson met Emmanuelle in Chicago on New Year's Eve at Cafe des Architectes located inside of Sofitel, one of Emmanuelle's favorite hotels. Jackson was having a celebratory dinner with his producer and co-anchor for having the number one up and coming sports news show. They beat the competition with back to back episode high ratings and had been rewarded with a multi-year contract renewal. Emmanuelle was having a celebration of his own, he had just birthed another Bistro that was due to open its doors on New Year's Day. Emmanuelle sipped his Hickory Smoked Bloody Mary and noticed from the corner of his eye, Jackson as he put his cell phone to his ear excusing himself from the dinner table. Emmanuelle grinned as he watched Jackson's slacks caress the curve of his derriere; boxer briefs, he thought. Jackson found a quiet spot near the staircase. A few stragglers noticed him from the FYT Energy drink Ads and Super Bowl commercials and waved while trying not to stare. Jackson denied them his attention and focused on his conversation.

Sandra was in Cuyahoga County tending to Bernard, who was in a losing battle to Lung Cancer. Jackson inquired about his father in law's condition and assured his wife of five years that he would be on the first thing smoking to Cleveland before checkout.

Bernard is a man's man, chivalrous, kind and attentive. His skin tone, the color of blackberry tea, the stroma in his eyes made them look hazel and gray; the same mystic eyes that Jackson avoided when he was lying to his wife. Bernard was proud and deeply rooted in his Caribbean heritage. Jackson was not winning any son-in-law of the year awards, but Jackson did not throw confetti at Bernard's feet either. *There's something about that boy, I can't put my finger on it, but I don't like it.* Bernard would protest to his only child and to anyone who would listen.

Jackson ended their brief conversation with loving and reassuring words. Emmanuelle waited until Jackson took his seat and indulged in his Yellowtail Tuna before sashaying over to address his entourage.

"Good evening gentlemen, my name is Emmanuelle, I own Emmanuelle's I, the Bistro over in Midtown. The grand opening for Emmanuelle's II is tomorrow, 1:00 PM sharp. We would love for you to be our guests. There'll be free drinks, samplers and press." Emmanuelle extended a business card with his picture on it and a smile to Jackson, taking notice of his naked ring finger. "Pardon the intrusion enjoy your meals."

Jackson read the front of the card out loud, "Emmanuelle Dubois, Private Chef and restaurateur. Maybe I'll hold on to this until next time."

Jackson's producer ordered a bottle of vintage wine and had it delivered to Jackson's suite as a last pat on the back before he left the hotel to return to his quiet life with his wife and new baby boy. Jackson stripped to his underwear and gulped straight from the bottle, slouched in the oversized chair then turned the television on. He checked his cell phone to make sure he had not missed any of Sandra's calls or messages. He slid his hand inside his boxer briefs then stroked himself.

"I have a big dick." His chuckle turned into a hearty laugh. "I could use something tight and wet on this dick right about now."

Sandra's assigned ringtone began to play drowning the timid ticking noise from the heater. Still stroking himself, Jackson answered the call. "You naked?"

"Jackson, I'm at the hospital. No, I'm not naked."

"I need you right now."

"Are you drunk?"

"Had a few drinks, you know I don't get drunk. Miss me?"

"Yes, I miss you."

"Show me how much. Take a picture and show me what's in them panties."

"I'm sitting in a room full of people who are worried that my father won't make it through the night. I just wanted you to know that I'm spending the night at the hospital with my mother, have a good night."

"Come on, Sandy."

"Goodbye Jackson."

"Sandy!"

Jackson could not hold his liquor and what little he could stomach made him obnoxious. Jackson called Sandra back, but his call was immediately forwarded to her voicemail. "Fuck!" He called his wife again and left a message apologizing for his tactlessness. It was almost day one of a new year. This was fit to be anyone's experience except Jackson's. He put his clothes back on hoping to stumble into something or someone to do. As Jackson stepped into the hall the door slammed shut, he patted his pants pockets. "Damn!" The room key was inside Jackson's wallet which was inside of his suit jacket pocket.

While Jackson waited on the gentleman at the front desk to program another room key, Emmanuelle, who was just leaving dinner lingered in the lobby entertaining a meaningless conversation with his business partner until Jackson's attention was undivided. Emmanuelle pretended to be engulfed in his text messages when he bumped into Jackson.

"I'm sorry. Me, with my clumsy self."

"It's ok. Emmanuelle, right?"

"That's right. Shall I expect you tomorrow?"

"I would love to come, but I have a few obligations to fill."

"That's too bad."

Emmanuelle briefly loaned his attention to the young lady who extended a compliment to his Orville Baptiste Fox fur Oxfords while Jackson checked out his small frame decorated in designer doll clothes. "Enjoy what's left of your night Mr. …" Emmanuelle paused, waiting for Jackson to formally introduce himself.

"Perry. Jackson Perry."

"Jackson Perry. Cheers to a prosperous new year."

"Hey, if you're not in too much of a rush, I hate drinking alone."

Two drinks led to an acquaintance, three drinks afforded the exchange of contact information, five drinks led to an invitation to room 326 C.

Emmanuelle reached inside Jackson's pants like a grab bag and pulled out a hand full of goodies. He kissed Jackson like it would be their first and last kiss. Jackson was positioned on his back, sheepishly watching as Emmanuelle crawled onto the bed. The sheets were damp, sticking to Jackson's back, his head sank into the stark white pillow. Emmanuelle was feminine and fastidious, he carried class like divas carried clutches with European designer names. Before Jackson could release himself, Emmanuelle raised up and curled beside his lover.

"Why'd you stop?"

"To be continued."

"To be continued. What the …?"

Emmanuelle interrupted Jackson, by putting his finger to Jackson's lips. "Shhh, if you've enjoyed what I have to offer, you'll want to see me again. If not well, at least I got mine."

"You're not gonna finish what you started, little boy?"

"Happy new year, stranger."

Emmanuelle slid into his panties then perched himself on the edge of the bed. "How long have you been sleeping with *little boys?*"

"What?"

"You heard me, how long?"

Jackson scoffed, "I'm not gay."

"You're not gay right now, but you were when I rode that stick honey. How long?"

"Why do you keep asking me that?"

"You're too seasoned, too comfortable. And there I was thinking I was snagging myself a newbie."

"Doesn't matter how long."

"Oh, my God! Oh, my God!" Emmanuelle covered his mouth with both hands, exposing his manicured nails.

"What?"

"You're the Powerhouse, kickboxer guy, spokesman for that energy drink!"

"How long have you been sleeping with men?"

"Darling, I'm an old queen. I was born this way, live this way and will die this way."

"I never do this. I just ..."

"Just got caught up. Just wanted a little company. Liar, liar, pants on fire."

Emmanuelle stood up and finished dressing, Jackson did not budge. Emmanuelle got back in bed fully dressed and deep throated Jackson.

Jackson's body shook aggressively as he reached his climax. Emmanuelle was pleased with the control he had inherited over this hard bodied, hardheaded, very married man. "Here's something to keep in mind, I always finish what I start."

Emmanuelle snapped his fingers twice at Jackson. "Hellooo! I'm talking to you, Mr. Perry. Are you cheating on me?"

Jackson was brought back to the present from his long-distance daydream.

"No, I'm not cheating on you."

"See how easy that was, daddy? All I ask is that you lie to me with a straight face."

Emmanuelle was to be seated in 11 B on a first-class flight back to Chicago first thing in the morning. Jackson was to return to his first life from a long day of renegotiating contracts and closing business deals. Jackson had driven three cities away to be with a man who had shared him with an unsuspecting wife for nearly two years. Emmanuelle dared not force Jackson to choose because he knew Jackson would never leave Sandra and Emmanuelle would never leave Chicago.

Jackson placed a call from the hotel phone before checking out.

"This is Jacob."

"I'm headed out in a few, meet me at the warehouse, you ain't got shit to do."

"I need to drop these packages off; you need some extra weight moved or something?"

"The packages can wait."

"And Susan?"

"Drop her off before you head to the warehouse."

"I'll catch you on the other side of sixty minutes."

Jackson disconnected the call then surveyed the room for any of his belongings that he may be leaving behind. He rehearsed in his head the play by play on where he had been and why he was late. Jackson checked the voicemail messages that sat idly in his inbox.

Jackson, we need to talk and if you're listening to this then you have time to call me back. Delete. The next message began to play, *I need to talk to you, you smug son of a bitch! Why do you treat me like I don't mean shit to you?* Delete. Jackson sighed with frustration, feeling trapped by his sexual gratifications.

One hour and thirty-eight minutes later, Jackson had finally pulled into the parking lot of the warehouse. Jacob was parked alongside the building in a no parking zone. He popped the trunk and grabbed one of the two backpacks.

The owner of the warehouse was the eldest brother of Jackson's mother, Daniel Kenneth Sr. When life served him hard times, Jackson bought the warehouse and turned it into a training facility. Jacob tossed the backpack over his left shoulder and followed Jackson inside.

There were four boxing rings strategically placed in the center of the gym. The smell of vinyl and canvas stood out like an erection, free weights and mirrors lined the back wall and framed pictures of kickboxing greats, Miguel Davenport, Marco Archuleta and Sti Pinnot hung behind the receptionist's area. Jackson unlocked the door to his office and sat on the edge of the principal's desk. Jacob pulled two plastic bags from the backpack and sat them beside Jackson. He watched intently as Jackson stacked the money in the money counter and confirmed the amount of three hundred thousand dollars. Jacob was paid twenty thousand dollars for a job well done. Jackson deposited the money into a safe that he kept hidden inside of an old locker that had survived a fire at a local Elementary School. The drop was successful. Jacob sat in his car until Jackson locked up and pulled off.

Once upon a time Jackson was heaven sent. He rescued Jacob from passed due bills and homelessness when he had given him a job and a lavish place to live. None of what Jacob had acquired would have been obtainable bartending. Jacob had been introduced to a sumptuous way of living, fast money and free pussy. But these days, Jackson was greedy and less benignant, a blatant liar and a bully. Jacob had become a prisoner kept on a leash that did not stretch past the truth.

Jacob scrolled through the call history on his cell phone and found the number that he had been saving since 8:22 PM Saturday, three months ago. Jackson had called Sandra from Jacob's phone because his phone died; a small detail sewn into an elaborate lie to cloud the three missing hours that he was unavailable. Jacob reluctantly added the number into his contacts and entered the letters J W, as the contact name. He considered calling the number just as headlights lit up the front seat of his car. Jackson had returned to the warehouse. He always backtracked once a drop was made. It was a waste of gas to the unsuspecting, but to

Jackson, it was sweeping the crumbs left in plain sight.

Jacob pulled into the driveway of the house where he and Susan resided. He shook his head in shame at the beautiful house that would never be a home. Susan heard Jacob pull into the garage, twenty minutes would pass before she opened the garage door to see what the holdup could be. She cupped her hands against Jacob's car window and peeked inside.

"Are we free yet?"

Jacob rolled the window down, disappointed in himself. "I didn't get the chance to talk to her."

"Don't tell me you're freaking out now."

"I said, I didn't get the chance."

"If you don't ..."

Jacob interrupted, "If I don't then what, Susan?"

"Calm down, do boy. If you don't then I will."

Jacob unlocked the car door then pushed it open, suggesting Susan get inside. "This ain't just about you, I want out just as much as you do."

"Then take care of it."

"Suddenly, your dick is bigger than mine?"

"Jacob, we're on the same side here. I just want my life back."

"What life? You're a fucking hooker!"

Susan slammed Jacob's car door then stormed inside the house. Susan was the only person that Jacob could trust, but her mouth was poisonous like venom which often made it hard to tell who he was at war with. If they could not keep it together, they would never recoup the freedom that existed from underneath Jackson's thumb.

Jacob stared in the rear-view mirror at the house directly across the street. He desperately wanted to be the man in Sandra's life. Her facial features were so soft, cheekbones high, her smile full and bright. Jacob had kissed her lips a thousand times in his mind. He wanted to know what her giggle sounded like, what her mean face looked like. What her touch felt like. Jackson had forgotten what it felt like to want her and need her.

Jacob stood in the kitchen archway, watching Susan angrily take dishes from the dishwasher then put them away. Having felt Jacob's indifference, Susan glanced over her shoulder. She was not used to the things that Jackson had exposed her to either. They were both trying to wake up from the same pipe dream turned nightmare. Jacob sat at the bar in the kitchen and asked Susan to get him a cold beer from the cooler.

"Jacob."

"What?" He snapped.

"Never mind."

"Then why'd you call my name?"

"No reason just forget it."

Susan sat a bottle of beer on the coaster, she had been scolded by Jackson about putting things on the counter without a guard.

Marble ain't cheap, respect my shit.

Susan leaned on the counter and stared at Jacob. "How come you've never tried to fuck me?"

"Excuse me?"

"You've never tried to take advantage of me. It's why I'm here, right?"

"I really don't know why you're here, Susan."

Susan mumbled under her breath, *don't tell me, you're gay too.* Jacob raised the bottle of his Berliner Weisse German Beer and took a swig. Susan watched his lips cover the rim of the bottle. Jacob sat the bottle down and wiped the condensation from his hands onto his jeans. "What are you looking at?"

"Why so defensive? It was a simple question."

Jacob sighed, irritably. "Because you keep doin' shit to get on my nerves, just shut the fuck up!"

"Jacob, I do everything around here like I'm the fucking maid, spreading my legs for puppets who couldn't afford this pussy without their puppet master. Jackson has you wrapped so tight that you're a fucking cocoon!"

"Susan, it's not you. I knocked on Jackson's door the other day. I knew his wife was in there, but she didn't answer. And even if she did, I didn't know what to say."

"Maybe we should leave this alone for a while, let a little time go by then try again from a different angle."

"And what angle would that be?"

"I don't know, the angle where you stick your dick in some pussy and give your palms a break."

Jacob took his brew to the head. "Suck my dick!"

"It's not like I haven't tried!"

Jacob kicked the bar stool from under the counter and rushed over to Susan. Susan's heartbeat sounded like a Carimbo Drum, she backed herself into the kitchen counter, trapped. Jacob grabbed a hand full of red hair, wrapped it around his fist and pulled Susan down to her knees. "Let go of me!" Susan screamed as Jacob unzipped his pants and exposed himself. Jacob grabbed the back of Susan's head and forced himself into her mouth.

"Shhh, listen... you hear that? That's the sound of you shutting the fuck up!"

Jacob pushed Susan to the floor by her face. He wiped his penis with the dish towel then tossed it on the counter. Susan stayed in the position that she was left in until she heard Jacob walk down the upstairs hallway and slam his bedroom door.

Headlights pierced the dining room windows. Susan crept across the hall to the formal dining room and watched Jackson step out of his Ferrari wearing clothes by designers she had never heard of. Jackson buttoned his suit jacket then dragged a bouquet of fifty long stemmed pink roses from the backseat and a big white box with pink polka dots and a big pink bow positioned in the center of the lid; the Pre-Show. Jackson was preparing to make up for his mess ups. He checked himself in the tinted car window then spit his gum into the Blue Muffin bush. The headlights winked then dimmed until they eventually shut off.

Showtime.

Vonceil Tubbs

CHAPTER THREE

"Dear God, I swear if you get me out of this I will never, ever speed again."

Blue and red patrol car lights pierced the back window of Jackson's car making deformed shadows on the ceiling. "Damn, what's taking him so long? Run my shit and let me go!" Jackson anxiously tapped his fingers on the steering wheel as he assessed the traffic that stood still ahead of him. By now, Sandra was out of view and had probably reached her destination. The officer tapped on the window with his knuckle then handed Jackson his driver's license, insurance card and a speeding ticket.

"You can call the number on the back for information regarding your ticket. If you won't be able to pay it by the due date or you if you choose to contest it and fail to show up in court just call the number on the bottom right."

"Yes ma'am, I mean sir. Sorry about that, thank you."

"Have a good day."

Jackson mumbled under his breath as he watched the officer walk back to his police car, *good day my ass!* Jackson sped off almost side swiping another vehicle. *If I won't be able to pay? I'm Jackson Powerhouse Perry!* He reached for his cell phone as it slid from the seat and onto the floor. He slammed on breaks to avoid hitting the car in front of him, who had slowed down for the railroad gate arms.

"Shit!"

***

The sound of wine glasses greeting the wooden dinner tables and futile conversation with old friends had become its own idiom. People were hungry for good company and juicy gossip. Sandra walked into La Casa de Los Alimentos and advised the hostess that she was meeting a friend and would like to reserve a table. After confirming Sandra's name, the hostess led her to the back-corner booth where her dinner date had been awaiting her arrival. Audrey hugged Sandra then kissed her on the cheek.

"I ordered water for you; I remembered the extra lemons this time."

"Thanks love, been waiting long?"

"No, not really. I had two people show up for class and they both decided to put me out of my misery and take a free pass for an earlier class next week."

"You're going to wear yourself thin. How many classes are you instructing now?"

"Just three."

"Four."

"Three and a half."

"And the stores, how are they coming along?"

"Business is good, no complaints. Enough about me, what's going on with you?"

Sandra slumped down in her seat and rested her head against the back of the cushioned booth and sighed. "He wanted to do it."

Audrey leaned in and smirked. "And you didn't?"

"I did, sort of."

"Sort of?"

"I felt so out of place and all we did was kiss."

"It's just sex."

"Sex with someone who isn't my husband. Just sex could change everything, everything that I know to be true about myself."

"Jackson hasn't been acting like much of a husband lately and please spare me the, *I took three credit hours of Psychology in college bullshit.* You don't know yourself; you only know what Jackson has programmed you to be."

"That's easy for you to say because you've been there, but you ain't happy and getting even is wearing your ass out."

Audrey threw her hands up. The truth always tastes different from someone else's plate. She shared a bed with her ex-husband for three years while he shared a bed with her best friend.

"All I'm saying is, you haven't been happy in over a year, that's like dog years in a marriage."

Sandra reached inside her purse and pulled out a folded sheet of copy paper. On it was a conversation via text message between Jackson and someone with a 773 Area Code. It was not the conversation that had Sandra's attention it was the unidentified phone number that Jackson provided and suggested his lover use for future contact.

"Read this."

Audrey took the paper, read then reread the short conversation between Jackson and an apparent lover. Jackson had given out a number that Sandra did not recognize to someone who called him Darling. "What if he has another family out there somewhere? I mean, it's not like I can give him kids. Oh my God! What if he has kids?!"

"I didn't know you couldn't have kids. Sandy, I am so sorry."

"I haven't actually been told that I can't, but I've miscarried twice, and doctors keep saying, there's nothing physically wrong with me. How many tests do I have to take before one comes back with a different result?"

"You should see a specialist."

"The last thing on my mind right now is bringing a baby into this mess. Lord knows it's not on Jackson's to do list, neither am I apparently."

"Get checked out just so you'll know. It's worth knowing what's causing these miscarriages, right?"

"It's easier to just accept it."

The waitress interrupted the small talk and realizations with dinner specials and freshly baked yeast rolls. Audrey ordered the Turkey and Blue Cheeseburger with Sweet potato wedges and Sandy ordered the opposite; a Sweet Potato Burger with an Arugula and Blue Cheese salad.

Sandra was grateful for the communion and the kinship; Audrey was the closest thing to a friend that she had in Renfro City. Sandra dreaded going home and having to pretend that everything was normal when everything was so strange and unversed. Audrey offered her a place to pity party for the night if she needed to clear her mind. Sandra declined the invitation due to previous commitments, drink half a bottle of wine, masturbate then finish off the bottle of wine. "I lied," Sandra confessed.

"About what?"

"I've had three miscarriages."

Audrey spoke with a mouth full of food, exposing the slight gap between her two front teeth, "If doctors say, there's nothing wrong then something is probably wrong. One miscarriage is too many, I'll text you the number of my good friend, she's great at what she does."

"And what if there really isn't anything wrong?"

"Then you'll know, but something is definitely wrong."

The two newfound friends parted once they had overstayed their welcome. Sandra closed her car door and revisited the number that stared at her from the piece of paper that she had been shamelessly carrying around for days in her purse. A call from Jackson dragged her emotions from hurt to anger; her answers were short and brusque. Jackson had to catch the next flight to Chicago to make the extempore meeting in the morning called by the producer of his sports show, he would be out of town for the next few days. Jackson apologized for not being able to spend time with Sandra before he left and promised to make it up to her once he returned. Sandra hung up before Jackson could complete his thought. She did not want to hear him say, I love you. She did not want the burden of reciprocation.

Sandra had finally made it home after contemplating a hotel stay for the night. She stepped out of her Gucci heels and absorbed her surroundings. The cars, the house, the jewelry, the types of wine she drank and the glasses from which she drank the wine, paintings purchased from private auctions, furniture that no one else owned because it was one of a kind, clothes that were popular in select countries, created by eclectic people with exotic names, she was for sale and she had been bought time and time again.

***

Jackson stuffed his duffle bag inside the overhead bin after unzipping the side pocket and taking his secondary cell phone out of it. There were five missed messages and three missed calls. Jackson grinned; this kind of attention complimented his control issues. A young lady sitting on the opposite side of the aisle took notice of how attractive Jackson is. She positioned her leg in a way that would cause him to bump her knee as he took his seat.

"Oh, sorry about that."

"Don't be, it's the most action I've had all day."

Jackson extended his hand and smiled. "Jackson."

Nina accepted the warm gesture. Jackson noticed his neighbor waiting for him to look up so that she could engage in prying conversation. Jackson texted Jacob and gave him instructions to follow for the next couple of days. Nina was still gawking as people walked through the narrow aisle preparing to take their seats. Jackson called Sandra and left a message, *Hey, baby. I'm on the plane, I'll call you when I land, love you.*

"Married?"

"Very."

"Happily?"

"Today, yes."

"Since when do married men flaunt bare ring fingers?"

"Since when do ladies ask strange men so many damn questions?"

"Since we needed answers to our damn questions."

Jackson offered half a smile but was over his fervent neighbor. Nina was too audacious for Jackson, he preferred the passive aggressive, silent thinker type. Jackson excused himself and pretended to be engaged in the unsigned contracts that rested on his lap. Nina took the unsubtle hint leaving Jackson to his business while waiting on the flight attendant to take center stage, so that she could educate the flyers on how to fasten a seat belt. Jackson wondered why Sandra had not bothered to return his call. He checked the time, *I called you almost ten minutes ago, where are you?* Jackson phoned his wife the way he used to when he was trying to learn her number by heart; he dialed all ten digits.

Sandra reached for her phone, trying to avoid missing another call. Strong arms gently held her close.

"Maybe I should leave, you seem preoccupied."

"I'm sorry, don't leave."

"Give me one good reason why I should stay."

"I don't want to masturbate tonight."

Sandra had not felt the touch of another man in over six years. Her body was programmed to respond to Jackson's touch. Omar took Sandra's hand and placed it inside his pants, she was more impressed with herself. This was so out of her character, but it was naughty, and she liked the way naughty felt. Omar took his duty belt off and laid it on the countertop next to the sugar and flour canisters. Sandra pulled her shirt over her head and without saying a word invited her guest to remove her bra. Omar kissed Sandra softly, but intentionally. He pulled his pants down to his steel toe boots; he had outgrown his boxers. Omar pulled his manhood out and stroked himself. Sandra thought to herself, *should I put my mouth on it? Maybe next time, will there be a next time? Is that a tattoo?!* Sandra was lifted off her feet and carried to the breakfast table.

Omar demanded, "Turn over."

Sandra turned over and laid on her stomach, waiting for the next order of instructions. Omar pulled Sandra gently by the waist until she was propped on her knees, she gripped the edge of the table for support as he spread her cheeks and licked inside. The feeling was intoxicating, she was ready to feel his tattooed bad boy. Omar turned Sandra over on her back then licked the bottom of her feet, he sucked her toes one little piggy at a time. Her body insatiably begged for a connection. Omar licked in between Sandra's thighs; she palmed the crown of his head, his tongue felt like a penis.

"Stop teasing me."

"Is this what you want?" Omar shook his hips.

Sandra retorted by biting her bottom lip. She gasped when she felt Omar, he was thick. Omar and Sandra were body to body. Culpability encouraged her to resist him, but Omar held her attention with his physical conversation. Each thrust was deliberate. Omar pulled Sandra to the edge of the table and placed her feet on his chest, he put his middle finger against Sandra's lips; she kissed and sucked his finger. Sandra's nerves caused her to her tense up.

"It's going to hurt."

"It's going to feel good."

"You promise?"

Omar put the head in. "I Promise."

Sandra dug her pedicured toes into Omar's hairy chest as she felt him make his way inside. "I wanna cum inside you," Omar moaned. Sandra was breathless, she gave him the green light when she arched her back and came on her breakfast table. Omar let out a growl as he released himself inside Sandra. He pulled out slowly, still partially erect then positioned himself in between her thighs. He spoke softly as if he were instructing a child, "I need you to relax for me."

"I am relaxed."

The tattooed bad boy was now flaccid. Omar opened Sandra's cheeks and watched his cum trickle down and disappear.

"It's a shame that I can't have you to myself."

"That's the sex talking."

"My dick ain't hard. This is me telling you how I feel."

"Maybe you can have me to yourself next weekend, if you don't have plans."

"So, you're gonna act like you don't know what I'm talking about?"

"Omar, right now I can't be anything more than …"

"… Than what?"

"Than this."

Omar pulled his pants up and sat on the edge of the table. Sandra sat up and folded her arms against her bare breasts. "I really like you. I just don't want to get in over my head."

"You don't think this is getting in over your head? Oh, let me guess, you love him, all of this will work itself out."

"I just thought we, you know, had an understanding."

Omar interrupted Sandra by holding his hand up. "Let's not ruin the night. I have to work security for the Autism Benefit in the morning. I need to rest up, it's gonna be a long day."

"So, next weekend, are we on?"

"I'll let you know."

Omar walked to the front door half dressed, Sandra followed. He hugged her with one arm and slapped her on the butt before walking outside. "Yeah, we're on."

Sandra felt liberated and in control for the first time in years. Omar had awakened a monster. Omar had crossed Sandra's path several times before she agreed to take his cell number. It would be another month before she would use it.

Sandra was reminded of the friendship she had abandoned so many years ago. Ariel was her soulmate. They did everything together even planning to lose their virginity on the same night. The one person that she needed and wanted to share this experience with, she could not.

Sandra sat the bottle of Mondavi Reserve Cabernet Sauvignon on the edge of the tub then sank into the hot, bubbly water. The milk and honey bath scrub had the bathroom smelling like aromatherapy. The steam penetrated Sandra's pores loosening Omar's grasp. *That man knows he fucked the shit out of me.* A painting of Sandra and Jackson hung over the Powder Bar in a Juliet Lacovi antique frame. It reflected such a dormant place in time, Sandra had experienced her second miscarriage while Jackson chose to ignore her emotional outreach. She shared with her husband her dreams of opening a bookstore and maybe a café too, something small to provide a home for underground writers, artists and freelance work of all kinds. She wanted something that she could call her own, something to give her purpose. Jackson told Sandra that he needed her by his side, he needed her full support at all times. But in practicality, the spotlight was reserved for a table of one.

Sandra gripped the neck and drank the wine from the bottle. Audrey's words rang loudly like a Catholic church bell. *You only know what Jackson has programmed you to be.* Sandra was tired of crying, but her emotions were disobedient. Sandra's phone vibrated twice; it was less intrusive than the latest R&B song.

"Hi, lover."

"Hi." Sandra giggled like a schoolgirl for the first time since she was a schoolgirl. "I take it you've made it home safely."

"Yeah, I did. I just wanted to let you know that your body is amazing, I can still taste you."

"You've left quite an impression yourself. May I ask you something?"

"Of course."

"How do you feel about kids? Do you want kids?"

"I love kids, I have six nieces and nephews. I want at least three of my own. How about you?"

Sandra was fixated on the painting. She took another sip of wine. "I would love to be a mother someday. All I need is one, but I wouldn't mind two."

"Where'd that come from?"

"It's good to know what your partner wants before things get too serious."

"Oh, so I'm your partner now?"

"I thought you wanted to be."

"What happened to in too deep and all you can offer me is sex?"

"I realize now that I'm worth more than just sex."

"What about your husband?"

"It's time he realizes that I'm worth more than just sex too."

"How about I give you a few days to think about what you're saying. If you still feel the same way when we revisit this, then I'll be whatever you want me to be."

"Fair enough."

"Get some rest and I'll call you after the Benefit. There may be a luncheon, but I probably won't go."

"Take lots of pictures… good night."

Sandra did not have time to collect her thoughts before her phone rang again. She let the water out of the tub and grabbed her robe. She sighed petulantly, "Hello?"

"Where were you when I called earlier? I left messages and everything."

"I went to a movie with Audrey, my phone was silenced. By the time I got your messages you were already in the air."

"Well, I'm here. I'm waiting on a car."

"Glad you made it safely."

"Maybe we can go out or something when I get back. Would you like that?"

"Sure, sounds nice."

"You pick the place."

"Baby?"

"Yeah?"

Sandra knew what she wanted to say, but the words would not come out. "Don't worry about it, it can wait."

"What's up?"

"I was thinking, maybe we can go to that hotel on Belle Hill Island, the one we went to about a year ago and work on a family."

"A family?"

"Yes, a family."

"You are my family."

"A real family. A mother, father … baby."

"Sandy, can we talk about this later?"

"It's either a yes or no."

"I don't know. I guess, but a baby is a lot to deal with right now."

"Thank you."

"For what?"

"Confirmation. Bye Jackson."

Sandra hung up the phone and began grabbing clothes from the closets and drawers. She stuffed clothes in one bag and shoes in another. Morning would not find Sandra in The Brigance Hills; she was headed to the Buckeye State.

CHAPTER FOUR

The air was so crisp that the dew on the lawn was crunchy. Single and two-family houses were staged along Pierson Street, boarding working class brown skinned people and retirees. Sandra parked in front of the house her parents raised her in. Annie Pearl still lived there, alone. Every now and then Mr. Willie would stop by and rest his hat, but let her tell it, he was a very good friend and nothing more. Annie Pearl was still very much in love and married to her deceased husband, she still wore her wedding ring. And even though her mother was just five hours away, it gave Sandra peace of mind to know that Annie Pearl had a very good friend around to keep her company, especially at night.

Sandra frowned when she noticed the gutter hanging on the side of the house and the bottom step cracked and wobbly. She reached for the screen door handle and noticed the screen was missing. Sandra could hear Annie Pearl coming down the rickety wooden stairs, she waited patiently for her twin to unlock all three locks and the chain.

"Baby! It's my baby girl! What are you doing here, is everything ok? Come on in!"

Sandra had not been home in over eight months. She gave her mother all her worries in one hug and Annie Pearl took them to the kitchen table to sort them out. "What brings you home? You look tired."

"I just miss you, mama."

"I miss you too, baby. What's the matter?"

"Nothing. Everything. I don't even know where to start."

"Start from the beginning."

Annie got up from the table and grabbed her cast iron skillet from under the stove. She poured oil from the oil can that sat in the middle of the cooktop. "Get the bacon and eggs from the fridge and grab those biscuits too. You want grits or oatmeal?"

"Mama, you don't have to go through all this trouble. I'm not really hungry... grits are fine."

"Orange or Apple Juice?"

"Tea. How's Ms. Denton? Is her daughter still staying with her?"

"Chile, her daughter, the kids and her daughter's new boyfriend. She can't get a moments rest in her own home."

"Really? What kind of able bodied man would move into his girlfriend's mother's house?"

A voice chimed in from the living room, startling both Annie and Sandra, "A sinner, that's who. Hey Pumpernickel! Come give auntie some shuga."

"Aunt Tootie!"

"Look at you. lookin' like your mama." Aunt Tootie stood back and assessed Sandra. "Annie Pearl, this is all you."

Aunt Tootie is a broad, busty, shit talker who could sing her ass off. The only things she feared were spiders and God. Aunt Tootie was Sandra's favorite aunt and the eldest of the five Murphy sisters, Annie was the middle child.

"What a beautiful surprise!"

"Your mama saw you out the window and texted me. Annie Pearl know darn well, I don't fool with texts on those tele'cell gadgets. Those things ain't Godly. I was around the corner dropping off tomatoes and green beans from my garden over to Cecilia's house. You know she uses a walker now. Poor thing still falling all over the place."

Annie chuckled and shook her head as she cracked eggs into the hot skillet. Her sister is her best friend. They took care of each other and kept one another in line. "Annie Pearl, you got it smellin' good in here. Add cheese to my eggs, I lost a couple pounds so, I got room."

"Auntie, how's Skip? I missed his call last week, but he didn't answer when I called him back."

"That sinner is fine, he probably needed someone to agree with him. Call him and let him know you're home."

"I will."

"How long you staying? Must be indefinitely since that heathen ain't tag along with you."

"He's out of town on business, I didn't want to be home alone."

"Mm hmm. Annie Pearl, I got to take my breakfast to go."

"So soon? Stay for a little while."

"You want me to?"

"Pretty please, I haven't seen you in months."

"Nope, got to go. I'll try and stop by tomorrow, but I probably won't. Call your cousin. Love ya'll."

Aunt Tootie had breakfast to go, a hug and kiss from her favorite niece and things to do. The sun was in full swing, piercing the clouds and invading the kitchen. Sandra checked her cell phone, no missed calls, no messages, no service. Damn. Annie sat across from her only child and felt her implicit pain.

"Baby, I know something is bothering you. Let's talk about it."

"I'm so tired of pretending that we're ok. Things are so different; Jackson is so unpredictable."

"Did he put his hands on you?"

"No. He put his hands on someone else."

Annie turned the grits off and put the bacon on a bed of paper towels to drain the grease. "Put it in plain talk for me."

"He's cheating on me. He has been for some time."

"Mercy. You know your father couldn't stand that man."

"And he let everybody know, he couldn't."

"I couldn't either, but I knew you loved him, and I didn't want to interfere."

"Mama, I never knew you didn't like Jackson. Why?"

"Cassandra, you know I love you and I would give my right arm for you, but you're not yourself when you're with him. He constantly takes from you and you continue to give to him. I know he's a celebrity and there are these protocols to follow, but sometimes I couldn't tell who he loved more, fancy things or himself."

"He used to be so loving and so down to earth. When did he change?"

"When he didn't need you anymore."

Sandra was faced with the cruel reality that her mother's perception was more than accurate. Jackson did not need Sandra for anything, and he made sure that she needed him for everything. "Oh, don't go gettin' in your feelings about that. Now that you know, what are you going to do about it?"

"I don't know."

"Whatever you do make sure you forgive him, but don't you forget."

"Mama, how about we go to the home store and get a new screen door after breakfast. I'll call someone about the gutter and steps Monday morning."

"Willie said, he would fix the gutter when he got a minute and redo the screen on the screen door."

"And what about the steps? It's not safe, we'll go pick out a new screen door and I'll call a professional to handle the repairs."

"Baby, don't waste your money on those things. Those gutters ain't bothering nobody."

"It's not a waste of money, I'm protecting your investment. While we're at it, let's freshen the whole house."

Sandra sat in the passenger's seat of her mother's Crossover after spending almost an hour and a half convincing her that spending this money was long overdue. Ariel had convinced Sandra to keep her college bank account before she had lost herself in Jackson. *You need your own money and he doesn't have to know you have this account.* Every dime that was gifted to Sandra over the years by Jackson was set aside in this account, she had over four million dollars of hush money, not including the sweetheart account that Jackson put allowances in. Sandra had allowed Jackson to damage so many opportunities and relationships, hers and Ariel's being one of them. Sandra wanted to reach out to her but was afraid that she would get the reaction that she deserved. Annie pulled into The Home Workshop parking lot then reached in the backseat for her purse.

"I got some peppermint. Want some?"

"No thanks. Mama, when was the last time you talked to ..." Sandra mumbled, "*Ariel*?"

Annie Pearl looked over at her only child. "To who?"

"Ariel."

"Well, she calls me every Sunday. So, last Sunday. I expect to hear from her tomorrow."

Sandra sat up in her seat, surprised. "She still calls you every Sunday?"

Sandra felt ashamed. This meant her ex best friend kept in contact with her mother more than she did.

"Yeah, we talk for at least 30 minutes. You know she's like my second daughter and a sister to you."

"Yeah, I know."

"Ready to go inside?"

Sandy wanted to ask so many questions, but she did not want to probe, she wanted her mother to feel her disappointment and volunteer the information.

"Yeah, sure."

"Cassandra?"

"Yes, ma'am?"

"Her number is still the same."

The day aged beautifully. Sandra had passed out on the bed in her old bedroom that was still decorated with LL Cool J and Salt-N-Pepa posters on one side, Cabbage patch dolls and pound puppy plushies on the other. Annie stood in the doorway and smiled when she thought back to the day, she held Sandra in her arms for the first time, she cried until she heard the baritone voice that would sing lullabies to her at night. In her eyes, Sandra was still the same little girl who would lose a fight with sleep waiting for her daddy to get home. Bernard promised to always protect her, but Annie Pearl knew that one day it would be out of their hands. Now, she hurt for her child.

Annie held both her hands up. "Oh God, protect my child. Only you know what she stands in the need of, Lord. Bind everything that troubles her and have her to know that you are still God, even in this."

The cell service was terrible. In the middle of the night a series of messages came through on Sandra's phone causing a string of uneven pitches. The sheets gathered under Sandra's body as she propped herself up on her elbow. Squinting at the bright screen, she quickly addressed the notifications before she lost service again. It was almost four in the morning, but she returned Omar's call anyway hoping to leave a message for him. He answered sounding wide awake and indifferent. Sandra had been unavailable all day. She opened the bedroom door and peeked down the hall. Mama still sleeps with her door cracked, she thought. The neighborhood was quiet except for the neighbor's dog, Beanie who could be heard barking at a can being bullied by the wind. Omar was still in his feelings even after Sandra explained why she needed this time to regroup. She did not have the patience to babysit Omar's feelings, it was too damned early in the morning. Sandra checked her remaining messages while Omar talked about the Benefit and how successful it was. There was a text message from a number that did not have a name assigned to it. Sandra replied, *who is this?* To her surprise, she received a response almost immediately. Omar was still marveling over a photo that he had taken with, Bryan Houston, a local talk show host who grew up with Autistic siblings.

"Sweetie, I can't talk long, I'm in bed with my mother. I don't want to wake her."

"Oh ok. When are you gonna hit me back?"

"I don't know what my day is going to look like, but I'll call you when I get a chance."

"Alright. Don't stay away too long."

"I won't."

Sandra decided that she was over Omar. The sex was good, but he was too emotionally attached. She let him hang up first then read the response from the unidentified number.

[I'll explain who I am later. I need to talk to you, it's important.]

[Later? Why can't I know who you are now?]

[Because I don't want you to assume anything.]

[How did you get my number & are u even sure u have the right person?]

[Yes, Sandra I'm sure I have the right person.]

Sandra completed a free number search, but could not get any pertinent information, she was slightly intrigued. The area code was assigned to a city in Illinois. Sandra stared at the message, what did she have to lose, a husband? Sandra had no choice, other than to accept that the upper hand did not belong to her. She locked the message thread and went back to sleep.

Annie put dirty dishes in the dishwasher and examined the functions of the buttons that lit up in royal purple. Sandra reached around her mother and pressed the express power wash button. In a matter of days, Sandra had the gutters and step repaired and had updated all the appliances in the kitchen. The new bedroom suite would be delivered in a few days and both bathrooms were getting new sinks and mirrors. Sandra leaned on the counter, flipping through sales ads from the Sunday newspaper.

"Ma, do you like this furniture set?"

Annie leaned in and tilted her head to get a better look. "It's nice."

"I'm getting it for you."

"Cassandra, you have outdone yourself. I don't need no new furniture set."

"The one you have has died. And I'm replacing those TV's."

"Now, you want to throw out my good TV's. What's wrong with my TV sets?"

"They're tube TV's. I'm going to get ready to visit daddy. The painters will here in an hour or so."

"Ok. Your aunt is on her way to be nosy."

Sandra had planned on replacing the kitchen cabinets too, but after a consultation with the Home Workshop interior designer, they both agreed that paint and new knobs would be just as refreshing and cost effective.

It was 71 degrees and not a cloud in the sky. Sandra sat in the driver's seat of her BMW and squeezed the steering wheel. She braced herself for the conversation she was going to have with her father.

Cleveland was not what it used to be. The faces of its people looked worn and starved for opportunity. Children grew up too fast leaving their parents to raise hope instead. Everyday people were in and out of grocery stores buying food for the week and speeding down Interstate 90 trying to get to their destinations before the church goers congested the streets.

Sandra turned into Lake View Park and followed the trail to the parking area. An older woman with toy trucks and colorful helium balloons squatting next to a headstone caught Sandra's attention. She tried to walk by without making eye contact, but the woman noticed Sandra and spoke. Sandra smiled sympathetically, waved and kept walking. In her mind, this lady was at the funeral. No one talks while you are viewing the body at the funeral. The toys were placed in front of the headstone and the balloons were placed next to the toys, held down by a plastic balloon weight. Sandra walked to the end of the breezeway, but realized she was in the N's, not the M's. She turned around reluctantly, searching for a short cut.

"Are you lost, sweetheart? I haven't seen your face here before, maybe I can help."

"You're familiar with all the faces that come through here?"

"No, just the ones that are regulars in the children's cemetery."

"Oh." Sandra looked around. "I didn't realize there was an area just for ..."

"For children? Yes, this side of the park was donated to the mothers of slain children."

"I see. I'll go out and make a left this time."

"Do you know the site number?"

"Uh, seven M dash three dash nine."

"Oh, you're a long way from the site. You have to exit the cemetery, turn left then make another left at the first light. Once you turn back in make a right and the M's will be straight ahead just walk to row seven."

"Thank you, I really appreciate that." Sandra pointed to the toys and balloons. "I feel like a bad daughter. I came empty handed."

The lady stood up and dusted the dirt from her white dress. "I'm sure your presence is gift enough."

Sandra was paralyzed. She wanted to walk away, but her feet would not move. "Is it rude to … ask, how …"

"Talking about it actually helps me deal with it. I was married to an abuser. A drug abuser, woman abuser, he even managed to abuse my thought process. We tolerated each other long enough to make Mikey, but we just couldn't find love for one another. One day, we had gotten into a fight because I wanted to send my son to my mother's for a while. He accused me of cheating and told me that if I had another man around our son that he would kill us both. He fought me like a man in the streets and kidnapped my son…"

Sandra tried to hold back her tears as she already knew the outcome. The lady sighed deeply. "Mikey was five. Today is his birthday, he loved toy firetrucks and balloons."

"How old is he today?"

"Twenty-two."

"I am so sorry for your loss."

"Yours too." Sandra stretched her arms out and the two strangers shared a hugged. "Don't let me keep you. Be sure to tell someone you love them today."

Sandra gave her assurance then left her to host her son's birthday party. She checked her eyes and lips in her rear-view mirror. There were no visitors on that side of the park, which made the conversation Sandra wanted to have a little easier. Sandra had not been to her father's gravesite since the day they laid him to rest. The pain soon wore the mask of the procrastinator then procrastination turned into indolence. Bernard's headstone was clean and the grass around it had been clipped, which meant regardless of his absent daughter, he had regular visitors. Sandra dropped to her knees and cried, she felt like the worst person on the planet. Bernard died almost two years ago; born earlier that morning at 8:57 AM, fifty-six years ago. A car drove by, causing Sandra to pull it together. She sat Indian style in front of her father and apologized. Sandra emptied her soul and told her father everything that was going on in her marriage. She told him about the specialist that was recommended by a good friend, she had even mentioned Omar. Even though, Bernard could not comfort Sandra, she felt his spirit and his chastisement.

Sandra looked over her shoulder when she heard leaves being crushed under footsteps. Her heart sank to the bottom of her feet when she saw a five feet seven inches, walnut eyed woman standing before her. Sandra stood up slowly, awestruck.

"Give a bitch a hug, you act like you've seen a ghost."

"Oh my God!" Sandra fell into her best friend's arms and rested her head on her shoulder. The embrace was confirmation of a revival. "Ariel, I am so sorry. I just need you to know that you're my best friend and I love you."

"I love you too. I talked to ma, she told me that you were planning to come out here. I wasn't sure I'd make it at first, but here I am. I sat in my car for almost an hour and just waited. When I saw you pull up, I decided to give you some time."

"We have so much to catch up on."

"Yes, we do. Take your time, I'm gonna go sit in the car."

Sandra turned to her father and blew him a kiss. "Daddy, I love you. Happy birthday."

Sandra decided to stay a few days longer so that she and Ariel could catch up on lost time. Ariel and Sandra sat on the couch and laughed, cried, gossiped and got yelled at when they were making too much noise. Sandra did not mention the mystery texter, she could not explain how someone had managed to attach puppet strings to her back. Ariel suggested Sandra keep their reunion to herself. Though Sandra was fed up, Jackson was more than capable of controlling any progress made towards her happiness.

The smell of homemade chocolate chip cookies made a trail from the kitchen to the living room. Annie Pearl was notorious for putting a scoop of vanilla ice cream and shaved ice in milk, topped with whipped cream and serving it with dessert, Sandra had named it the Snowball Frosty. It accessorized the reunion like red wine to cheese. Sandra's phone buzzed with back to back text messages. It was the mystery texter. She decided to wait until she returned home before sending a response. Annie Pearl's house was a drama free zone.

"So, who are you dating, now?"

"A tall, dark and handsome mistake."

"Let me guess, his ex is his best friend and he lives at home, only until he gets on his feet, but he's been getting on his feet for the past five years."

"The past three."

"Let me hook you up with somebody."

"No, thank you."

"I've hooked you up with a couple of good guys."

"Name one."

"Earl."

"The drug dealer?"

"He was a businessman."

"A businessman with two kids and a wife."

"I didn't know he was married until after the fact."

"He wore a wedding ring!"

Ariel reached inside her purse and handed Sandra a letter that was sealed inside of a white business envelope. She told Sandra to read it when she had time to herself. Sandra needed this trip more than she realized. She had driven three hundred miles for healing and restoration.

She made a promise to Annie Pearl that she would never stay away this long again, and she promised to pick up the phone more often.

Night fell upon the day. Sandra fell asleep in her clothes stretched out across the bed. No service, no calls from Jackson and not one care in the world. Annie Pearl's alarm seemed to linger right outside of Sandra's door. She grabbed the pillow and covered her head. Annie Pearl volunteered at the Direct Care Center on Wednesdays from 6:00 AM to 11:00 AM, assisting new patients with registration and setting appointments. Before she left, she opened Sandra's bedroom door; Sandra pretended to be asleep. With tears in her eyes, Annie Pearl did what she knew how to do best, she prayed over her child. She knew that Sandra was headed back to the storm that she had sought refuge from. She could not go with her, but she could keep her covered in prayer.

Sandra closed the trunk on her luggage then sat on the porch and listened to the sound the car tires made as they rolled over the wet bricked streets. It was the only thing that kept her from being upset with her husband who only called her once in the two weeks she was gone. She did not want much, just for him to do the things that he promised he would do, to have and to hold, for better or worse. Annie pearl pulled into the driveway, smiling. She did not want her daughter to leave, but life is for the living.

"So, you all packed up and ready to go?"

"Yeah, I'm gonna miss you mama. I'll be back for Thanksgiving."

"Very good. Baby, thank you for everything. It looks so good in there."

"You're welcome. Don't forget to register the appliances… mama?"

"Hmm?"

"I forgot daddy's birthday."

"I know."

"Why didn't you … you didn't even tell me."

"You still found out, didn't you?"

"I ran into a lady who lost her son, she was at the cemetery."

"Anyone I know?"

"No, but we talked for a few minutes, she told me that her son's father decapitated him then killed himself. All I want is to be a mother, but I don't feel like I married the right person to start a family with."

"What makes you say that?"

"I can't get Jackson to say that he wants a child, but he won't admit that he doesn't."

"Cassandra, if you want to have a child, have a child."

Sandra looked at her mother in astonishment. "Just like that?"

"If it's one thing I know, happiness will take any avenue to reach its destination." Annie Pearl chuckled. "Your father said that to me that when I turned him down after he asked me out."

Annie Pearl's words were always clear and uncompromising; and always right on time. Sandra pulled into a gas station to fill her tank before heading back to Brigance. A little boy holding a toy pickup truck struggled to keep up with his father. He looked Sandra in the eyes, smiled then stuck his tongue out. Sandra removed her phone from the car charger then turned the radio down.

"Iredrove Technologies, how may I direct your call?"

"Hi, my name is Cassandra Perry. I'm calling to speak with June Orton."

"Sure, one moment please."

Sandra was placed on a brief hold while the receptionist connected her call to June Orton's extension.

"This is June."

"Yes, hi; My name is Casandra, Audrey Blake gave me your number. I'd like to make an appointment."

CHAPTER 5

The streetlights came on at 5:36 PM, the same time as yesterday and the day before that, like clockwork. Jacob pulled into the warehouse parking lot and parked alongside the building in the no parking zone. He grabbed two backpacks from the trunk and threw them both over one shoulder, like clockwork. Once Jacob was inside, he turned on lights that could only be seen through the back windows of the warehouse. He unbuckled the crowbar from underneath Jackson's desk then went into the men's restroom. The fourth stall had been turned into a utility closet because of its irregular size. Jacob lifted a piece of the wooden floorboard revealing a safe the size of a seven-gallon trash can. Jacob took several stacks of money from each backpack totaling over four hundred thousand dollars. The money was secured in the safe and the square piece of flooring was positioned back in its place. Jacob returned the crowbar to its designated area then as instructed, unlocked the bottom drawer of Jackson's desk to collect his pay. Jacob sat in his car for a couple of minutes and composed a message to Jackson, letting him know that the drop had been made then he pulled off. Like clockwork.

The black car that was parked across the street in the hardware store parking lot was gone. Once Jacob crossed the first main intersection the black car pulled behind him and flashed his patrol lights. Jacob forced the backpack under his seat then pulled over. Two plain clothed police officers approached Jacob's car, one stood on the driver's side while the other looked inside from the passenger's window. Jacob rolled his window halfway down.

"May I help you officers?"

"I sure hope so. Mind stepping out of the car?"

Jacob was reluctant to step out of the car. He quickly looked in the back seat to ensure there was nothing there that needed to be explained. The second officer walked from the passenger's side to the back of the car and rested his palm on the trunk.

"Are you employed at the warehouse?"

"Yeah, I am."

"What do you do there?"

"I'm the manager."

"Who's your boss?"

Jacob realized that this was not about him. This was not about traffic violations, but this was about Jackson. Jacob stuck both hands inside his front pockets.

"My boss is the owner."

"And who is the owner?"

"I have a feeling you know who the owner is. May I ask what all of this is about?"

"It would be a pretty good idea to answer these questions very carefully. Who is the owner?"

"Mr. J. Perry."

"We have reason to believe that there's been drug related activity inside of the warehouse."

"I don't … "

The second officer held his hand up. "Careful, what you say now can bite you in the ass later."

"Sir, I don't have anything to do with any drug related activities."

"Why were you at the warehouse tonight?"

"I was doing my routine stop to check on things."

"Check on things?"

"Yeah, there's been reports of knuckleheads breaking into small businesses."

"Your alarm system broke?"

"I am the alarm system."

The officer had finally moved from the back of the car and stood next to Jacob. "Owner can't afford an alarm system, but you can afford this car on your manager's salary?"

"I inherited it."

"Who died?"

"My father."

"If we wanted to look around the warehouse, would you have a problem with that?"

"Not at all. Would you have a problem getting a warrant?"

"Not at all. We'll be in touch."

"Have a blessed night officers."

Jacob waited until the officers pulled off before he got back into his car. He banged his fist against the steering wheel. "Fuck!"

***

Susan was beyond ready to leave the life that was malevolently created for her by Jackson. How hard could this be? she thought. Susan had silver and gold, higher end this and that and no bills; yet, she still did not profit nearly enough for the sale of her soul to the devil. Jacob began to notice that Susan stayed away from Brigance at least two nights a week. He was convinced that she had met someone. Jacob invited Susan to dinner in the kitchen. He wanted to talk, hoping she would bring worthy input to the table. Jacob called her twice but did not leave any messages. They were well aware that Jackson was still checking their voicemail. Susan walked into the house, apologizing profusely for being late. She peeked in the pot and frowned, Damn shame, she thought. Jacob did not cook anything that excluded a microwave option. Jacob untwisted the tie on the paper plate bag and placed two plates on the counter. Susan watched in disgust.

"I know we're having pork and beans and wieners, but you asked me to dinner at least feed me on a real plate."

"It's Gumbo!"

"It's the special on the menu at a daycare!"

"I worked hard on this meal."

"You cut the plastic pouch and dropped the wieners into the pot!"

"Fine, don't eat it!"

Susan picked up the phone and dialed River Bottom's to place a delivery order. One of the few things she and Jacob had in common was their love for authentic Jamaican food. Jacob dumped his boxed gumbo into a trash bag then took it outside.

Susan had changed into sweats and a tank top, feet propped up on the ottoman with a beer raised to her lips. Jacob sat next to her and turned the television down.

"Where do you stay when you're not here?"

Susan sat her beer on the floor. "You really wanna know?"

"Yeah, I really want to know."

"I go home."

Susan sat up and reached for her primary cell phone. She proudly showed Jacob pictures of a beautiful thirty-two hundred square feet ranch style home. It was not as lavish as the one she had been provided, but it was hers. Jacob noticed a Mercedes parked in the driveway.

"That your car too?"

"Actually, it is."

Susan took power walks downtown every Tuesday and Thursday afternoon and noticed a house for sale in the Business District. The couple who owned it wanted something more accommodating to their swanky lifestyle. Jacob scrolled through the pictures. The neighborhood looked like a national park with benches and man-made ponds, geese and shade trees.

"Those houses are ridiculously priced. When did you do all this?"

"The guy's wife wants to move into the new penthouses they're building downtown. He said he needed to hurry and get the house from under him because units were selling fast. I personally think he rushed the sale because his mistress found out where he lives."

"Why would you think he needed to move because of a mistress?"

"Because I showed up unannounced and he had no idea that I knew where he lived."

"Let me guess, a judge?"

"Councilman."

"And the car?"

"Just a little *homeowner's* insurance."

Although, Jacob had not thought about securing a place to live once this bridge was burned, he had a crush on a majestic looking house made of Brick and Stucco that sat in midtown; stunning features from the landscaping to the antique mailbox. Jacob would drive by and flirt with the idea of buying it and maybe even starting a family there one day. It had been for sale for over a year. The inside was destroyed by a cheating husband who was ordered to turn the house keys over to his ex-wife in a divorce settlement. She did not want the house, she wanted to hang his balls around her rear-view mirror. Jacob decided to look into it next week, if his schedule permitted. "Can I ask you something?"

"Yeah."

"If we're lucky enough to avoid jail after all of this is over, what are you gonna do?"

"Bartending is all I know."

"You can't go back to bartending, that's like me going back to the street corners."

"Remember Smitty?"

"Yeah, fucks like a rabbit."

"Shit! Is there anybody you haven't fucked?"

Susan licked her lips. "You."

"*Anyway*, he can't keep up with the bar. Asked me to turn it around for him."

"What did you tell him?"

"I told him; I can't put that kind of work into something that's not mine."

"And he said?"

"Told me to make him an offer."

"Did you make him an offer?"

"Before now, I wasn't sure if I wanted to, but I think I will."

The food had arrived finally, smelling like a Jamaican cookout. Susan and Jacob talked and plotted until they covered every possible escape route from their unorthodox threesome. Susan curled up on the couch and fell asleep. Her prepaid phone was lying on the floor just under the ottoman. Jacob reached for the phone slowly while keeping his eyes on Susan. He swiped upwards as the instructions on the screen suggested to unlock the phone. Susan was in constant conversation with someone named Big T. The text messages were inconsistent as if parts of the conversation had been deleted. Jacob looked through Susan's picture gallery. Susan had over sixty nude pictures of herself. Not bad, he thought. Jacob checked her internet browser history; she had recently searched for information on Jackson and the statute of limitations. Jacob realized that Susan was smarter than what he gave her credit for. He scrolled through her contact list. Everyone in her contacts were listed as initials. *Big O, JS, Big T, Big M.* Jacob took a picture of her contacts to do a little investigating of his own. He quickly put her phone back under the ottoman when she stirred in her sleep, making herself more comfortable.

Jacob closed his bedroom door and locked it. He reached under the bed until he felt the strap of his backpack. Fourteen thousand dollars for half a day's work ain't bad, he smirked. Jacob could afford to buy and fix up that house and now he had the will to do it. The phone rang, it was Jackson. He had gotten a heads up to meet his distributors at the pier, there was another shipment coming. This happened every seven to nine months; the Thomas boys would cheat their way into an extra shipment which meant more work for the little guys, but bonus time for the

Kingpins. These off-schedule transactions were never simple, and they took a lot of time.

Jacob was responsible for dropping batches off to several businesses in and outside of the city limits and collecting payments. The Quick Stop and Shop grocery store in Columbus was his favorite drop. The owner let him have anything from the store he wanted, including his stepdaughter. Phillipe got high off his own product, puffing woolah on the rooftop of his establishment, but the money was always fifteen minutes early.

Jacob took all his clothes off including his socks then sat on the toilet. He kept a pack of cigars and a book of matches behind the toilet. Jackson had locked him out of the house for two days because he had smoked in the kitchen. *I don't want my house smelling like a bar. If you miss the bar so damn much go and beg for your job back.* Jacob opened the window and fired up a half-smoked Boris Sadyne Apple Cigar. Susan had made a good point, Jackson is sloppy. He will eventually hang himself, but they did not have time to wait on eventually. Jacob did a courtesy flush when he heard Susan knock on his bedroom door.

"I'm in the bathroom!"

"I'm going home."

"Susan, I don't know … what if Jackson comes sniffin' around and he can't pick up your scent?"

"I'm getting my locks changed, I'll be back before you take your morning piss."

***

Sandra sat in her rocking chair thinking about her trip home. She put the letter that Ariel had written her back inside its envelope. She had her best friend back, and all was forgiven. She was whole again. Jackson had been home for three hours then he was back in the streets. On any given day, Sandra would have reasoned with herself until she was justified in the excuses she made for her husband, but not today. Today, she was unbothered. Jackson left dirty dishes on the counter and an open container of Chinese food on the table. Sandra smiled when she thought about what happened on the table. She snickered when she thought about Jackson eating his dinner there. Sandra put the dishes in the dishwasher then put the food in the refrigerator. She had never questioned Jackson's love for her like she had lately. Jackson barely kissed her, sex became monotonous and he always had an excuse for why he missed her calls. Sandra took the dishes out of the dishwasher and sat them back on the counter, she sat Jackson's food back on the table, opened.

Sandra leaned against the counter and thought back to the day Ariel told her that she needed to talk, and it was very important. Sandra could not see past her wedding ring or her happily ever after, so when Ariel told her that Jackson had sent her pictures of his penis and asked her to come to his hotel room that night, it fell on deaf ears. Ariel stood next to Sandra on her wedding day, dressed in crimson, smiling in adornment; brokenhearted.

Sandra replied to the mystery texter.

[If you're free, I have time to talk.]

[Cool, give me a couple mins]

[Ok]

Sandra walked outside on the back patio and looked out at the mini forest of trees. Why couldn't I just be a tree, she thought. Sandra was nervous. She contemplated saying, hello. *Or should I say, Hi?* She did not want to sound too concerned or not concerned enough. *Should I sound sexy or go for the professional white lady?* The night air had a little bite. She went inside to get a sweater from the coat closet when her phone rang. Startled, Sandra answered both nervous and slightly out of breath.

"Hello?"

"Hello."

"I'm listening."

"Thanks for agreeing to speak with me."

"I don't mean to sound rude, but can we fast forward, please?"

"Jackson is involved with …"

"Someone else, I know."

"Yeah, but …"

"Look, I appreciate you feeling the need to make me aware of what's going on in *my* marriage, but please just mind your business."

He turned out the light then peeked out of the window. He wondered if Sandra was pacing back and forth or sitting on the couch while she reprimanded him. "Who is this anyway?"

"This is Jacob."

CHAPTER 6

Sandra held tight to her umbrella, trying to keep it from turning inside out while dodging rain that fell sideways. The guest entrance camouflaged with the front of the building, which was huge with windows everywhere, it looked like the Kunsthistorisches Museum in Vienna. Sandra looked around for a receptionist. There were two uniformed and armed security guards stationed at either side of the entrance doors and a large service desk with two women sitting behind it to the left of the black elevators. As Sandra approached the desk, her phone rang.

"Where are you?"

"I told you, I have a dentist appointment."

"Do I have one too?"

"Did you make an appointment?" Sandra rushed Jackson off the phone, perceptibly irritated by him. "I just got called back, I'll talk to you later."

The receptionist observed Sandra and offered her assistance by smiling. Sandra turned the volume down on her phone then dropped it in her purse. She advised the lady behind the desk that she was there to see June Orton. The receptionist tapped a few keys on her computer then handed Sandra a visitor's badge. This was no ordinary doctor's office. Sandra took the badge and clipped it on her purse.

"Please ensure the badge can be seen for the duration of your visit." The smiling receptionist pointed to the pocket on her work shirt. "You can clip the badge in this area, or you can borrow a lanyard."

Sandra clipped the badge on her jacket pocket then wrote her name on the visitor's sign in sheet. Sandra was also asked to provide her car make and model along with picture identification. "You're going to bypass these two elevators and walk down the hall until you get to the blue floor. Follow the blue floor until you arrive at the two blue elevators, take those elevators to floor four. The floor receptionist will take care of you from there."

"Thank you."

"You're welcome and enjoy your visit."

Sandra was directed to a room that looked like a high school principal's office with its own laboratory. She sat in one of the three mesh chairs that surrounded a round glass table. There was no television, no old magazines and no broken coffee maker. Eight minutes had passed before a thin, white woman walked in wearing a white lab coat and safety glasses that guarded her perfect bun.

"Hello, I'm June Orton. You must be Cassandra."

Sandra stood and extended her hand. "Yes, hi."

"Please, have a seat. What can I do for you?"

"Well, I'm able to conceive with no problem, but I'm not able to carry to term."

June raised her brows in wonderment as her specialty was not fertility. "Have you seen a doctor about this?"

Sandra felt like the Coyote chasing the roadrunner. "I have. I came to you because Audrey told me that you may be able to help."

"Are you familiar with what we do in this building?"

"Apparently, not."

Sandra proceeded to walk towards the door in tears. What was Audrey thinking? Sandra had her hand on the doorknob. "I am so sorry for wasting your time."

"Cassandra, maybe I can help."

Sandra threw her hands up. "How?"

"Let's talk, please have a seat. What we do here is exploit biological progressions and we specialize in genetic manipulation. Maybe we can figure something out."

Sandra sat down, her hands resting in her lap. "I'm sorry, I'm so embarrassed."

"Don't be, let's start with your diet." June removed a silver tin storage clipboard from the wall and handed it to Sandra. "If you can remember, I'd like you to write down the things that you ate, drank or craved during your pregnancy or pregnancies."

Sandra picked up the pen that was attached to a chain on the clipboard. Her diet never changed. The same things she ate prior to her pregnancies were the same things she ate during her pregnancies. She did as she was instructed and made a short list. Sandra observed the microscopes with three and four objective lenses, beakers and burettes, some filled with colorful liquids others waiting to be used. Everything was so clinical and sterile, and June was so neat and manicured. There were stacks of boxes of blue gloves and tall hamper looking garbage bins for hazardous waste all strategically placed around the room. Sandra read over her list then handed the clipboard to June.

"How is this going to help, exactly?"

"It'll allow me to start a case study."

June rolled her chair over to the file cabinet and pulled a single sheet of paper from the top drawer then two more from the middle drawer. She placed the papers in front of Sandra. "The first form will allow us to test anything that you bring to us that is not poisonous, considered drug paraphernalia and that has not been obtained illegally. All items to be examined must be in a sealed and labeled container. The line on the bottom requires your signature as confirmation that you understand the above statements." Sandra signed the form feeling like a step towards progress had been made. June rolled back to the file cabinet and took a manila folder from the third drawer. She wrote the date and a seven-digit number on the outside of the folder then placed the form inside. "The next form says; you won't sue us if the results aren't what you'd like them to be. These results will be shared within the company should it fit the subject of research. Please sign and date the last line." Sandra's heart was pounding. June added the second form to the folder, she smiled at Sandra. "Last one. This form is for you to provide your contact information. Include the best times and days to contact you."

Once Sandra had provided the requested information, she took a deep breath. What's next? June stood and collected the third form. She made copies for Sandra to take with her and per protocol, asked if there were any questions. June explained that the seven-digit number written on Sandra's file is a generic reference number. All information pertaining to her case will be assigned to that identifier.

"I appreciate you going through these lengths to help me."

"Cassandra ... "

"Sandra, please."

"Sandra, we'll just call it a favor, but there is one more thing that I'm going to need from you."

"Sure, what is it?"

"I need you to get pregnant."

***

Jackson pulled into the alley behind the warehouse. It had rained all morning and part of the parking lot had flooded. Trainers were in the boxing rings with their fighters, hoping to create champions, weightlifters were battling it out with cast iron dumbbells and the beginners were skipping rope and building stamina. Jackson shared a firm handshake with one of his former trainers who was responsible for the success stories of a few boxers who had managed to headline a couple of fights outside the gym. They entertained small talk until Jackson's cell phone gave him an excuse to retreat to his office. He locked the door behind himself and took Emmanuelle's call while he counted his money.

Emmanuelle threw a birthday bash for himself at his Bistro, Emmanuelle's II and petitioned Jackson's presence. No was not an option. Jackson told Sandra there was a business meeting that he needed to attend in Chicago, and he would be gone for a few days. Jackson knew that this gem of a lie was losing its shine. He wished he could be the man that Sandra had fallen in love with years ago, but that man did not exist anymore. Emmanuelle was beginning to demand more of Jackson's time. They both knew that the lines had already been crossed and what was understood did not need to be explained. That was good enough then, but now Emmanuelle wanted a return on his investment.

Emmanuelle was going on and on about how exhilarating and perfect his birthday party was. Jackson admittedly had a good time but was considering letting Emmanuelle go. Their association was too much like a marriage. Jackson had given Emmanuelle a Rolex Yachting watch for his birthday, a watch gifted to Jackson a year ago from the very married with children and curious Vice President of Strategic Sales over at Bowser and Associates. Emmanuelle crowned it acceptable with his response; *Beloved, I'm in love! Is this my promise ring?*

Jackson sat the first stack of bills aside and noted the amount on the top bill with an ink pen then sat two more stacks inside the tray of the money counter. The sound of the machine was like a serenade.

"Let's plan a rendezvous."

"Here we go with this shit again."

"Oh Jackson, sweetheart let's not quarrel. I want to take a trip."

"I can't afford to spend any more time away from Sandra for a while."

"You can afford to do whatever you want to do."

"Well, I don't want to go on a trip."

"Why do you insist on taking the long and hard roads, hmm?"

"Where do you want to go?"

"I thought you'd never ask. South America. I want to dance on Lagoinha do Leste in the night and eat breakfast on the balcony of an ocean view penthouse in the morning."

"Sounds nice."

"Nice? Honey, it is the perfect recipe for a little piece of heaven on earth."

"I gotta get out of here. I haven't eaten yet. Shit, I gotta stop by the bank before they close."

"You know I hate it when you cut me off."

"How could I cut you off when you were done talking?"

"Your response should have acknowledged my statement about the beach."

"You dictate what I say now?"

"No, I *dick take* and you tell me what to do, daddy."

"Don't do that."

"Don't do what?"

"Call me that. I ain't your daddy."

"I swear ever since your side piece ran her ass home to mommy, you've been so sensitive. If she wants to leave then open the door, honey. You weren't worried about playing house when I sent you that first class plane ticket and you certainly weren't worried about her feelings when I …"

"Emmanuelle…"

"When I sucked the confession out of your dick."

"You're about to piss me off little boy. I really don't have time for your bullshit."

Jackson's tone was chiding, but Emmanuelle was far from intimidated. "Oh, honey wrap it in ice the truth hurts, doesn't it?"

"My wife …" Jackson began to protest.

Emmanuelle threw his head back and laughed. "Your wife? Let's be honest, you've seen my pussy more than hers lately."

Jackson hung up and threw his prepaid flip phone in the trash. Emmanuelle provoked Jackson because he was good at it. He took the phone from of the trash can, broke it in half then smashed it into pieces with the head of a ten pound weight. Emmanuelle was not the problem; Jackson's gluttony was.

Jackson collected the stack of money that sat on the tray, kissed it then put it back in the safe. He put the stack that had been counted in a gym bag under some old workout clothes and running shoes that he kept in his office. Jackson pulled around to the front of the warehouse to assess the puddles in the parking lot before he left. He made a mental note to remind Jacob to have it taken care of before the customers filled the suggestion box with complaints.

A black car was parked across the street almost hidden by a Staghorn tree. When Jackson pulled into the right lane the black car followed. Jackson realized he had forgotten to lock his office door. He made a U-turn when traffic allowed and headed back to the warehouse. The black car was unable to follow without being noticed and kept with the flow of traffic.

The rain fell intermittently. Jackson went back into the warehouse only to find that he had locked his office door after all. He sat in his car for a few minutes listening to the rain falling with no coordination on his windshield. Emmanuelle had boldly stepped into the ring with Jackson and targeted his weak spot. A good fighter never shows his opponent his emotions.

Life-1, Jackson-0.

***

Omar pulled up to the drive through window and handed the cashier six dollars and eighteen cents in exchange for a number six, upsized then pulled into a parking space to answer his phone.

"This is Omar."

"I almost had your boy."

"Who, Jackson?"

"Yeah, I couldn't tail him long enough to clock a destination."

"Todd, I thought we said, we'd wait until we got word on the Thomas boys."

"We ain't say that, you said that shit. If we get him, we get the Thomas boys."

"All we have is speculation and no plan. I'm working on it and when it's time, we can clean the whole house."

"Oh, I see. The plan is to keep fucking his wife."

"This has nothing to do with Sandy."

"Sandy? She's *Sandy*, now? I told you to leave her alone, now you got your head up her ass."

"You're just mad cause your head ain't up her ass. I'm doing my job."

"You gave him a speeding ticket, which he probably paid with the loose change from under his couch cushions and that's doing your job?"

Omar put his car in reverse. "I'll catch up with you later."

"Are you headed to the precinct?"

"In a few, I need to drop something off first."

Todd pulled into the parking space next to Omar. "Let me guess, you bought her lunch."

"Damn, you tailing me too?"

"The question is, what makes you think she appreciates those greasy ass sandwiches and cold fries? She's married to Jackson Powerhouse Perry, you're about as fast food as she gets."

"Todd, there's nothing wrong with treating a friend to lunch."

"A friend? I need you to focus, Omar. You're getting in the way of what I got going on."

Todd pulled off and stuck his middle finger up at Omar. The same streets that fed Todd were the same streets he was in a battle against.

The Thomas boys had marks on their backs that stretched from California to the New York Islands. The authorities had been waiting patiently for them to leave one strand of hair out of place. The Thomas boys were primitive in their thinking, careful in keeping their noses clean; they were loyal to the family business. The faces of the Thomas boys were high school dropouts and fatherless knuckleheads who traded education for four hundred dollars a day. Their jail time was served by the hoodlums who worked the same corners as the prostitutes. Omar was convinced that he could strip Jackson of his bride in exchange for his freedom. District 14 had other plans.

Jackson barely had a career when he met Loren Thomas. He was still fighting in local gyms without accredited training and no chance at a title. Loren approached Jackson with the opportunity of a lifetime to kickbox overseas. *Let me make a household name out of you and introduce you to money you'll never see without me.* Jackson was flown to the most beautiful countries; Italy, France, Portugal and had access to the most beautiful things; women, private planes and yes men. He was trained by professionals and was matched with title holders that he could not beat without wagers being placed under the table. Jackson was an international headliner with an undefeated score card. When Europe had given Loren Thomas all it had to offer, he led Jackson stateside to recreate the phenomenon. Jackson was a commodity; his obligations to Loren were exhausted five years later when he chose to retire from kickboxing. The Thomas Boys placed a new opportunity on the table and Jackson was attracted to their proposal, after all fast money is sexy. Jackson made millions of illegal dollars for himself and even more for the Thomas boys, but he was still just a plan B.

Todd walked into the station house with his head down avoiding eye contact and conversation with his fellow officers. He moved a few papers from one side of his junky desk to the other looking for a single stick it note with a phone number written on it. He frowned at the grease stained fast food bag and chocolate milkshake that had spilled in the trash can because of a loose lid. Todd moved the trash to the left side of the can with a pen, but was unsuccessful at spotting the yellow, square piece of paper.

"Damn!"

Todd glanced at Omar's desk. Nothing was out of place. *Sissy*. Todd rushed out of his office to the parking lot. He rambled through his glove compartment where he had stashed opened junk mail and receipts that needed to be thrown away. The paper was stuck to the polystyrene of a Mastercard envelope.

Todd used to believe he could make a difference by cleaning up local neighborhoods, but temptation slept on his doorstep too. It was easier to clean dirty money when it was done behind the comforts of a badge. Todd dialed the number hoping he had enough time to get all the information he needed in one call. The phone rang a few times then abruptly connected to voicemail. A knock at the door startled Todd. A few officers from Homicide were taking lunch orders and wanted to know if he had a taste for anything. Todd dialed the number again and left a short message. He shook his head at the thought of Omar. *She's sexy, but the pussy can't be that good. Dumb ass.* Another knock robbed his focus.

"It's open."

Steven, an officer assigned to the Thomas boys take down handed Todd a memo. "Someone called looking for you, said you left a message."

"Shit, I forgot my number is coded. Go ahead and transfer the call, thanks Steve." Todd took a legal notepad and ink pen from the top drawer of Omar's desk. "Hey, this is Todd. I spoke with you a couple weeks or so ago. I was wondering if you have time to answer a few questions for me."

"Depends."

"On what?"

"You know what."

"You'll be completely excluded from investigation."

"And…"

"And what?"

"I remain invisible and I only talk to you."

"Deal."

"What can I do for you, officer?"

"I need to know everything you know. Jacob, who is he, exactly?"

"Jacob. Can I add him to this deal?"

Todd tossed the pen on the desk. "What do you mean?"

"I need to protect Jacob too."

"The deal was to cover your ass, not every ass you randomly throw in."

"Understood. Good day officer."

"Why don't I just open all the cells and turn a blind eye?"

"I need him covered. Just us, no one else."

"I need you to be my eyes and ears. Everything you know, I know. If Jackson takes a shit, I need to know what kind of toilet paper he used."

"Deal."

"Now, who is Jacob?"

Omar walked in and tossed his keys on his desk. "Hey, I appreciate your time, we'll be in touch." Omar sat on the edge of Todd's desk and inquired about his call. Todd told him that the sprinkler system guy finally returned his call to confirm a date and time for a consultation and estimate. Omar accepted the little white lie and took a seat at his own desk. Omar had Q and A in a few minutes with the Lieutenant. He had missed roll call twice last week and was tardy once this week. Todd pretended to be concerned with a best practices document that had been on his desk for two weeks. A strong fist pounded on the office door three times.

"Battle! Let's go!"

Omar tucked his shirt in and saluted Todd. "I'm going in."

Todd watched as he followed Lieutenant Johns down the hall to his office.

[Hey this is Todd, can I hit you back for those answers?]

[Waiting]

Before Todd could return the phone call, Omar walked in and took the best practices document from Todd's desk, leaving the office door cracked.

"Hey, uh, I was wondering if we could meet some place. My office is pretty busy right now."

"Some place like a restaurant?"

"Or a park or we can go to the Pin Wheel."

"The Pin Wheel?"

"Yeah, it's a good place to go and talk."

"It's a baby dump."

"Lots of adults go there."

"To get rid of their kids."

"Ok, how about Mardi Center? There's plenty of adults, not a lot of kids."

"Or a restaurant that serves grown up food that I can order, and you can pay for."

"I wasn't asking you out on a date, I just need to get some information from you."

"Don't you know anything about women? You don't have to date me to romance me. I have something you want, now how are you gonna get it?"

Todd threw his hands up. "Ok, a restaurant." He checked his watch. "Can we get this thing started."

"Slow down. If we pace it right, we can arrive at the same time."

"Look, I don't have time for games."

"Yureka's."

"What?"

"Yureka's. We can meet there."

"Yureka's? Hell no! A glass of water costs five dollars! Meet me at World of Burgers in fifteen minutes."

"A burger joint?"

"They have a pretty good menu."

"Of just burgers."

"Or you can enjoy the delicacies from the jail cafeteria menu."

"Typical."

"Fifteen minutes."

"Twenty."

"Fifteen. I know this is a bit backwards, but what's your name again?"

"It's Susan."

"Susan what?"

"Just Susan."

CHAPTER SEVEN

Sandra sat on the couch with her legs crossed at the ankles, hands clasped together between her thighs; her disposition was calculating. Jackson stared at the receipt that Sandra placed on the coffee table. The top of the receipt read, Emmanuelle's Bistro II with a Chicago address and phone number to the eatery underneath. Sandra turned the worn piece of paper over to reveal the number that was written in purple ink. *Sandra had threatened Jackson's King, now she had him in check.* Jackson sat uncomfortably across from his wife and could not think of anything to say. Had she called the number on the back of the receipt? Had she called the restaurant? Had she noticed the last four digits of Jackson's credit card number or was she saving her one in the chamber for the finale? Jackson had no doubt that this would be the result of a short wick on an atomic bomb. Sandra asked Jackson who the number belonged to.

"A friend of mine."

"Is this the same friend who was given a separate number to use?"

"What number are you talking about?"

Sandra responded with the phone number including the area code, date and time the text message was sent. *Jackson was forced to analyze his strategy; he had underestimated his opponent.* "I don't even have that number anymore."

"I didn't ask if you still had the fucking number!"

"What am I supposed to say? Nothing happened!"

"Bullshit!"

Jackson dropped his head. "Ok … ok, but baby, she don't mean shit to me."

Sandra twisted her wedding ring until it was removed from her finger. "It's apparent that I don't either."

Jackson failed to eradicate the threat of capture. Checkmate!

***

Sandra turned the television on and opened the blinds; the telephone cradled between her shoulder and her cheek. She had given the front desk permission to let Omar up to her room. Her clothes had been stuffed into her luggage and stored in the bedroom closet; her cellphone was charging on the nightstand. Omar brought steak subs and French fries, soft drinks and wishful thinking to Sandra's hotel room. He sat the food on the kitchen counter and took a look around.

"So, this is what they call taking time to yourself?"

"Some would say, yes."

"Taking time to yourself is more like a queen sized bed and free WIFI. *This...*" Omar spun around. "is a luxurious two-bedroom apartment."

"You're overreacting."

"Overreacting? There's a horse and carriage out front!"

Omar leaned in to kiss Sandra and just caught the curve of her cheek. He reached for her hand as she walked to the center of the room to give her dismissal speech. Omar was eager to take his place in Sandra's life. The last thing Sandra needed was another relationship that had the potential of heartbreak and emotional decay. She grabbed Omar's hands as he attempted to slide his arms around her waist. Sandra asked him to have a seat. He declined.

"Please, I just want to talk to you."

Omar sat uncomfortably on the edge of the chair. Sandra told Omar that it was not a good idea to keep seeing one another. She offered him friendship, but she would need some time. Her life had become unfamiliar, like she had been written out of the script. Omar stood confidently, choosing to ignore the obvious, waiting to hear that he was the exception. Women did not break up with Omar, they kept themselves relevant by giving him access. Sandra spoke softly, "I'm sorry."

"Yeah, I'm sorry too."

"You understand, right?"

"You think I can't buy you the things that you're used to and splurge on fancy hotels, don't you?"

"Omar, I'm not concerned with what you can and cannot do for me."

"Then what is it?"

"It's me. *I've* been missing from my own life. I haven't lived for me since ..."

"Since that night on your kitchen table."

Omar did not give Sandra the satisfaction of seeing the discontent on his face. He walked passed her and let himself out. No goodbyes, no pleading. Sandra wanted to feel something, but she was empty. Omar spoke through the door, *I love you.*

"I love me too."

Annie Pearl was calling. Sandra washed down a mouthful of cold fries with the watered-down soda before answering. She frowned at the greasy steak subs that were beginning to stain the brown paper bag.

"Hey."

"What's going on?"

"Mama, what are you talking about?"

"Little girl... "

"I left Jackson."

"I know."

"You talked to him?"

"He called me, asking if I had talked to you. Said, he hadn't talked to you in days."

"What did you tell him?"

"I told him it's not unusual for me to talk to my child. Is there something wrong?"

"He called you, but he hasn't picked up the phone to call me. He doesn't even know where I am."

"Where are you?"

"I'm at a hotel."

"How long are you going to stay there?"

"Until I close on the loft. A friend of mine knows the owner, she practically gave it away."

"Cassandra, you bought a new place to live?"

"And a new car."

"Mercy."

"The house, the cars, those things are in Jackson's name. I didn't want him trying to keep me from leaving."

"When will you close on the loft?"

"In a few weeks or so."

"A few weeks? Baby, that's a long time to be staying in a hotel."

"It's free."

"What do you mean by *free*?"

"Jackson mentioned the DeMarca Swartz Suites on his show a few times, they sent him a thank you card a few months ago. He didn't realize they had given him two months of free stays. I just held on to it."

"I just need you to be ok. I love you."

"I'll be fine mama, I love you too."

Sandra replayed the conversation that she and Jacob had the other day in her head. He sounded like a white man who grew up around black people. Sandra contemplated messaging him. She was curious about what he had to say that night. Sandra did not want to hear the truth, but now her peace of mind relied on it. After considering poking the bear, Sandra sent a text message to Jacob.

[Hi, this is Sandra. Can we talk?]

[Sure. I can give you a call in a few minutes.]

[I was hoping we could talk face to face.]

[Face to face? That would be ok I guess.]

[12913 Biscauf Main. Ask for me at the desk.]

Sandra nervously waited for Jacob to arrive. On the other side of the door were so many missing puzzle pieces. Thirty minutes had passed and no Jacob. Sandra threw the steak subs that Omar bought in the trash bin just outside the door. Just as she took her clothes off to relax, the hotel telephone rang.

"Hello, Mrs. Perry there is a Mr. Jacob here to see you. May I send him up?"

"Yes, thank you."

Sandra peeked through the peep hole; Jacob was standing with his back to the door. Sandra gasped when she came face to face with the man who she had secretly fantasized about. The man who lived across the street in the house with the pretty red double doors. Jacob tried to avoid looking Sandra in the eyes. She was even more beautiful up close. He focused on his grandmother to avoid the erection that almost embarrassed him twice. Sandra tried to keep her eyes above Jacob's waist. "You're Jacob? The Jacob that's associated with Jackson?"

"Yes."

"But you live across the street, what's going on?"

Jacob collected his thoughts so that he could start from the beginning. "May I?"

Sandra did not know what to feel or what to think. She offered Jacob a seat on the couch. Reluctantly, she sat next to him. "Yes, I live across the street, but I'm not who I appear to be, and neither is Jackson. Sandra took a deep breath.

"Go on."

CHAPTER EIGHT

Jackson's legs hung over the arm of the couch; his head buried between the couch pillows. There was a trail of empty beer and wine bottles from the kitchen island to the living room floor. Sandra's wedding ring sat in a glass of white wine on the coffee table. The sun was intrusive, splitting its rays between the blinds and the transom windows. Jackson stood up unable to keep his balance, he knocked the glass of wine onto the floor.

"Shit!"

He got down on his knees and began wiping the carpet with his hands. Jackson had lost the one thing that made the most sense in his life. Control. Jacob banged on Jackson's front door. There was no answer.

"Jackson! Open up!"

A driver slowed down, observing as Jacob banged on the door again. "Whatcha looking at nosey? Move on!" Jackson had finally opened the door, squinting trying to block the sun from shining directly into his eyes. He looked like shit and reeked of alcohol. "Where have you been? I've been calling you."

"You sound like a bitch. I thought I told you not to come to my house. My wife could have answered the door."

"How am I supposed to reach you? You ain't answering your phone."

"Figure it out."

"What the fuck is your problem?! You need to get your shit together, man!"

"Who the fuck is you talking to?! I own your lily white ass!"

Jacob was afraid of Jackson's bite; his bark did not mean shit. Jacob was a bartender at the Broken Bottle, a pub on the lower end of the South side. The hustle was real, and a dollar bill was hard to come by.

"Somebody needs to take that nigga down a peg or two. His shit stank just like mine. I'ma rob this janky toilet bowl cause Dre owes me money, charging full price for these watered down dranks."

Dre was the cocky bar owner and Jacob's boss. Jacob barely brought home three hundred a week, but the Broken Bottle was the only place that paid under the table. When Jacob was fired without an explanation, he became desperate for money. Stix boasted, "You know he fired your ass cause you fuckin' his baby mama. He told everybody in that toilet bowl, let's see how he keep her with no gat' damn job."

Jacob waited outside the bar one night until Stix staggered out. Stix would do anything to get his hands on the curves of a full-bodied bottle of Hennessy. It took two weeks and three bottles of Cognac, before he was on board with Jacob's plans to rob the bar. Jacob knew how to get into Dre's safe without a key and he knew that bank deposits were dropped on Wednesday mornings. Stix and Jacob waited until the last customer was served and the strip was shut down till morning. They broke into the bar and emptied the safe. Stix took the VHS tape out of the recorder and cut the cords with his pocketknife while Jacob searched the backroom closet for anything of value. Once they were finally outside, they ran to Jacob's car which was parked at the end of the alley. Jacob counted five thousand dollars. He kept four thousand for himself and offered Stix a stipend.

The next day, Jacob drove by the bar to access the damage. Stix was outside talking to Dre; panicked, Jacob turned his car around and joined the gentlemen on the sidewalk.

Stix pointed to Dre. "Somebody robbed this man. Can you believe that, shit?" Stix looked passed Jacob and smiled with two missing bottom teeth. "Heyyy, look who it is; Powerhouse Perry Jackson! Let me hold something nigga, I know you got it."

Jacob recognized Jackson from the barbershop he owned up the street and his cable Sports Show. Dre became tensed, he saw a manipulator, Jacob saw an opportunity.

Jackson approached Dre. "You ready to sell yet?"

"If I sell you my bar then I got nothing, man."

Jackson frowned at the ugly building. "You ain't got much more than that now."

Jacob held his hand out. "Pleasure to meet you."

"You don't know that yet."

"Hey, if you need someone to help out around your shop or anything let me know."

Stix motioned for Jackson to *come into his office.* Jackson gave Jacob a business card and told him to give him a call. Jacob disappeared once the police had arrived. Jackson humored Stix and walked with him to the corner.

"Powerhouse Perry, I got some red hot goods."

"It's Jackson Powerhouse Perry. Look old man, I have places to be." Jackson pulled out his wallet and gave Stix a one hundred dollar bill. "Take care of yourself."

Stix put the money in his pocket. "Christmas come early, thank ya, kindly. Look here, I know who robbed this toilet bowl."

Jackson looked Stix in his red, strained eyes, he was so drunk that blinking gave him motion sickness.

"Now, how do you know that?"

"Because I did that shit. Me and white boy flushed that toilet bowl!"

"Why would you rob this place? You could have just asked for the petty cash."

"White boy stiffed me, and he kept most of my share. The economy is bad, I needs all my coins, plus I got the tape."

Jackson grabbed Stix by the arm and walked him around the corner. "You have the tape as in the surveillance tape?"

"That's gat' damn right, Mr. Powerful Jackson, sir."

"Where's the tape?"

Stix patted his chest. He had the tape inside of his dirty, trench coat pocket. The stench from his clothes was starting to stain the air. Jackson wanted to view it. "How much do you want for the tape?"

"Two million dollars."

"I'll give you two hundred dollars."

"Two hundred dollars and some pussy."

Jackson agreed and told Stix that if the tape did not have white boy on it, he would come back and take his refund out of his old drunken ass. Stix was struggling, trying to keep his balance. "When I get the pussy?"

"How did you get your hands on this without him knowing?"

"I was in the bar sittin' in my assigned seat the same day white boy got fired. Hustle man Mel came in and tried to sell Jimmy a s'curity system, said no monthly payments and …"

"You talk too much. You do realize that your purple ass is on this tape too, right?"

"Then Dre said, my man, let me see you outside. I knew then it was sooold!" Stix swung his imaginary gavel.

"Unbelievable.

"So, when I get the pussy?"

"Let me work on that for you."

"Let me give you my 'quirements."

"I'm sure it'll be *her* standards that'll be compromised. I'll uh, I'll be in touch."

Jacob stood still, staring Jackson in the eyes. They both knew that Jacob had the strength to overpower Jackson, but Jackson stood strong behind his security blanket in the form of a VHS tape.

"Remember that! I fucking own you!"

Jacob pointed at Jackson and spoke through clenched teeth, "Handle your fucking business."

Jacob walked across the street, steady pace, body erect. Sandra had asked Jacob to keep their meeting between the two of them. She knew Jacob would not mention it to Jackson, but she wanted him to know that she had no intentions of mentioning it either. Jacob walked into the house throwing punches in the air, cursing Jackson's name and kicking the furniture.

"Keep fucking with me and I'll be going to jail for more than robbery!"

Jacob opened his wallet and pulled out a few business cards that he had kept over time. He went upstairs and dumped the nightstand drawer out onto the bed. *Yes!* Smitty's business card was stapled to a receipt. Jacob dialed the cellular number on the front, but it now belonged to someone else. Jacob heard the front door close and quickly stepped into the hallway to see if Jackson had come to play Billy bad ass. Susan had come to recover the rest of her belongings. Jacob stood in her doorway.

"I didn't think there was anything left to pack."

"Well, I started to leave this stuff, but ..." Susan shrugged her shoulders. "It's my stuff."

"Did you know Sandra left Jackson?"

Susan gasped and turned to face Jacob. "Really?"

"I guess she found out he cheated."

"Wow! How do you know?"

"I know a lady who gets her hair done at the same salon as Sandra."

"You buy into gossip now? How little girlish of you."

"It's true."

Susan stopped what she was doing for a minute and asked Jacob to come inside. Jacob closed the bedroom door then sat on the dresser.

Susan lowered her voice. "While you were gossiping, did you hear anything about Jackson's sexuality?"

"His sexuality? What about his sexuality?"

"So, you haven't heard?"

Jacob hopped off the dresser and sat on the bed. "No, what have you heard?"

"He sleeps with little boys."

"He's a child molester?!"

"No, no, listen. He sleeps with men."

"Not little boys, but men?"

"He's sucking dick, focus Jacob!"

"I don't believe that. Jackson sleeping with men. Where'd you hear that?"

"From the same salon Sandra gets her hair done."

Jacob dismissed Susan's absurd accusation and inquired about her new beginnings. Susan had escaped The Brigance Hills, but she still resided in debt to Jackson. She turned her back to Jacob and proceeded packing her reprints of Marilyn Monroe and works from Henri de

Toulouse-Lautrec and a few journals that she had purchased some time ago, but had no intentions of writing in. "Everything is good, no regrets."

Susan had a million regrets, but her biggest regret was saying, yes to a man who would not take no for an answer.

Boy meets girl, girl falls in love with boy. Boy breaks girl's heart. That was the rotation of the hamster wheel for Susan. Her first sexual experience was with a Priest. Physically, he was six feet tall with broad shoulders and piercing green eyes. Publicly, he was a man of faith and a pillar in his community; biologically, he was her father.

Susan left home at age sixteen because her father could not keep his hands off of her or her little sister and her mother was more concerned with perception than deception. Susan met a man who promised her the world, he was thirty-seven and she was seventeen. He pimped her out to men who wore their pants above their navels and smoked Lucky Strike cigarettes. He used most of the money she made to support his drug habit. Susan left once the abuse became more frequent and she found herself turning tricks for free. She held down a disposable job that covered her bills and provided a few wants too but quit after the owner of a pet supply chain solicited her services. Susan introduced him to the wheel barrel, and he introduced her to clientele that could afford to keep her heels off the concrete; from clerk to courtesan.

Susan walked into the Check into Cash place where she had worked as a clerk and demanded her final pay from Phil who was still upset because she would not fuck him for free. Jackson walked into the tension prompting Phil to lower his voice.

"I'll mail you your check."

"Open the damn register and give me my peanuts!"

Phil grabbed himself by the crouch. "You can get these peanuts!"

Jackson took a half empty box of Snickers and ten bags of BBQ potato chips to the register. The Mike and Ike boxes had dust on them and the skin from the bottom of the Twinkies were stuck to their packages. Susan had gotten over the *Ooh! It's Jackson Powerhouse Perry!* Syndrome. She was more interested in what he had in his wallet. Phil counted the bags of chips. "You don' bout cleaned me out!"

Jackson observed in indifference, while assessing Susan.

"Somebody needs to, you haven't sold anything since you've been open."

Susan interrupted the small talk by pointing to the register and holding her hand out. Jackson waited patiently while Phil bagged his junk food. "Phil, give the lady her money. She worked for it, stop being an asshole." Phil gave Jackson his bag then opened the register and threw four hundred dollars at Susan. She stuck her middle finger up at Phil and told him to choke on it. Jackson followed her outside. "Hey, why'd you quit?"

"That's none of your business."

Jackson held his hands up, arrested. "Not trying to get in your business, just thought you'd like to make some extra cash."

"You thought right."

Jackson looked around. "I have a gentleman friend who needs lady company."

"Name, age, status, must be drug and disease free, type of service and half is due before I even see a dick print."

"His name is Steven, but his friends call him Stix."

"Stix?! The shit stain that can drink an ocean under the table? No thanks!"

"I'll clean him up for you."

"I fuck men for good money, but I'm not desperate."

"It's an insult, I know. I apologize. Know anybody who may be on the desperate side?"

"You know what? One of my girls …"

"You have girls?" Jackson threw his head back and laughed. "You a pimp now?"

"I'm a boss and a run a tight ship. My girls are clean, pretty and talented."

"Talented huh, did you find that out reviewing their resumes … or?"

"I have two girls and yes, I've fucked them both."

"So, give me one of them."

"My girls aren't for sale to Stix, but there's a new girl I have in mind."

Stix smelled like sewage. Jackson booked a suite for the night and purchased toiletries, a pack of men's underwear and an outfit from the super center.

Jackson yelled from the other side of the bathroom door, "Wash your hair too!"

Susan showed up with a young lady who had just celebrated her nineteenth birthday. She was a runaway at seventeen and never looked back once she crossed state lines.

"She didn't want to be alone, so …"

"Well, I paid for the room so I'm not leaving either."

"I charge extra if you want to watch."

Jackson gave Stix two bare skin, lubricated condoms. He and Susan stood in the adjoining room peeking from behind the cracked door. Jackson pressed record on his cell phone. Susan made the money gesture. "I'll make her stop and we'll leave right now." Jackson laid three hundred dollars on the nightstand.

Stix had not touched a woman in almost eleven years. Nineteen turned her head when Stix tried to kiss her lips.

Stix scratched the nappy hairs on his chest. "Take your clothes off."

She hesitantly undressed while he struggled to put the condom on. Jackson turned to Susan and shook his head in shame. Susan just wanted this circus act to be over. Stix wouldn't last five minutes, she thought. Nineteen could be heard telling Stix to take it easy. "Shut up, bitch!" Susan peeked in the room and saw Stix trying to force his limp penis into Nineteen. He yanked the condom off and grabbed her by the head. "Put it in your mouth, come on!" Susan reached for the doorknob to intervene, but Jackson held his hand up. Stix slapped Nineteen then grabbed her by the neck. Susan pressed past Jackson and grabbed Stix by the shoulder.

Having lost his balance, he stumbled to the floor. Embarrassed, he got up and struck Susan in the face. Nineteen grabbed her clothes and tried to run into the bathroom. Stix grabbed her by her ponytail and slung her to the floor. He stood over her, waving his penis in her face. "Put it in your mouth!" Susan grabbed a concrete rock that she kept in her handbag and bashed Stix across the back of his head so hard that he fell forward, hitting his head on the corner of the desk. Jackson rushed over to Stix and stood over him but did not want to touch him. Susan instructed Nineteen to get dressed.

"What the fuck was that?!"

"I don't know, he's a drunk and he takes crazy pills too, I think."

"We gotta get outta here."

"What am I supposed to do with him?"

Stix stirred a little as if his limbs were involuntarily reacting. Jackson and Susan sighed with relief. They dragged Stix to the elevator, he was in and out of consciousness. Susan suggested the outdoor pool exit to avoid spectators. Jackson put him in the backseat of his car and gave Susan an extra two hundred dollars to help him get Stix into his apartment. By the time they had arrived at Stix's deprived shed, he was non-responsive. His eyes were glazed, his chest was not moving. Jackson opened the car door and dragged Stix by the arms from the curb to his front door. It began to rain. Stix's door was locked. Jackson kicked the door in and dragged him to an old, worn recliner that sat in front of a closed door. Susan held her nose and stepped over stains that had caused the carpet to become matted and badly discolored.

Jackson frowned. "Is he dead?"

Susan knew the truth but held on to the possibility of him being in a stupor. "Maybe he's just … knocked out."

Jackson kicked Stix, there was no movement. Susan took a compact from her purse and handed it to Jackson. Stix was gone. "Let's go before someone comes."

"Who's gonna come? He lives in a fucking graveyard. Look at this place."

Susan covered her mouth. "Can we leave please! I'm going to throw up!"

Jackson told Susan not to contact the police. He had too much going on and this would be a very much, unwelcomed distraction. Susan did not want to leave the situation this way and told Jackson that he was a fucking idiot. Had he been a man and stopped Stix, none of this would have happened. Jackson kindly reminded Susan that she is a prostitute who had just killed a man and he had it on video.

"Susan… Susan!"

"Yeah?"

"I said, I talked to a Realtor about a house. It's a fixer upper. I figured I could get it at a steal then take my time with renovations."

"You found a house? Good job, Jackie!"

Jacob called the number on the receipt. Smitty's grub and pub had been around for over twenty five years. Smitty wanted someone who was an innovative thinker, someone who was in touch with the young crowd to pass the torch to and someone who would love the business just as much as he does. Smitty told Jacob a long drawn out story about how he got started and how Smitty's is not a bar, but a home and the customers are family. Jacob listened attentively. He had a soft assessment done on the bar and dropped Smitty a number. It was acceptable. Smitty had one request of Jacob.

"Promise me you won't turn it into some teeny bopper hangout and lose the loyalty of the seasoned family members."

"Don't worry, I put out fires. I don't start them."

CHAPTER NINE

After Jacob left the warehouse, he drove to Midland, a small town that housed a community of Italian Artisans. They made their own clothes, grew their own food, bartered and bought from one another. Jacob drove to Midland at least once a week to check on Eloisa, his grandmother. He recognized the black car that had been parked across the street from the warehouse for the past few days. It was the same black car that had pulled him over. When he noticed the car tailing him, he drove twenty-five minutes out of his way taking the officer down a two-lane country road that led to a small neighborhood grocery store and a gas station with one pump. The black car slowed down when Jacob pulled into the parking lot then sped off when he got out of the car. Jacob went into the grocery store and bought buttermilk, salami, tomatoes, a jar of peanut butter and Ciabatta bread. An older guy begging for money outside of the store, staggered over to Jacob and pointed up the road. Jacob kept walking.

"Hey son, that car there, that was a cop."

"I assumed as much."

"Gimme ten dollars and I ain't never seent cha."

"Have a good day sir."

Traffic was stalled by an eighteen-wheeler trying to turn onto the junction. Jacob took a short cut in the opposite direction. Finally, he turned into the graveled driveway and pulled around to the back of the cottage house that looked like it was built from a model kit. A petite, dark haired, olive toned woman walked out onto the back porch. She clapped her hands and smiled.

"Ciao il mio bel nipote!"

"Ciao bello."

"Doni, tu porti?"

"Groceries, mamma."

"I don't need anything, you spoil me."

"It's just a few things I noticed you were low on."

"Grazie."

Jacob carried the groceries inside the house and sat them on a small kitchen table with metal legs next to the back door. He took five hundred dollars from his pants pocket and extended it to his grandmother. She denied the handout three times before finally accepting it, like always.

"Mamma, I need to take this call. Tornerò."

Jacob sat on the passenger's side of his car with both feet on the ground. He feared that Susan called to discuss how much her freedom would cost. She told Jacob that he would be getting a visitor and not to be alarmed. She would not explain in full detail over the phone, but she needed to give him a heads up. Jacob's plate was already top heavy without having Susan add to it.

Jacob plopped down on the couch next to his grandmother, who was watching a TV game show. She turned the volume down.

"Nipote, che cosa è sbagliato?"

"Nothing's wrong, I promise."

"Il tuo volto dice diverso."

"So, what does my face say?"

"Your face says, you got a problema, sì."

"Mamma, I found a house that I really like. Nothing's in stone yet."

"Beautiful! You need a nice lady friend to live happily ever after with, primo."

"I agree."

"How's your new job?"

"Oh, I almost forgot to tell you, I'm going into business for myself."

"My beautiful boy, I am so proud of you. Your padre would be so proud too."

"I know mamma."

Jacob spent an hour repairing the cladding on the side of Eloisa's house, hoping the officer had better things to do than to sit idle alongside the road waiting for him.

Night had fallen in Midland; the only light came from the high moon. Jacob could not leave his grandmother's house without taking a plate of her home-made Ravioli. He kissed Eloisa on both cheeks and confirmed their standing date for next week.

The gravel bounced from the ground and into the tread of Jacob's tires, leaving white residue on the street as he pulled off. There was a blue sedan parked on the shoulder of the road. Jacob checked it out in his rear view. The people who stopped on 'Battle Alley' were not familiar with this road and the people who were only took it in the daytime.

Against his better judgement, Jacob drove to the warehouse to pick up a bundle that Jackson generously gave him for picking up groceries and his dry cleaning. The blue sedan pulled into the warehouse parking lot behind Jacob. Jacob reached under his seat and grabbed the handle of his

.380. A man wearing baggy blue jeans and a Nike hat to the back walked up to the car and tapped the window with his keys. Jacob rushed the car door open, pushing the unwanted visitor back a few steps.

"Easy, white boy."

Jacob ran his fingers over his window, ensuring that it had not been scratched.

"What do you want man? You ain't got no pussy to fall into?"

"Brotha, I didn't come for trouble."

"Oh, we're *brothas* now?"

"Let's take a walk inside."

"Let's not."

"I just need a few minutes."

"Wow, I hope whatever you're on becomes available over the counter."

Jacob got back inside his car and closed the door after realizing the visitor was not leaving, he rolled his window down. "This doesn't end with a kiss good night."

"Take my card, get back to me."

Before Jacob could roll his window up, the visitor tossed his card inside. Jacob headed North on Piney Road, checking his rear view to see if the blue sedan had pulled off. *Where do I know him from? His face looks so familiar.* Jacob looped back around, heading South on Piney Road, blue sedan was just pulling out of the warehouse parking lot. Jacob looked at the card that was still resting on his lap. He pulled into a gas station and parked under the light post. The card read; Todd Augustine, Detective, Renfro Police Department. *Detective? That's who he is, the nark that pulled me over!* Jacob scrolled through his photo gallery and found the picture that he had taken of Susan's contacts. The number that was on the card matched the number under the contact, Big T. Jacob called Susan, when she did not answer, he texted her, *call me ASAP!*

Jacob pulled into the old Lincoln Post Office parking lot and waited after messaging the detective. Blue Sedan pulled up and parked in the space next to Jacob.

"Long time no see."

"You gonna arrest me or what?"

"I want to make you an offer."

"An offer?"

"A job offer."

"I have a job."

"Oh, you mean your little paper route. Making drops for petty cash. Look, I know you want to get from under Jackson."

"I don't know what you're talking about."

Todd leaned against his car and sighed. "Listen closely white boy because I don't want to repeat myself. My badge is at home. I'm Todd, not Detective Augustine. I gave you my card to create some trust here."

"You talked to Susan, didn't you?"

"The Thomas boys no longer care for the way Jackson does business. So, you can go down with him or you can work for me."

"Wait, go down?"

"You did know that drug laundering is a crime, right?"

Jacob knew that drug affiliation was considered a crime, but he wondered if the officer of the law standing before him knew this. Jacob thought to himself, petty cash? He brought home in one month more than he brought home in a year working at the bar. It was not loyalty that kept Jacob on Team Jackson, Jacob did not need two thumb prints pressed against his back.

Todd was in pursuit of Jackson to curb the attention from the Thomas boys. The Thomas boys had positioned Jackson on center stage, targets were easier to hit that way. Jacob's phone rang, it was Susan. He ignored her call with an auto message, created just for her; loose lips sink ships.

"So, what exactly are we talking about here? Did you offer Susan a job too?"

"You ask too many questions. You want the job or not?"

Jacob assumed Susan had already accepted the ransom money and now her soul belonged to two devils.

Todd tapped his finger on the face of his watch. "Time is a lot of money."

"Let me get back to you."

"Jacob, your other option is going to jail. Period. You'll make more money, you won't have Jackson to deal with, you'll be on the right side of the law, literally. It's a win, win, win."

"Ok, so what now?"

"Is that a yes?"

Jacob shrugged his shoulders. "Yeah."

"Congratulations, you start Monday."

"Monday? I have a …"

Todd held his hand up. "Chill out white boy, it's a figure of speech." Todd laughed then got inside of his car which was still running. He rolled the window down. "I'll call you tomorrow and we'll set something up."

"Todd, I'm a grown man. If I called you black boy, you'd be ready to fight. Sono Italiano."

"Fair enough." Todd extended a handshake. "Italian boy."

What had just happened? The Police were still protecting the Thomas boys and chopping their flunkies off at the kneecaps.

Susan always answered her phone even during sex. Her phone rang until her voicemail picked up, which meant she was either playing tag or ignoring Jacob's calls.

Jacob scrolled through his text messages and tapped on the conversation between him and "J W". He wanted to be headed to her hotel room with wine and an erection. Jacob told Sandra that her husband is a drug dealer. To which she responded, *I'm not surprised. What I want to know is how you got my number? Are you a drug dealer too?* Jacob admitted that he did not own the house across the street, he was renting it. Sandra advised Jacob that she preferred the truth. It was not as delicious as the lies, but it was healthier. Jacob informally mentioned that

Jackson owned the house across the street with the red double doors and offered him a job and a place to live after he had been fired. *Is she your wife?* Jacob quickly demolished any notion that he and Susan were connected by anything other than circumstance. *Do you have kids?* No. *How old are you?* Twenty eight. *Are you from around here?* Something like that.

Jacob's phone rang. He realized he was still sitting in the Post Office parking lot with his foot resting against the brake pedal. It was Susan.

"Are you staying in Brigance tonight?"

"Already in my nightie."

"You got some fuckin' explaining to do."

"*You got some fuckin' explaining to do.* Get a clue Jacob! We're in a real life maze. We're trapped, and the only way …"

Jacob hung up on Susan. He was not in the mood for her ranting dramatics tonight. *Whatever she signed us up for had better come with a bonafied insurance policy.* Jacob turned the radio volume up; Keith Sweat was crooning, How Deep Is Your Love. Jacob sent Sandra four random letters in a text message. *Hit me back. You know you want to.* She replied shortly after. *Yes!*

[Is this supposed to mean something?]

[My bad, my phone was in my back pocket. Guess I need to put a lock on it.]

[Good idea.]

Jacob was enthused with his juvenile gesture; he did not expect Sandra to respond. Her response let him know that at least she did not despise him. He composed a response, *Can I come over?* Then deleted it. Jacob updated the contact in his phone from J W, which stood for Jackson's wife to Sandra.

[Didn't mean to bother you.]

[No worries.]

[Have a good night.]

[U 2.]

"Damn, girl."

CHAPTER TEN

Sandra pulled up to the resident entrance gate and swiped her access card. The green light flashed twice then the gate arm leading to the parking garage lifted. There were two men dressed in suits walking towards the elevator. Sandra waited until they were secured within the hoist way before getting out of her car. She unlocked the door to her peace, her sanctuary, her space. Sandra had never owned anything, and it felt so liberating. She twirled in the middle of the Mahogany wood floor and cried happy tears. As coveted as happiness is, it was so anti-social. Life will not wait for you to live it and happiness will not wait for you to find it. Sandra took pictures of the newly remodeled bathroom and open concept bedroom and the rustic style kitchen then sent them to Ariel. Ariel replied with two sets of travel dates and told Sandra to pick one.

Sandra stepped onto the small patio that overlooked the courtyard, it looked like a Botanical Garden, hosting a beautiful array of colorful flowers and foxtail agave plants. She stood in the corner of the room and looked out in approbation. But, instead of choosing a color scheme for the living room and choosing the perfect piece of art for her accent table, Sandra was preparing for the bullshit.

***

There were fresh Calla Lilies on the console in a beautiful glass lined wooden vase, they were Sandra's favorite. The house was spotless and smelled like day old regret. Jackson had spent a month studying his opponent's moves and had put together a fool proof strategy. Sandra pulled into the driveway, fighting to keep her emotions at arm's length. She backed out of the driveway and parked in front of the house. She recalled the very first time Jackson approached her. *Damn, you're beautiful. Whoever he is, tell him bye, bye.* Jackson has always been cocky, and always got what he wanted. Sandra still had keys to the front door but felt more comfortable ringing the doorbell. She looked around as if she were a first-time visitor. Jackson took a seat on the small sofa in the keeping room, Sandra sat on the opposite side occasionally glancing over at the kitchen table. There was no excuse good enough that Jackson could offer to blur all the disappointment. Sandra asked if there were multiple women and if there were children involved. She asked if he loved her and if their marriage was worth the trouble of putting the broken pieces back together. Jackson told Sandra that he ran into an old friend who held his attention years before they met. She was on business and he had been drinking. It meant nothing. Sandra wanted to believe him, but she knew it was a lie.

"Jackson."

Jackson scooted to the edge of the sofa. Sandra unequivocally, admitted to cheating. "I slept with someone." She hated when people said, *slept with* when the truth was, "He and I... had sex."

Jackson could not stomach the taste of his own medicine. His wife was admitting to him that she let another man penetrate a part of her that used to only belong to him.

"How many?"

"How many what?"

"How many men, how many times?"

"One man, one time."

"Were you staying with him this whole time?"

"No."

Jackson had been bolo punched in the gut. His opponent had pulled a trick move. He was back in his corner reevaluating his approach. The thought of someone else in between Sandra's thighs made him nauseous. Another man's hands, another man's sweat, another man's penis stealing pieces of her that could never be recovered. Jackson strode out of the room. Sandra waited several minutes before walking into the living room where Jackson was standing in front of the window. She stood in his personal space. "Maybe this is too much for the both of us."

"Whose car is that? Is that your car?"

Sandra peeked out of the window. "Yes."

"You don't like the car I got you?"

"Jackson, I think this is too much for us. It's too much for me."

"If you want to throw in the towel then throw in the towel."

"I don't know what I want to do."

Jackson treaded back into the center of the ring, confident in his next move. He pulled Sandra's wedding ring out of his front pocket then reached for her hand. Sandra held back tears remembering the day she promised to never take it off. She walked back to the keeping room and grabbed her purse. Jackson met her under the archway as she positioned her purse strap on her shoulder. "I'm going to go ahead and leave."

"So, we're done talking?"

Sandra walked past Jackson but stopped short. "Jackson, how hard is it to say, I'm sorry. Not one time did you offer me a simple apology. I've heard every excuse. You don't love me, I'll learn to live with that, but treating me like shit, I can't live with."

"Sandra, the truth is, I was feeling myself. She was the girl who rejected me, I saw an opportunity and I took advantage of it. I'm sorry."

Jackson sounded well-rehearsed. *The truth is*, normally meant the next words out of my mouth are lies with the intent to tell half the truth. Sandra dropped her guards just enough to be coaxed into having a seat. Jackson had gotten his opponent's attention. He was back in the fight. "I'll do whatever it takes to make this work."

"What do you think it takes?"

Jackson grabbed Sandra's hand. He positioned her wedding ring on her ring finger. "First, I have to be a good husband."

Jab!

Jackson led Sandra upstairs to one of the guest bedrooms. The door was closed and there was a big yellow bow hanging on the doorknob. Jackson stood aside. "Open the door." Sandra opened the door and burst into tears. It was a nursery, fully furnished. There were baby clothes hanging in the closet and even a rug that read, baby on board. "Do you like it?"

Left hook!

Sandra nodded, as she picked up the oversized teddy bear wearing a bib and bonnet. Jackson picked up the baby booties that were sitting on the changing table and hid them behind his back.

"I don't know what to say."

Jackson held up the blue and pink booties one pair in each hand. "Which one do you want, boy or girl?"

Right hook!

Sandra wondered who this man was. She would not have recognized Jackson had it not been for the horns and pointy tail. Sandra took the booties from Jackson's hand. He pulled two matching outfits from the closet.

"Versace, really Jackson?"

"Is that a smile?"

Knock out!

Jackson walked Sandra down the hall to their bedroom. Sandra gently pulled her hand away before Jackson opened the door.

"What are you doing?"

"I figured you'd want to get started right away."

"Jackson ..."

"Stop fighting me woman."

Jackson pulled Sandra close to him and kissed her on the neck. She allowed it. He kissed her forehead then her nose. She was content with that. He kissed her lips, but she did not make eye contact. He lifted her chin with the curve of his pointer finger. "Kiss me." She did. He opened the bedroom door to a bed full of rose petals, both red and white. Robes drawn across the couch with matching house shoes. Annie Pearl's wisdom reminded Sandra to forgive, but never forget.

"I can't stay. I promised Audrey; I'd be there when the HVAC guy came. I should probably get going."

"We start filming this week. I'll be in Chicago for two weeks then back home for two."

"Congratulations on the new season."

"Thanks for encouraging me to go for it."

"Jackson."

"Yeah?"

"Is all of this for show or do you really want to start a family?"

"Yeah, I'm ready."

Jackson followed Sandra back down the stairs. They conversed briefly in the foyer. Jackson tried once more to coax his wife out of her clothes and into their bed before they were to be separated for weeks. "You sure you don't wanna stay a little while?"

"I'll see you when you get back."

Jackson watched Sandra strut in her high heels to her new BMW X6. He stood guard at the window until a faint jingle broke his attention. He searched the couch cushions thinking maybe Sandra had left her cell phone. The jingle stopped then started again. Jackson took the stairs three at a time and followed the sound. It was his burner phone it had been powered off for over a month. Jackson only powered it on when he had business to take care of in Chicago. That ten digit number was the thin line that kept two worlds from colliding. There were over forty missed calls and over sixty text messages. Emmanuelle had called and left several hostile voicemail messages followed by, forgive me messages which Jackson ignored. The phone rang in his hand. Jackson peeked out of the bedroom window to confirm that Sandra had left then sat in her rocking chair.

"Yeah."

"Oh, so you do exist, huh?"

"What do you want, Nina?"

"I want to know why it took you a month to take my call and why did you leave and not come back?"

"I told you, I was in Chicago on business and I had strict deadlines."

"You're so full of shit. I know you're cheating on us, but when you're with me, I expect your full addiction."

"Baby, there's no need in worrying your sexy ass about that anymore."

"Good."

"Because my *addiction* is no longer available to you."

Jackson hung up on Nina. She was one of his biggest regrets. He should have let her go on her way once they exited the plane, but Jackson's luggage was delayed due to weight requirements and was due to arrive two hours later. Nina was checking into her hotel room with a delay of her own. She invited Jackson to her room for adult conversation so that he would not have to sit in the unreceptive airport seats for hours. Jackson accepted the invitation and indulged in more than adult conversation. Nina was intentional, she took charge and dragged those who were unable to keep up. Except when it came to Jackson. Jackson was her Merlot after sitting for hours in board meetings. Jackson had a way with words without opening his mouth. To Nina, they spoke the same love language. To Jackson, they were just a couple of cheaters.

Jackson threw extra pairs of socks and underwear into his travel bag. His suits were already in route to the studio. He lifted the pillow on Sandra's side of the bed and opened the box that he had placed there. Sandra smiled at him today. Just hours before that she cursed his name. Jackson put the two thousand dollar tennis bracelet back under Sandra's pillow, he left the rose petals and robes undisturbed. Jackson had won the title match. Now it was time for him to accept the championship belt. He sent a message to his opponent.

[Sandra, thank you for giving us a chance, I love you.]

[Luv you 2.]

Life-1, Jackson-1.

CHAPTER ELEVEN

Four... Three ... Two ... The studio lights flashed then rotated in a circular motion indicating big news in today's sports. Jackson turned to camera 3 ready to report.

"Big Redd Claiborne Jr. is now a member of the Chicago Buckhorns, the defending NFL champions sealing a deal with the former Panthers linebacker after the Panthers waived him on Friday. He cleared waivers on Saturday and Monday. He's currently in Marshall City waiting to join Casey Hendricks and the gang anticipating winning a fourth super bowl in five years. Gerald, how does this effect the Buckhorn's defense?"

"Well, Claiborne would come in as a vet on the defensive side of this team. He was defensive player of the year; they need him in the most critical way. Smitts is out, Jones is out, Pace is playing with an injury. This guy has strong legs, no injuries. Not to mention the excitement from the rivalry showdown the fans would see if these teams cross paths in the AFC. I can't wait to watch."

"You heard it right here, folks. Football party at Gerald's!"

"Twenty dollars a head."

The gentlemen shared a laugh as Jackson closed out the show. "This has been All in Sports News, I'm Jackson Powerhouse Perry."

"And I'm Gerald Whittaker. Thank you all for watching."

A voice from behind the monitors yelled out, *clear!* Jackson took his microphone off and shook the hand of his new co-anchor. Production was a wrap. Lilian came out of the control room just in time to catch Jackson before he headed to stall four to have his makeup removed. *Show review, conference room one. Grab Gerald on your way.* Jackson checked his phone. No calls or messages from Sandra. Typically, he would have at least two from her by the end of a show. He briefly checked his burner phone. Nina. She knew he was in Chicago because the new season of All in Sports News premiered today. Everyone gathered in the small room and chipped in their two cents on how the show went and what minor tweaks would be in place for the next taping. A thin white male with moussed hair wearing headphones around his neck came and tapped Jackson on the shoulder. Jackson followed him out and was directed to a call in the OCC room.

"This is Jackson."

"Hello darling."

Jackson took the phone from his ear and mouthed a few curse words. "What do you want?"

"Oh, sweetie is that any way to talk to your baby girl?"

"We don't have anything to say to one another."

"And who decided that?"

"Goodbye."

"No goodbyes, we'll see each other soon."

Jackson hung up the phone and regained his composure before walking to his dressing room. The studio was starting to thin out. The associate producer was in deep conversation with Aaron from the research department. They waved blindly at Jackson as they compared notes on the NBA Draft picks. Gerald left immediately after the show review; he had a lady friend waiting for him at the apartment that the show provided during the season. Jackson opened the door to his dressing room, he hesitated, shocked to see an unwanted guest. "See, I told you we'd see each other soon." Jackson threatened to call security if Emmanuelle did not leave. He sat on Jackson's lounge chair and crossed his legs. "Tattle tell. What are you going to tell them, that your lover is picking on you?"

"Why are you here?"

"I'm pregnant."

"Get out!"

"And it's yours."

Jackson took his suit jacket off and hung it in the closet. He cracked his knuckles and turned to face Emmanuelle. Emmanuelle dismissed the subtle threat. "Jackson, we both know I'm not going anywhere until I get all my questions answered. Now, we can do it here or we can have dinner like two civilized human beings. Frankly, I could use a stiff drink."

Jackson grabbed Emmanuelle by the shirt and yanked him out of his seat. He strong armed Emmanuelle until his back was against the wall, the heel of his shoe left a black scuff mark on the paint. Jackson spoke paradoxically to his actions, ensuring that Emmanuelle did not misunderstand his intent. Jackson's forearm was pressed against Emmanuelle's neck.

"Sir, I have no dealings with you. Either you can walk out of my dressing room or I can call security, and have you thrown out."

Emmanuelle was astounded. Jackson picked up the courtesy phone and alerted security that Emmanuelle was leaving and was to have his access to the studio revoked. Within what seemed like moments, security burst open Jackson's dressing room door and removed Emmanuelle. Jackson smirked then waved bye, bye. He was daft to believe that this would be the end of Emmanuelle. Jackson took his burner phone out of his pants pocket. He decided it was time to lay it to rest. Five people, five on and off again affairs, two men, three women and a wife who was starting to smell his bullshit.

Jackson deleted Nina's number then Emmanuelle's, two down, three to go. He texted Mia, a twenty something elementary school teacher and told her that he did not want to be alone tonight. She responded with a picture of her vagina and a short message; *we would love to have you cum by.* Before destroying his little black book, Jackson voraciously texted Oliver, a double jointed, financial advisor who made his own clothes and set up a dinner date for tomorrow evening. One last hurrah.

***

Sandra had no intentions on staying in Brigance while Jackson was in Chicago and she had no intentions on sharing her new home address with Jackson. Audrey was on her way with Chinese takeout, ready to gossip. Sandra had ordered the bed that she saw at Dixon's a few weeks ago, she was so excited to finally roll up her sleeping bag and put it away for good. The doorbell sounded like a gong. Audrey was dressed in workout clothes carrying gift bags and food. She walked around and toured her new; I need to get out of the house, are you free? get away spot. The two friends hugged and giggled in spite of themselves. Audrey told Sandra about a guy she met at the stoplight. The light lasted longer than their courtship. Sandra told Audrey that it was over between her and Omar and even though Jackson put on a stellar performance, she was curious about someone.

"Wait, Jackson professed his eternal love and you have your eye on someone else? I knew there was a naughty girl in there somewhere."

"It is possible to be married and find someone else attractive."

"True, but I believe the word was, curious."

Sandra blushed as she nibbled on her sweet and sour chicken. She sipped her gas station wine while Audrey waited on the juicy details. "Well, who is he?"

Sandra reminded Audrey of the well-dressed neighbor that lives across the street. Audrey gasped, "The hot guy who drives the bad boy car?"

"Yeah."

"Wait until his wife leaves the house then go over there and ask him out."

"He's not married and who does that?"

Audrey raised her hand. "Hey, you only live once."

"It would seem so … awkward."

"Why?"

Sandra shrugged her shoulders. "Because he lives right there, literally across the street."

"Well, technically, he lives across town. Jackson lives across the street."

"I'm crazy for even thinking something like this wouldn't blow up in my face."

"It could, but you'd have some hellified memoirs."

Sandra and Audrey toasted to hellified memoirs and finished off the bottle of white wine. They both fell asleep on the small corduroy sectional watching The Golden Girls reruns. Audrey woke up in the middle of the night to get a glass of water. "Sandy, your phone's ringing."

"Who is it?"

"It says, Jax."

Sandra sat up and spoke through her yawn, "What time is it?"

"It's almost 2 in the morning. I'm gonna head on home, hun. I made a couple of commitments that I'm sure I'm gonna break. Don't get up, I'll lock the handle."

Audrey kissed Sandra on the top of her head, and they said their good nights. Sandra cleaned up the kitchen then laid across the couch. Jackson called back. She had not heard from Jackson since he had arrived at the studio yesterday morning. Hearing his voice was going to erase what little progress they had made. Sandra answered anyway. Jackson sounded as if he had been awakened from a deep slumber. Sandra held the phone while he rambled off a few excuses as to why he could not find the time to call his wife. There was a knock at the door. Sandra muted the call and peeked through the peep hole. It was Audrey, she had forgotten her wallet. Audrey asked if she was talking to Mr. Hottie from across the street. Sandra shook her head no, to which Audrey gave her a thumbs down. She whispered, "Hang up and call him. You only live once." Sandra locked the door behind Audrey. The Golden Girls were still on. Sandra let those words sink in. Those old ladies always got their men. Hell, even Sophia got served every once in a while.

"Hello?"

Sandra had forgotten to unmute the call. "I'm here."

Audrey made plenty of sense. She did not mind ruffling a few feathers in the name of happiness even if it meant taking the long roads alone.

"What do you have on?"

"Pajamas, I'm going to sleep."

"You don't want to talk to me? Hang up and call me on video."

"Jackson, you've spent all day giving yourself away. It's two in the morning and I'm supposed to be excited because you're offering me what's left of you?"

"Sandy, I told you, we all went …"

"I'm so over this shit."

Sandra was done wasting her time and her tears. She hung up the phone and turned the television off. She sat in the middle of the couch, Indian style and scrolled through her text messages until she found Jacob's text thread. Sandra snickered at how nervous she was. She texted Jacob four random letters then realized how late it was. "Great, I suck at this."

[Is this supposed to mean something?] Jacob included the smirk emoji.

[My bad, my phone was in my back pocket. Guess I need to put a lock on it.] Sandra included the lock, smile and embarrassed emoji.

[Or you can just text me anytime you want.]

Sandra scooted to the edge of the couch with her mouth open. Help! How do I respond to that? She thought.

[Anytime?]

[Anytime]

[What if I want to call?]

[Then you should call.]

[When should I call?]

[Call now.]

CHAPTER TWELVE

Todd stuck a piece of bubblegum in his mouth to mask the smell of the onions from his World of Burgers, double onion and extra pickles cheeseburger. He let out a loud belch after gulping down the rest of his Dr. Pepper. He started his car as soon as Omar walked out of the precinct. Todd blew the horn twice.

"Hurry up! Walkin' all slow."

Omar got in the car and fastened his seat belt. He barely spoke. Todd looked over at his pitiful partner and smirked. "You still sulking over that girl? It's been like a month, man."

Omar looked out the window and waited for Todd to pull off.

"This ain't about Sandra. It's been a long day. Drive."

"We're back to Sandra, now? I'm your boy, I'm here for you. What happened?"

"Just didn't work out. Will you drive, please?"

Todd finally pulled off and dropped Omar off at his quaint apartment compound. Omar got out of the car and thanked Todd for the lift.

"Hop back in, let's go have a drink."

Omar waved his hand. "Nah, go ahead. I need to clean up my place."

"It's Friday night and you wanna clean? Come on, drinks on me."

"Maybe next time."

"Ok, but next time the drinks are on you."

Todd had one friend and she drank from the toilet. He kept relationships at arm's length to keep from having to pretend that he was something he was not. He teased Omar, but from time to time he would entertain the thought of getting involved with someone that he could be himself around and spend a little money on. Jacob called Todd to let him know that he had just met up with Yandy and they were good to go. Yandy reminded Jacob of himself. He knew the ins and outs of the drops and the pickups; he knew the habits of the customers and what he could and could not get away with. He was from the streets and knew how to connect the dots without instructions, he was an honest liar.

Jackson had been caught keeping portions of the profit from distribution totaling approximately eleven percent per drop; drops were anywhere from one hundred to four hundred thousand dollars. This had been going on for months. Loren Thomas, the human calculator, let Jackson get away with stealing until his plan to cut him off was finalized. The Thomas boys offered Jackson a new position. He would work directly for Dana and Loren Thomas and oversee the whole South West side of town. This included product going in and out of two grocery stores and three furniture stores. A takedown on the three furniture stores was on the brink of execution. The Thomas boys gave Todd the head nod to clean house. They were beyond ready to let that area go; South West business had not been good in months; the poor kept getting poorer. And what better man to take the fall than a liar and a thief? Once they get in rotation, Jacob would not have to push the product anymore and would answer to Todd. Jacob's thoughts were focused on the aftermath. Susan was already nesting, but Jacob was staring at the chess board with a pocketful of strategies and no moves.

"Wanna go have a drink?"

"With you?"

"Yeah, Italian boy, with me."

"You buying?"

Jacob invited Todd to Smitty's. Surprisingly, he had never heard of it. It was crowded and the one television set that hung behind the bar was fuzzy. Orders were going in the kitchen and taking forever to be served. The jukebox that sat in the corner was charming, but it only played half the song before abruptly cutting it off. The atmosphere was sociable, and the beer was cold. No one had complaints except Todd.

Jacob knocked on the bar, which was the house signal for a new order. "Two darks."

"Darks?"

"Unless you want lite beer."

"What kind of basement juke joint is this?"

Jacob picked up the two mugs and handed one to Todd. "It's mine. Let's grab these two seats."

"Yours?"

"Yeah, I own it."

Todd looked around. "Beer is good, but this place needs some work, Italiano."

Jacob observed the wobbly table. "It does, but I have big plans for this place."

By the third beer, Todd seemed like less of an asshole. He waved the waitress over and placed an order for a slice of chocolate cake. Jacob raised his brows. "I wouldn't take you for a flour and sugar kind of guy."

"I'm not really, just had a taste for something sweet."

Jacob pulled his chair up to the table and leaned in. "I hate to bring business to the party, but what's going to happen when Jackson realizes his load is weak?"

"He'll reach out to Loren and Loren will take it from there."

"Boom, just like that?"

"Yeah, but I need everything to look normal on the outside. Keep doing whatever you're doing on his end."

"So, I still work for Jackson?"

"Just think of it like this, you're working your new job and still getting paid from your old job."

Todd finished his beer then pushed the mug aside to make room for his cake. "Hey, what's up with Susan?"

"Susan?"

"Yeah, what's her story?"

"You're interested in Susan?"

"Not interested, just inquiring."

"That's the same thing."

Jacob assumed Tod was not familiar with Susan's work history. Susan is visibly attractive; long legs, small waist, long bouncy red hair and green eyes. But Jacob knew where her mouth had been.

"Ok, I'm a little curious. She got a man?"

"No, not that I know of."

Todd leaned in to speak but was interrupted by the chipper waitress. *Chocolate cake for the handsome gentleman. Anything else, love?* Todd winked and shook his head, no.

"So, you hittin' that?"

"I'd rather stab myself in the eye with broken glass."

"So, Jackson got ya'll playing house and ya'll ain't *playing house?*"

"We bump heads more than anything."

"I ain't never dated a white girl, but she's sexy."

Lance the bartender and host came over to Jacob and Todd's table. A gesture that was suggested by Smitty to make sure the guests felt accommodated. He asked if there was anything they needed and if they were having a good time. Jacob took the opportunity to change the subject. He asked Lance if Smitty was in the back, he wanted to introduce Todd. Smitty had agreed to have his office cleaned out by this weekend. Jacob assured him there was no rush. Lance mentioned that he left the keys to his office but had not been in today. "You don't think she's sexy?" Todd inquired.

"I think you've had enough to drink." Jacob put a one-hundred-dollar bill on the table and unenthusiastically answered Todd, "Sure, she's ... you know, attractive. Shoot your shot."

"I'm feeling froggy, I just might."

Jacob chuckled. "Make sure you wear your bullet proof vest... she's like a boomerang."

Jacob sat in his car and scrolled through his contact list. He did not have a number for Smitty other than the bar's contact number. Jacob went back inside and gave Lance his cell phone number. He instructed Lance to have Smitty call him if he came by and to keep the number for himself. Jacob looked around his bar and envisioned all the changes that he wanted to make. The chipper waitress walked by carrying empty beer mugs and dishes.

"Back so soon?" She flashed her pretty smile. "Let me know if I can get you anything."

Jacob touched her back lightly and returned the smile. "I'm good, thanks."

Todd dropped his keys on the kitchen counter and finally flipped through mail that had not been touched all week. Bills, bills and potential bills. *Yes! World of Burgers coupons!* He opened the back door for Sophie who greeted him with her cheeseburger chew toy in her mouth. Todd was not the courting type and he did not care for the cutesy talk and lingering on the phone with nothing to say for hours. But he was tired of being lonely and detached, which he graciously accredited to life and his ex-fiancé. He opened a card from his grandmother. It had a picture of a bear holding balloons that spelled out, happy birthday on the outside and a five dollar check on the inside. Todd played a voicemail message from his mother. *Hello son, today is the day I rejoice in the Lord, for he has given me a beautiful baby boy. I want you to know that life is for the living, so live your best life. Happy birthday, enjoy the chocolate cake, love mom.* The message was three years old, but the pain from losing her was fresh. Sophie scratched at the back door, ready to come inside.

"Hey boopsie boo! All done?"

Sophie wagging her tail was confirmation of her contentment. She ditched Todd for her chew toy and comfy bed. Todd channel surfed until his buzz began to wear off. He was in a tug of war between doing something he may regret and doing something that may enlighten him. Susan won the coin toss.

"Yes, officer?"

"What's up?"

"You tell me, you dialed my number."

"Just calling to see if you had plans next weekend."

"Plans? Oh, God is this a drunk call?"

"I ain't drunk."

"But you've been drinking courage, I see. What are your intentions, officer?"

"I just wanna hang out. What's wrong with that?"

"You and I are what's wrong with that. "

"Forget it, you're making this shit too hard."

"That's a shame."

"What's a shame?"

"You seemed so much tougher than this. Alcohol softens you, call me when you're sober."

"I knew this was gonna be a bad idea. If you don't wanna go out just say you don't wanna go out."

"I have plans next weekend." Susan could be heard smiling over the phone, "But I'm free tomorrow."

***

Jacob received a text message from Lance telling him to stop by Smitty's as soon as possible. Jacob wiped the shaving cream from his face with his bath towel and threw on a pair of dirty jeans. It had rained all night and the morning air was cold. Jacob pulled into the handicapped parking space next to Smitty's car and rushed inside. The bar was not open for business yet, but Lance often did inventory early on Saturday mornings. Jacob had promised the staff that he would not put them out, in fact he wanted to keep a few of them on board.

"What's with the crowd outside?"

Lance sat a box of cocktail straws on top of the bar.

"When I pulled up, I saw Smitty's car, I figured he came to clean out his office. I called his name when I got inside, but he didn't answer me. So, I went to the back and called his name again and that's when I saw him on the floor."

"What?! Is he ok?"

"I don't know. I don't have a number for his wife, but he kept emergency numbers in his office somewhere, I think."

Jacob rushed to the back of the building. Smitty's old office was turned upside down. There was a cardboard box sitting on the desk where he had begun packing his family photos. There were old newspaper articles that had turned sunset yellow pinned to a cushion board, plasticware and paperclips were scattered in the top drawer and empty cigar boxes were stacked in the corner. Jacob did not see anything with emergency numbers on it. Lance stood in the doorway and told Jacob to let him know if there was anything he could help with. He tossed the office keys to Jacob.

"Where'd they take him?"

"Missionary Central Hospital."

Jacob was nervous, he did not know what to expect. Smitty was like that favorite uncle who gave you your first sip of beer then told you not to tell your mama. He and Smitty would sit in the bar after hours and talk about everything and nothing over cold beer and leftover food from the day's end.

The hospital parking garage was packed. After the voice inside the metal box gave a lecture on how the parking garage operated Jacob choose a level based on parking availability. Thankfully, there was room on the first level. Jacob walked through the automatic sliding doors at the emergency medical center and asked if Mr. Samuel Stakes had been admitted. Before the lady behind the administration desk could key in Smitty's name, a young lady approached Jacob.

"Jacob? Hi, I'm Brianna, Smitty's daughter."

"Wow, look at you, you're all grown up!"

Brianna held her hand out. Jacob dismissed the handshake and gave Brianna a hug. The scrawny little girl with braces and braids was now a grown woman. Jacob expressed his concern. "Is he ok?"

Brianna began to cry and shook her head no. "He didn't make it."

Jacob walked Brianna to the double doors leading to the corridor and offered his condolences, "I am so sorry. I didn't even know he was sick."

"He didn't want anyone to know that he was battling heart disease. That's why he was so eager to have you take over the bar. I was a little offended when he said, he'd hand-picked someone and it wasn't me. But I couldn't love that bar the way he did or the way you will."

"I'll definitely do my best. We tried to get in contact with your mom, but no one had a number for her."

"My father kept my number in his wallet on a piece of paper that says, call my daughter if something happens to me. He was funny that way."

"Brianna, if you need anything, anything at all please let me know. Take my number and keep me posted on everything."

"I will and thanks."

Wow, Jacob thought. Uncle Smitty is gone. Within a blink of an eye, he was no more. Jacob drove around the city and thought about life, the way death often makes us do. He decided right then that he would take more chances and live out loud on purpose more often. He reached over on the passenger's side of the car and grabbed a business card from the glove compartment.

"Brennen Realty, how can I help?"

"Hey, I spoke with Gabriel the other day about a house on Canston Circle. Is he available?"

"He just got in a few minutes ago, hang on and I'll connect you to his office line."

"Thanks."

CHAPTER THIRTEEN

Men in white caps with splashes of slate blue and cranberry paint smeared across the front of their overalls moved furniture from the open space before the kitchen into the living area. The chocolate gentleman who wore his locs in a bun eyeballed Sandra as she signed the merchant's copy receipt for the pizza delivery. The painters were supposed to be done yesterday afternoon, but they painted the living and dining areas the wrong color and failed to paint the accent wall. Sandra was ready to cancel her check and go with another black owned company. The owner was a young man who had just earned his bachelor's degree in business management and decided to start his own painting company. The painters apologized profusely; the young entrepreneur made Sandra whole by offering to paint an additional room free of charge. Locs pretended to be preoccupied with the lid of a can of paint when Sandra walked by. He nudged his partner and nodded towards Sandra. The two painters marveled as if to say, *if they could, they would.*

"Mrs. Perry, we ..."

"Sandra."

"Mrs. Sandra, we're done. Come take a look and let us know if everything is the way you want it."

Sandra had finally gotten rid of her corduroy sectional that used to be the center piece of her studio apartment way back when and welcomed a new Dove Gray leather sofa and chair with a matching ottoman. The colors were stunning, and the furniture flattered the space. "I noticed you have some artwork over there. I have some adhesive hooks in the truck, I can hang them for you."

"Everything looks beautiful, you guys have outdone yourselves. And if it's not too much trouble, I wouldn't mind your help hanging the paintings."

Sandra tried to tip locs for his added assistance, but he would not allow it. He handed Sandra a mini portfolio of her living space in different colors; a keepsake for all customers to keep them in mind the next time they decide to freshen their sanctuaries. Sandra locked the door behind the painters. She unrolled her silken shag silver rug and positioned it in front of the sofa. She opened the pizza box and threw her hands up. They delivered the wrong pizza. Sandra did not bother complaining, Audrey was stopping by later to pick up some things that she had claimed from Sandra's storage.

A 216-number popped up on Sandra's cell phone. It was not stored in her contacts, but she assumed it was someone from home and answered regardless.

"Hello?"

"This is my new cell phone number. Your cousin told me I needed to update, so I have a new phone too."

"Aunt Tootie!"

"Hey pumpernickel, how's everything?"

"Good, everything is fine. Why did you need a new number?"

"Well, I didn't, but that sinner didn't tell me that. And those heathens at the cell phone company didn't even ask me why I wanted it changed, but they sho' charged me."

"What phone did you get?"

"Chile, I don't know an iRobot or something."

They shared a warm laugh and talked about Annie Pearl's home makeover then gossiped about family business. "I got something for you."

"For me? What is it?"

"It's either a birthday gift or a housewarming gift."

"Auntie my birthday was five months ago, you gave me a …what did mama tell you?"

"Tell me why I have a housewarming gift for my married niece."

"He cheated auntie and I moved out. I considered leaving him a year ago, but I just needed something more tangible than my suspicions."

"Have you talked to him?"

"He's been in Chicago for the past two weeks; I'm supposed to go over there tomorrow."

"Uh huh, give me something I can take back to your mama."

"He's agreed to go to counseling."

"Now give me something that's between pumpernickel and Aunt Tootie."

Sandra sighed, "I've been having … conversations."

"Is that code talk for you know what?"

Sandra giggled. Aunt Tootie still used code talk for s-e-x.

"He's so different from what I'm used to. We can fill up a whole day talking about nothing. He sends me good morning messages and ..."

"Mmm hmm. Just remember you still wear someone else's ring and until you don't anymore ... no conversations."

***

Sandra did not feel at home anymore. She ran her fingers across the clothes she had left in her closet. She nosily walked around to Jackson's side of the closet and slid the doors open. There were new garment bags and a stack of shoe boxes, which meant he had gone shopping and easily spent a few thousand dollars on a whim. There is a sitting area between the two sets of sliding doors separating his and her closets, Sandra sat on the double chaise lounge and reasoned with herself to let her guards down a little. She stood in the bedroom doorway and smiled at her rocking chair. It was the only thing that made her feel welcomed. She sat down and ran her hands across the arms of the chair, a force of habit, then rocked.

Jackson wanted to go out to eat at Chef Amandi's, but Sandra did not feel up to embracing the fake smiles and the romanticized lifestyle. Jackson's show was back on the air, so she would get the short end of his attention stick.

"Maybe we can cook together."

Cooking made Jackson tolerable. He drove thirty minutes to a fresh food market and purchased asparagus, sweet potatoes, lamb chops and gourmet carrot cupcakes for dessert.

Jackson made the best Rosemary glaze, he seared the lambchops then finished them in the oven. Sandra baked the sweet potatoes and tried a Parmesan and garlic recipe that she saw on a cooking show for the asparagus. The kitchen smelled like dinner time at Chef Amandi's house. The conversation was fluid, they even reminisced over a few fond memories. Jackson was genial, and Sandra dropped her guards. Dinner was delicious and filling, leaving no room for dessert. Jackson cleared the table and put the dishes in the dishwasher. Jackson's primary phone buzzed, he ignored it. No one associated with business or bullshit had the number. They sat on the couch and watched The Color Purple; Jackson had never seen it. By the time Celie was fixing to shave Mister, Jackson's head was in Sandra's lap. She tried to move without waking him, but he slowly opened his eyes then smiled at her. He was so handsome. Sandra smiled back, burying her fingertips in his dark curly hair. Jackson sat up and inquired about what was going on in the movie.

"I'm not telling you."

"Come on, please. This movie is like two days long."

"It is not, watch it."

Jackson kissed Sandra on the cheek. "Please."

"I don't wanna ruin it for you."

Jackson kissed Sandra on the cheek, once more. "Pretty please."

Sandra looked at Jackson and shook her head no. He touched Sandra lightly on her cheek then leaned in to kiss her lips. They looked one another in the eyes and embraced a morsel of what used to be.

Sandra responded softly, almost in a whisper, "Just watch it."

Jackson scooted closer and kissed Sandra intensely, he bit her bottom lip playfully then lifted her on top of him. He played in her hair and smelled it. She still uses pomegranate and vanilla shampoo, he thought. He unbuttoned her shirt and kissed her defined collar bone. Sandra sat up, exposing a full view of her blue laced bra. "I should get going."

Jackson stood up and grabbed Sandra by the hand. "I don't want you to, but if you have to…"

"It might be best if …"

Jackson intercepted Sandra's defense with a kiss, he unbuttoned the last three buttons and slid her top off of her shoulders. She pulled Jackson's Karate Kid T-shirt over his head and revealed the results of his early morning workouts. She unbuttoned his jeans; reunited with an old acquaintance. Jackson's phone buzzed. He left it unattended in the front pocket of his Saint Laurent distressed jeans that were now draped around his ankles. He tried to obliterate every touch that another man had left on his wife's body. They made love on the couch, fervently. Sandra arched her back when Jackson went deep, and Jackson took nothing for granted. The color purple was still playing on the television.

Sofia, Sofia. That sure is a pretty name. How can a pair of pants that fits Sofia, fit me?

You're just going to have to try them on.

Sandra had fallen asleep on her stomach; Jackson used her backside as a pillow. His phone buzzed. Jackson sat up sluggishly, watching Sandra all the while, ensuring he did not disturb her. He had six new messages. His heart was snatched from his chest when he viewed the pictures that were waiting for him in a vicious text message. The first picture was of Jackson's cell phone lying on the hotel desk next to two empty beer bottles showing an incoming call from Sandra. The second picture was of him sleeping naked, lying on his stomach, an opened condom wrapper could be seen on the nightstand next to the remote control. The third picture showed Jackson on his back with his eyes closed while his lover engaged him in oral sex. Jackson tip toed down the hall to the guest bathroom and locked the door. He was infuriated. The last message suggested Jackson return the missed phone calls or wifey would have her very own copies of these pictures and there were plenty to share. Jackson was shaking, it took him thirty minutes to finally calm himself down. When he returned to the living room, Sandra was sitting on the couch half dressed.

"Is everything ok?"

Jackson grabbed his boxers and put them on. "Lamb chops got me. I was hoping I didn't wake you."

"It's fine, I didn't expect to fall asleep."

"Did you want to go get in the bed?"

Sandra slid her jeans on and looked for her top. "No, I have an appointment tomorrow morning. I've probably overstayed my welcome."

"Your shirt is behind the pillow."

"Thanks. Jackson, I know we're in this ugly place, but …"

"Sandy, you don't have to say anything. I have a lot of work to do to regain your trust. I'm aware of that. You still staying with Aubrey?"

"Audrey. And yes."

"I got you something. Well, I ordered something that I thought you would like."

Sandra buttoned her top. "What is it?"

"You always talked about how nice those red doors are across the street and how this house would look nice with them. So, I ordered the red door."

"You ordered the same door?"

"Well, ours will have that door grill that we both like."

"I don't know what to say. I can't wait to see it."

Jackson left the front door open until he heard Sandra's ignition. He closed the door when she had finally pulled off. Jackson had received another message. He grabbed the cordless phone out of the hall closet; a safety net in the event of an outage. He plugged the cord into the phone jack behind the Barcelona chair in the den. The receiver needed to be charged. Jackson yanked the cord out of the wall and found the old school desk phone.

"You have a lot of fucking nerve to think you own me because you have a few pictures."

"Well, hello darling. I've missed you, too. And fifty is hardly a few."

154

"What the fuck do you want?"

"You."

"I'm not an option."

"You know they say; it's a small world and we're only separated by six degrees. So, you can imagine my surprise when I caught up with an old friend who said, he had just been dumped by his lover. Well, let's drink to the blues honey, I said. We dined, we drank, we talked …"

"Emmanuelle, keep your soliloquies to a mi …."

"Hush child, mommy is talking. He poured his little broken heart out to me and I recognized myself in his story. Oliver, I said, my man has cheated on you. Oliver, you remember him. You fucked him senseless before you crushed him into pieces."

Jackson felt heat thread itself around the strands of his hair and through his pores on down to the tips of his toenails. He wanted to strangle Emmanuelle until his flamboyant life drained from his petite body. Emmanuelle had become disenchanted with Jackson.

"I think you should move on and leave me the fuck alone."

"You know I absolutely love the photo of Sandra under the covers, showing just enough breast to be tasteful yet naughty. She is undeniably beautiful!"

"She has nothing to do with this. If you do anything to …"

"To what? To hurt her? Beloved, no one can hurt her the way you have. Me and Oliver, both agreed."

"You and Oliver should go kill yourselves."

"And why didn't you tell me, wifey is half Cuban? Those eyes, beloved!" Emmanuelle screamed with excitement. "The picture of her wrapped in the Cuban flag, flawless honey!"

"I need you to listen and listen good. Sandra is off the table. I will fucking kill you then send pictures to your mommy of her lifeless little girl."

"My mother died from a broken heart years ago and my father hasn't spoken to me in decades. Send the pictures to him, it would probably be the best Christmas gift I could ever give him."

"What's his number?"

"My sweet Jackson." Emmanuelle sighed, "I deserve to be treated with respect whether you want me or not. You and papa have the hardest time understanding two-way streets. Wifey is off the table, but you have till the first of the month to tell her about me and I'll know if you do because she won't be surprised when I call her. Don't let your time run out, daddy."

Emmanuelle hung up the phone leaving Jackson crippled by self-inflicted wounds. Jackson growled, tormented. He punched the wall leaving the stud behind the drywall visible. The second punch; blood sprayed the wall as the flesh separated from the tissue around his knuckles and opened up.

Jackson woke up on the den floor still in his boxers. He did not remember flipping the furniture over or breaking the legs on the chair. His knuckles were the size of super bowl rings. He wished it was all a bad dream, but reality met him on the other side of yesterday and she had morning breath.

Sandra sent Jackson a good morning message thanking him for dinner and for everything.

Jackson cleaned the dried blood from his hand and wrapped it the way his trainers did before a kickboxing match. Jackson was due back in Chicago next week. He had no plans on seeing Emmanuelle and he had no plans on telling Sandra about his outlandish affair. Jackson replied to Sandra's message. He told her that she had made his night and that he missed her. He reminded her that he would be leaving town Thursday and would be back in a couple weeks.

Jackson sat his phone down on the table and made a cup of coffee. *Damn, no creamer.* He poured the black liquid out of his championship title holder mug into the sink. He smiled at the box of green teabags that sat abandoned in the cabinet next to a box of unopened minute rice. Jackson made a cup of hot green tea like he had done so many times before for Sandra.

Jackson checked his phone. He had received another text message.

[Tick tock.]

CHAPTER FOURTEEN

"Welcome home!"

Jacob looked from the high ceilings with missing recessed light bulbs to the dirty walls to the badly scratched wood floors. "So, good news! The seller had most of the damages repaired when I told her we had a serious buyer. The only thing you'd need to do is …"

"Paint, buy appliances, buy toilets, light fixtures, kitchen cabinets and buy doors for every room. Who takes off with all the toilets and light fixtures?"

"You'd think that Oliver and Barbara Rose used to live here, but it is a beautiful home. Oh! I almost forgot! She also agreed to leave the theater seating."

Jacob hiked up the winding staircase avoiding the wobbly banister. Sad faces were drawn in black paint on the hall walls. Obscenities in red paint were displayed on the bedroom walls and there were piles of trash in the corners of what looked to be a theater room. The theater seats were not physically damaged but were covered in something sticky like dried spills from fruit punch. Gabriel handed Jacob a half full glass of optimism. "You're getting a six hundred-thousand-dollar house for half that price and two free rows of theater seating. Call up a cleaning crew and let them handle the hard part."

Jacob sighed with contentment, he had his very own Bar and grill and now he was going to be a homeowner. The gentlemen walked down the stairs to inspect the back of the house. A faint knock at the front door caught Gabriel's attention.

"Go ahead, I'll get that. I let the owner know that we would be here today, maybe she forgot." Gabriel answered the front door enthusiastically, "Hello there! May I help you?"

"Sure, I'm supposed to meet Jacob here."

"Oh! Ok, right this way! We were just about to go out back." Gabriel held his hand out. "Hi. I'm Gabriel."

"Sandra."

When Jacob saw Sandra walk through the front door, he imagined just for a moment that she was coming home to him. Gabriel excused himself to take an important phone call. Jacob offered Sandra a tour, she accepted. They covered all six thousand square feet, decorating and coloring each room. Sandra walked into the mother-in-law suite and stumbled over an uneven plank of wood. Jacob grabbed her by the waist to keep her from falling. They briefly held eye contact.

"You ok?"

Sandra smiled nervously. "Yeah."

"You know, I didn't think you were coming."

"Why not?"

"I don't know. You seem more comfortable with texting."

"Doesn't everybody?"

"Nope, not everybody."

"What are you more comfortable with?"

"Hearing your voice and seeing your face."

Jacob hooked his pointer finger around Sandra's pointer finger. They stood in awkward silence looking at everything, but one another. Gabriel called for Jacob to come and take a look at the two riding mowers that were left in the garage, they were practically brand new. Sandra watched Jacob walk from behind. He was slightly bowlegged. She wanted to pinch him on the butt. He smelled so good and It was obvious that he worked out. The muscles in his arms flexed when he talked with his hands. No conversations, she thought.

Smitty's had been opened for thirty minutes and it was already packed. Jacob hoped the momentum would endure once the new changes were implemented. Jacob introduced Sandra to Lance.

"Lance this is Sandra. Sandra this is the best bartender on the planet, aside from myself."

Lance smiled and nodded. He was showing a customer some work he had done on his father's farmhouse. Jacob glanced at the pictures. "You did that?" Proud of himself, Lance took credit for sanding and staining his father's hardwood floors. "I need to talk to you later." Jacob grabbed a two-seater by the restrooms. "I'll be right back." Sandra looked around the bar, noticing the black art on the walls and the soulful atmosphere. She had concluded that Jacob was a black man dipped in white chocolate. Jacob returned to the table shortly after. "Sorry, about that."

"So, this is your heartbeat."

"Yeah, this is my baby."

"Nice." Sandra glanced at the television set behind the bar.

"There's a few updates coming soon."

A waitress wearing a pin with Smitty's face on it walked up to the table. *Hi, family! May I take your drink orders?* Sandra noticed Lance was wearing the same pin. She ordered Ginger Ale and Jacob ordered iced tea with lemon.

"May I see a menu, please?"

Jacob interrupted, "That'll be all Carlee, thanks."

Sandra's facial expression asked Jacob to explain what had just happened. "I have a little surprise for you."

As Sandra inquired about the surprise, Carlee was back by their sides. She sat Jacob's iced tea in front of him along with a small dish of freshly cut lemons and a frosted drinking glass in front of Sandra then poured half a glass of Ginger Ale. *I'm going to sit this over here so that it's not in your way.* Lance was not far behind. He served two full plates of hot food and thanked Sandra for dining with them today. Sandra's eyes lit up. She told Jacob that Annie Pearl made the best fried green tomatoes and she could not find anyone who came close since she planted her feet in Brigance. Jacob ordered baked chicken thighs, fried green tomatoes and macaroni and cheese for them both. "I hope you like it."

After one bite, Sandra was in love. "Whose grandmother is in the back cooking? My compliments to the chef!"

Jacob was impressed with how down to earth Sandra is. They both liked watching old school cartoons and hated surfing the internet from a cell phone. They both liked eating dry fruity cereal with a glass of milk and they hated to hear people chew their food. Jacob watched Sandra eat the skin from her chicken first then the meat. "This isn't weird for you is it?"

Jacob sipped his tea to wash down the macaroni and cheese. "What?"

"Me, you, fried green tomatoes."

"You mean because you're someone's wife?"

"You can't even say his name."

"Sandra…"

"Yes?"

"I may regret saying this, but it's more evident than I realized."

"What is?"

"I really like you. I really like you a lot. I know you're … with him, but …"

"I really like you too, Jacob."

"I like you in a way that, I wouldn't mind having dinner with you more often or maybe catching a movie sometime and kissing you goodnight."

"I'd like that."

"Seriously?" Jacob could not contain his smile.

"Yes."

"Aren't we foolish for opening this can of worms?"

"Yes."

"I don't care."

"Me either."

***

Jacob walked into the house singing loudly and off key. *Rockets, moon shots spend it on the have nots. Money, we make it. Fore we see it, you take it. Make me wanna holla the way they do my life.*

Susan was sitting on the couch in wide legged dress pants and a blouse watching a movie.

"Shhh!"

"This ain't livin' this ain't livin. No, no baby, this ain't livin'. What are you watching?"

"The Curious Case of Benjamin Button. It's almost over."

"Benjamin dies in the end."

Susan threw two of the four oversized throw pillows at Jacob. "I hate you!"

"Daisy dies too."

"Fucktard!"

"Congratulate me."

"Congrats."

"You don't want to know why you're congratulating me?"

Susan turned around and looked Jacob from head to toe. "Oh my God! You got some pussy!" Susan stood to her feet and applauded.

"Why is everything about …"

"Oh, shut up. What's the good news?"

"Why are you dressed up? Was there a hooker awards ceremony downtown today?"

"No, curious case of the missing dick print, I went to the funeral."

"Smitty's?"

"Yeah, why weren't you there?"

"I was, I couldn't stay for the whole thing."

"Ok, ok. Why are congratulations in order?"

"I got the house!"

"About fucking time! Congrats, Jackie, I'm proud of you or something like that."

Jacob sat on the couch and conversed with Susan for hours. They compared notes on Jackson, the Thomas boys and Todd. Susan covered her face with a pillow at the mention of Todd's name. Jacob told Susan that Todd had inquired about her but did not think he would actually give her a call.

Susan agreed to go on a date with Todd. He picked her up in his Porsche 911 and took her out to Yureka's. Susan was used to paying for dates with her nature card, but Todd picked up the tab and went to bed alone that night. Jacob was impressed, Todd seemed like the kind of guy who bopped his women over the head and carried them over his shoulder.

Susan mentioned that they had gone on a second date; a lunch date at World of Burgers. She was not looking for anything serious, it just felt nice to be treated like a lady. Jacob replied to a message from Sandra. That was the third time Jacob's phone took his attention away from Susan. Susan snatched Jacob's phone from his hand.

"Give it back!"

Susan held the phone in the air playing keep away from Jacob. She ran into the kitchen and looked at Jacob's message. Susan covered her mouth and gasped. Jacob reached for his phone as Susan switched hands. "Can I get my phone back, please?"

"Ooh! Is this *Jackson's* Sandra?!"

Jacob grabbed his phone. "It might be."

Susan read the text out loud, "*Today was nice and the food was delicious. Looking forward to next time.* Be careful, Jackson is a lot crazy.*"

"It was just a late lunch."

"You mean the last meal of the day? I believe it's called dinner with Jackson's wife."

"He doesn't have a clue about what to do with a woman like that."

"But you do?"

"Yes, I do. Hey, let me ask you something…"

"No, me and Todd haven't …"

"Not that. I'm curious, what does Jackson have on you?"

Susan walked out of the kitchen to answer her cell phone. She returned soon after. "What does he have on you?"

"I asked you first."

"I asked you second."

Jacob had earned Susan's trust and she had earned his. They had become the perfect dysfunctional network. Jacob took a beer from the cooler and poured it in a chilled mug. He thought about the countless hours he had spent wishing he could undo that night.

"Robbery."

Susan slid on her blazer. "Do I look ok?"

Jacob gave a thumb's up. She made sure her wallet and identification were in her handbag then unlocked the door to the garage. "Murder. Don't wait up."

CHAPTER FIFTEEN

Sandra sat her phone on the small kitchen island while she put groceries away. She used her knuckle to put Jacob on speakerphone. She had bought all of Ariel's favorites, Cheetos, Blueberries, thinly sliced turkey from the deli and crab cakes. Sandra turned the volume up on her phone and stepped out of her Prada high heels, a guilt gift from Jackson. She walked upstairs to her bedroom and stripped to her panties and bra. Sandra yelled over the railing that served as a wall and a balcony, allowing her to view the open space below.

"Hang on a second!"

"Huh?"

"I said, hang on a second!" Sandra rushed down the stairs and took Jacob off speakerphone. "Sorry, about that."

"I'm going to miss you this week."

"I'm going to miss you too."

"No, you're not. You're going to have your best friend all to yourself, I don't stand a chance."

"That's not true. I think about you more than I should."

"Good."

"How long are you going to be at the bar?"

"It's going to be a late night tonight, inventory." Jacob had inventory with Todd. Yandy had made his first round of drops, now it was time to play the numbers game. "Maybe we can meet for breakfast in the morning."

"I have a hair appointment."

"Before I forget, one of my customers gave me two tickets to see Fantasia, he can't use them. You and Ariel should go."

"Are you serious?"

"As serious as two fifth row seats."

"I *love* Fantasia! I owe you a kiss for this, thank you so much!"

Jacob muted his phone then knocked on Sandra's door. "You expecting someone?"

"No, not at all." Sandra looked through the peephole and smirked. "I should probably put some clothes on."

"I'll be a good boy, I promise."

Sandra took Jackson's shirt out of the dryer and wore it as a robe. It had gotten mixed up in her things when she packed her bags and left. Sandra stood behind the door until Jacob was inside. He took in the atmosphere and nodded with approval. "This is really nice. I love these colors together." Sandra could not stop staring at how Jacob's biceps stretched the fabric on his short-sleeved shirt, making it look like he would have to cut the shirt to get out of it. His five o'clock shadow barely covered his dimples. He opened the to go box that he was hiding behind his back; fried green tomatoes, southern fried porkchops and garlic mashed potatoes.

"Thank you, it smells like sin! I thought tonight was a late night."

"I'm on a break."

Sandra took the food to the kitchen and sat it on the stove. Jacob watched her backside massage the fabric of Jackson's shirt as she walked away from him. Sandra folded her arms across her chest, realizing her provisional robe was unbuttoned. Jacob stuck the Fantasia tickets inside her front pocket then took Sandra by the hand and unfolded her arms. He opened her robe and laid his eyes on every curve. Sandra smelled the cologne on his neck as he outlined her ear with his nose. "I can't stay long."

"I understand duty calls."

Jacob rested his cheek against Sandra's cheek and spoke directly into her ear, "Don't you owe me something?"

Sandra ran her fingertips up Jacob's tattooed arms until her hands were clasped behind his head. Jacob turned his Cleveland Indians baseball cap to the back and kissed Sandra's lips for the first time.

***

Jacob opened the passenger door of the blue sedan and got in. It smelled like onions and old French fries. Loren wanted to lay eyes on Jacob since he would be overseeing four times his normal product weight and hundreds of thousands of his dollars. Jacob was nervous, the Thomas boys were confederates. They were people you heard about, but never met. They drove two hours to Burrows City, a small city outside of Fort Wayne. A slight right off of highway exit 213 A eventually connected to a narrow paved trail with a forest of trees on either side guarded by a wooden fence. Tall, bright light posts met the travelers at the end of the trail. Todd parked in the cul-de-sac in front of what resembled a library.

"Here we are."

"This is where they live?"

"Not they, Loren."

Jacob unfastened his seatbelt and looked to Todd for a little reassurance. Todd reached under his seat and handed Jacob a brown leather toiletry bag. "The job comes with paid training." Jacob unzipped the bag. There had to be over thirty thousand dollars inside.

"I'm supposed to chop this right?"

"No, Italiano. That's all yours."

Jacob thought to himself, if he had just made thirty thousand dollars for delegating workloads without having to pay Yandy, how much does Todd make and how much did Jackson stiff him for? Jacob would get paid again once Loren made sure the numbers were big and round. "Oh, I need you to park your old school Jag. It's too flashy. I need you to blend in, get something practical."

"Like a sedan?" Jacob chuckled.

"Unless a sedan is not suitable enough to play footsies in with your boss's wife."

"Did your girlfriend tell you that?"

"Watch it Italiano."

A stout man wearing expensive mom jeans and a Heathcliff Huxtable sweater tapped on the car window. He motioned for Todd and Jacob to get out of the car.

"What are you two doing, waiting on the red carpet? You got my alarm system going bananas, it didn't recognize your license plate."

"My Porsche is being serviced, should be ready in the morning. Loren this is Jacob. Jacob, Loren."

Jacob opted for the handshake, Loren patted Jacob on the back and motioned for his street jockeys to follow him inside.

The foyer did not seem like it would ever end. It looked like something out of a gangster's movie; stained glass windows with tall columns and mosaic flooring. Jacob was waiting to see men wearing dark shades in black suits with big guns strapped to their backs standing guard. Loren gave Jacob a tour of his eight bedroom eleven bathroom mansion. There was an outdoor and indoor pool, the laundry room simulated a laundromat and there was a room down the hall from the main kitchen that was decorated like a small diner equipped with a full kitchen and bar seating. Loren received a call. He instructed Todd to take Jacob up to the conference room and he would meet them there shortly. Jacob took a seat at the glass table. Loren favored glass so that he could see the hands of his visitors at all times.

Todd pulled a big book from the bookcase. It looked like an encyclopedia, the spine was worn, and the pages were antique white. He flipped through it until he reached his preferred page then sat it down in front of Loren's seat. A little girl peeked into the conference room, startling both Jacob and Todd.

"Your grandpa is gonna get you."

She giggled and shook her head, no. She stared at Jacob. Todd told her to go and find her favorite doll and show it to him. She shook her head; no. Jacob pulled a lollipop from his pocket that he had taken from the candy dish at the bar and waved it at her. She shook her head, yes. Loren walked into the room and apologized for taking up their time. He held his arms out and his granddaughter ran into them.

"This is Polly. Polly, you know Todd and that guy over there, that's Jacob."

Polly was hugged and kissed then ushered out of the room and asked to join Helena downstairs in the family room. "Stingy kids I have. Five kids…" Loren held up one finger. "only one grandchild." Loren and Todd did administrative work while Jacob observed. Loren sat back in his chair and smiled when the numbers matched, he was not a fan of remainders. "Jacob, your sir name is?"

"It's Rossi."

"Ah, Italiano. I fell in love with a Spanish woman once, she grew me up and still, she dumps me. She says, Loren you ain't poop, but she didn't say poop. She goes, Italian men are too cocky. I say, well it must be hereditary, my mama says my pops ain't poop either."

They shared an icebreaking laugh that had perfect timing. Jacob finally exhaled. "I'm sure it's her loss."

"What loss? She's down in the family room with our only grandchild. Oh, I failed to mention, she came back."

Loren removed four books from the shelf exposing two deadbolts and a keypad. He slid the bookcase to the left, revealing a room with wall to wall built in safes. He opened one of the smaller safes and removed five stacks and sat them on the table in front of Todd. "Gentlemen, I think we're done here."

Jackson closed the door to his dressing room to give himself more privacy. He had just arrived at the studio with just under twenty minutes to spare before someone put a script in his hand. He straightened his tie in the full length mirror before returning his attention to the phone call.

"Yeah."

"I got a call from Frank, he asked me if we had a hand in rotation. J R and Duke are waiting on product. What's the hold up?"

"I've been busy with a real job."

"Jackson, we're talking about the sum of eight hundred thousand tax free dollars here."

"You broke or something? I can give you a loan. But it won't be tax free."

Jacob was over Jackson. He just wanted one round outside the ring with *Jackson Powerhouse Perry.* A text message from Sandra popped on Jacob's screen. It was poetic justice. Jacob smirked, when he thought to himself, that's why I had my tongue down your wife's throat. "Look, there's a production crew waiting on me. Tell Frank, you haven't heard anything."

"You know as well as I do, it doesn't work like that. Who's Frank's contact?"

"What does his contact have to do with this?"

"If his rotation is slow. We may be able to steal business from him."

"You know what? Let me see what you workin' with. If you can get Diablo to run weight our way, I'll put you over distro."

Frank worked for Diablo. Diablo is an African drug Lord that has connections from the mother land to the mainland. Loren wanted him in his back pocket. Frank was running his own weight, including him in rotation was not worth the crumbs on the table. A haircut acquainted Diablo with Jackson, an investment made them associates.

"Text me his number."

"I sent you his contact card. I need to hear from you by the end of the week. It's gonna take you that long to get him to pick up the phone. If he asks how you got his number, you better tell him you stole it."

Jackson hung up the phone. Jacob looked across the table at Todd who was nursing a bottle of beer and grinned. Todd unzipped his leather messenger bag and slid two stacks across the table to Jacob, totaling one hundred thousand dollars.

"I'm impressed Italiano. If we get Diablo, there will be a very nice bonus with your name on it. I need Diablo's information before I pull out of the driveway." Todd finished his beer then got up from the kitchen table. "Be sure to pay Yandy nicely. Loyalty ain't cheap."

Jacob stripped to his socks. He lit his cigar and dragged it, cracked the bathroom window then sat on the toilet. The number two posed inside of a circle at the top of Jacob's phone indicating two unread messages.

[Thank you, everything was really good.]

[Glad you enjoyed it. I almost pulled over and ate it, it was smelling so good.]

[I was referring to the kiss.]

CHAPTER SIXTEEN

They stood embraced in a hug, promising that no amount of space or circumstance would keep them apart this long again. Ariel was considering accepting a transfer to Renfro City. Nacada Technologies was building a new Engineering Firm just thirty five minutes from Brigance. She would be the Senior Manager over the Network Security department. Sandra had already offered her a place to stay for as long as she needed. The lady behind the customer service desk called for the occupants of the next set of seat numbers to board the plane. Ariel assured Sandra that she would call as soon as her plane landed at Hopkins International Airport. Her ticket was scanned then she was instructed to enter through the door leading to the boarding bridge.

Sandra adored the comradery between her and Ariel and how supportive and honest she has always been even if it meant hurting her feelings. *Friend, if you have feelings for Jacob and you've fallen out of love with Jackson, you owe it to the three of you to disconnect your ties with Jackson.*

Sandra knew Jackson was a cheater the first time he confused her with someone he had gone to an outdoor concert with in Springfield. Sandra had never been to Springfield and she had never made love outside. Aside from what Jackson was willing to do the night before their wedding with her best friend, he was good to Sandra and she was in love with him. A year ago, Sandra contacted a divorce attorney and told him, her sob story. He painted an unflattering picture of what a divorce looked like when there were millions of dollars up for grabs. Ariel told Sandra that she would support whatever decision she made, but life was bigger than being the unwelcome mat of Jackson Perry.

Sandra sat in her parked car for thirteen minutes listening to talk radio before finally going into the drug store. There were so many rows packed with something for everything, all kinds of creams for your feet, ointments for your rashes and drops for your eyes. Drug stores carried the best snacks. Sandra walked back to the entrance, grabbed a red basket then put two tin containers of peppermint bark and a bag of jalapeno popcorn inside of it.

Sandra walked up one isle and down another until she found what she was looking for. There were so many options. A lady in a blue and white smock wearing a name tag that read, Angie walked up to Sandra and asked if she needed help with anything. When Sandra was slow to respond, the store associate picked up a couple boxes and began explaining why one was better than the other. Sandra put both brands in her basket and thanked Angie for her help. Sandra waited until she was alone then grabbed two more pregnancy tests.

"God, I hope Ariel is wrong."

＊

Jackson's flight was delayed which denied him the opportunity to get home a day earlier. Although, he had successfully avoided Emmanuelle for the past two weeks of taping, Jackson's thoughts were haunting him.

"How could I have been so fucking careless!"

Emmanuelle knew that Jackson had another phone; he was pleased to learn that there was no password. Jackson always kept it hidden in between clothes in his luggage or locked in the safe when he was with Emmanuelle. One evening, following a pitch meeting, Jackson was surprised with a late dinner in his hotel room. A peace offering to soften the harsh words Emmanuelle spewed because Jackson did not want to title their involvement. Jackson had fallen asleep, like most men do after good food and bounteous sex. Emmanuelle noticed Jackson's phone on the chest of drawers just under the television when an incoming call from Sandra came through. Emmanuelle had contemplated answering the call and introducing himself as the other woman but decided not to ruin the polish on his afterglow. Jackson had only eighteen contacts in his main phone. They were the numbers of those closest to him. Emmanuelle sent a file to himself containing all eighteen numbers including a folder that was renamed 'wifey' containing pictures of Sandra. He deleted the forwarded messages from Jackson's thread then put his phone back in its resting place. Emmanuelle had confessed his love for Jackson as often as possible. Jackson would always elect to acknowledge his presence, but not his feelings. After rambling through Jackson's luggage and suit jacket pockets, Emmanuelle climbed on the bed and took pictures of a sleeping, naked Jackson. He massaged Jackson's chest then sucked his nipples. He turned the flash feature off on his camera then held his phone slightly above his head and took pictures of himself pleasuring Jackson. He gently laid on top of his lover and took a picture of himself kissing Jackson's lips. Emmanuelle held the power to destroy Jackson in the palm of his hand, but revenge is not fast food. It is Chateaubriand.

Jackson left his luggage in the laundry room. Clothes from his last trip were still in the washing machine. He had never been away from Sandra this long; he was convinced that she was not coming back home. When he called her, she responded with a text message. The health of their marriage was questionable and there was no trust. She had broken the code and found a way to live without him. Jackson paced from the kitchen to the butler's pantry thinking about Sandra being with another man. Where were they when they had sex? Where was I? Was he better than me? Did she like it?

The silence was suffocating. Jackson did not realize that he had fallen asleep until curiosity woke him up. He checked his phone out of habit. There were no messages or calls from his estranged wife. He called her immediately, but she did not answer. He called again and left a concerning message for her to call him ASAP. He sent two angry texts following the last call and waited impatiently. No response. He had plans to follow Sandra to see who she was spending time with at night, but she made it hard for him to uncover her tracks. Jackson opened the doors to the den and sighed irritably. The mess was a living witness to the aftermath of his emotional explosion. He dragged the broken furniture through the wide utility doors and down the long driveway to the curb. Jackson stood passively with his arms at his sides, absorbing the structure of the houses and realizing that every door was an introduction to a story, some fairytales, some nightmares. Each house sat on a hill. Sandra loved that about the neighborhood. The windows looked like piercing eyes staring down from the top of the hill in disgrace.

Jackson felt a sense of triumph when he saw messages waiting for him. "Damn, I gotta throw my weight around just to get a response from my own wife." Jackson's smile expeditiously turned into a scowl.

[I know it's late, but we both know you do your best work during tiptoeing hours. I missed my handsome man last week. We have a new item on the menu, and I was unable to dine with you and hear your honest critique.] Another message came through before Jackson could finish the first. *[And remember, just because I've postponed your homework assignment, doesn't mean it isn't due.]*

Jackson considered changing his numbers, but that would only add fuel to the flames. Emmanuelle had a Glock 17; 9 mm and he had threatened to use all seventeen rounds. Although, he had not fired any fatal shots, Emmanuelle knew his warning shots had Jackson's attention, despite his indifference.

[What do you want? A hug? Validation?]

[Darling, I want you to open your closet door and love me out in the open.]

Jackson called Emmanuelle because he wanted him to hear the promising threat in his tone. "You will never have my love. You could save my life; you could save my wife's life and you still wouldn't mean shit to me!"

"I don't believe you. I can feel it in your thrusts, you have feelings for me."

"What talk show quack got you believing that bullshit?"

"You know, I've dated a few and I've loved a few. Hell, I've even turned a few, but none in as much denial as you. Answer me this, how does your dick stay hard when you fuck your wife?"

"You have the pictures, even your dick got hard when you saw her. I'm flattered, but I don't want to be with you. I don't know what else I can do to make you understand that."

"Beloved, it's not me who's failing to understand, but guilt does have a way of pulling your pants down in pubic."

"We can go back and forth until we're blue in the face, but that won't change the fact that I don't love you and I don't want you. If you're going to send her the pictures, send them then go kill yourself!"

Jackson hung up the phone and accepted that he had received all this day had to offer. He marched upstairs and crawled into bed, fully clothed. Jackson did not have anyone to turn to. His father was available to him all day and every day as long as it was to put a little something in his hands. He was too young to remember when a drunk driver snatched the stability from the hands of two unsuspecting children. Jackson and his sister were sent to the North side of Turtle Creek, West Virginia to be raised by their grandmother, who was already raising three of her seven grandchildren.

At the age of twelve, Jackson's older cousin, Dank Jr. molested him and introduced him to prostitutes. Five years ago, Dank Jr. was arrested on child porn possession and human trafficking. When Jackson found out about the arrest, he drove twelve hours with a special delivery for his first cousin, *I hope sucking twelve year old dick was worth it. I hope they rape you every single day until you die then I hope they rape your corpse. You sick son of a bitch!*

Jackson stared at the ceiling for hours. The sun was beginning to shed light on a brand new day. Jackson was not taking no for an answer, he wanted to talk to his wife and beg her to come back home. Sandra was the line in the sand between sanity and putting a gun to his head. Jackson took his clothes off and showered until the hot water turned cold. His eyes were red, he needed a haircut. Jackson got dressed and headed to his barbershop for a shave and edge up. Before leaving the house, he made sure that his attitude and appearance complimented the facade that he had worked so hard to build.

When Jackson arrived at the shop it was crowded just the way he liked it. Jacob was in Marvin's chair getting his hair cut, just like the rest of the bros did every week. Jackson made his rounds and spoke to everyone; kids ran up to him looking for candy and money. He gave all three of them five dollar bills and a bag of cotton candy. Marvin removed all the excess hair from around Jacob's neck and shoulders with his neck duster then placed a mirror in his hand. Jacob decided it was time to have a conversation with his old boss. Dre had finally decided to talk numbers to get the bar from under him. Jackson told Dre that his asking price is way too high. When Dre decided to take Jackson's offer, it was already off the table. Jacob over tipped Marvin like he always did and told Jackson, he would be in touch.

Jackson began composing a text message. Just moments before he pressed the panic button, his phone rang.

"I've been trying to get in touch with you. You act like you can't pick up the damn phone. What's up with that?"

"We need to talk."

CHAPTER SEVENTEEN

Opened containers of White rice, Oxtails, Curried and Jerk chicken were stinking up the kitchen. Empty bottles of Pepsi and Gatorade were staged on the new counter tops. Painters were coloring the upstairs walls and bags of trash were being taken to the dumpster. The light fixtures provided their own charm to their respective spaces. Jacob had chosen an English chestnut stain color for his revived hardwood floors and Lance and his crew created magic. The toilets, vanities and bathroom mirrors would be installed tomorrow along with new doors. The cleaning crew was on their third day of duty; they had cleaned everything from the garage to the theater seating. Jacob grabbed a garbage bag and began throwing away trash and leftover food that he graciously treated the contractors to. Jacob heard high heels cat walking across the floor in the front of the house. He anticipated seeing her face, waiting until her footsteps were closer before he spoke.

"Is that my baby?"

Sandra beamed when she saw Jacob's face and spoke timidly, "Hi."

"Hey gorgeous!"

Jacob helped himself to a kiss and then another. Sandra used her thumb to remove the lipstick that transferred from her lips to his. Jacob took Sandra by the hand and showed her most of the progress.

"Wow, it looks amazing in here! It won't be much longer before everything is done."

"Yeah, hats off to these contractors. They worked their asses off. The painters are still upstairs."

Jacob slid his arms around Sandra's waist. "What's on your mind?"

"Nothing."

"I don't believe you."

Sandra rested her head on Jacob's chest. "Do you believe in love at first sight?"

"I do."

"You believe that you can love someone with all that love means, just by looking at them?"

"Yeah."

"Have you ever fell in love at first sight?"

"Yes."

Sandra looked into Jacob's eyes with tears running down her cheeks, she had nothing to lose. "Jacob, I'm in love with you."

"You ought to be."

Jacob softly kissed Sandra's lips. He wiped her tears and kissed her again. The painters stalled on the staircase to enjoy the tender moment. The lead painter cleared his throat and coughed to get Jacob's attention. "Fellas, how's it going?"

"We're all done Mr. Rossi. Whenever you're ready, we can go take a look and if you're satisfied, we can go ahead and get you closed out."

"Great, let's take a look."

Sandra grabbed Jacob by the hand. "Go ahead and handle your business. I'm going to take off."

Jacob instructed the painters to give him a minute and he would be there to inspect momentarily.

Jacob poked his lip out. "But you just got here."

"I know, but I have a few errands to run. I just wanted to see your face before you headed to work."

"Ok. Will I get to see you later?"

"Maybe."

"Maybe so or maybe not?"

"Maybe."

"I'll hit you up when I leave here."

"I'll be waiting for your call."

Sandra began walking towards the foyer. Jacob held her hand until their arms could no longer support the distance.

"Sandra."

Sandra turned around. "Yes?"

"I'm in love with you. I loved you at first sight."

***

Jackson did not know what to think when he pulled up to the Bamboo Sticks Diner off of Peartree and Iroquois. They had not been on this side of *ghost* town since the new World of Burgers was built. Now there were plenty of restaurants, places to live and shop. Sandra was sitting in a booth by the window stirring creamer into her coffee. Jackson placed his drink order before taking a seat. He looked at Sandra with fresh eyes. She was poised, confident and in control while Jackson was clothed in the opposite. Sandra thanked Jackson for meeting her on short notice. Something came up yesterday that she could not put off. The waitress stood by their booth, prepared to take their orders. Jackson cancelled his order of loaded potato skins and buffalo wings when Sandra declined the special of the day and suggested that her coffee was more than enough. Another waitress brought Jackson's strawberry lemonade to the table.

"May I have a straw, please?"

The waitress took a straw from her apron and sat it in the middle of the table with a few napkins. Sandra took a sip of her coffee then pushed it aside. "How have you been?"

"Honestly, I've seen better days. How about you? You look absolutely beautiful."

"I'm well, just trying to make sense of some things."

"So, here we are. What do you want to talk about? You ready to come back home?"

"Jackson, I've loved you for a long time. I thought that even when it didn't feel like love, I had enough in me to carry the both of us. But, I'm tired."

"What does that mean?"

"It means, I can't live like this."

"Live like what? I give you everything. Tell me what you want and it's yours."

Sandra could not hold back her tears. The pain on her face told a familiar story that Jackson already knew the outcome to. "Talk to me. What's wrong?"

"I deserve all of you. We've been married almost seven years and I still don't know what that feels like."

"Let me fix it. I can fix this. We can go on dates. Gerald was telling me; he goes on these date nights. Maybe we can go somewhere next weekend."

"You've had seven years to fix it. This isn't about spending time together. This is about me always having to compromise, and you getting to do whatever you want."

"Sandy, I'm sorry. I'm sorry for everything."

"I am too, Jackson."

"I love you. Don't you know that? I don't think this is so bad that we can't work it out. Married people go through things, but they ..."

"Jackson."

"They make it work. You want to throw it all away, just like that?"

"Jackson..."

"Tell me what to do and I'll do it."

"I'm not in love anymore. I want a divorce."

Jackson furiously burst through the diner door causing the cow bell to make a loud clanking noise against the glass. He stormed up the street heading nowhere in a hurry. Sandra put a ten dollar bill under her coffee mug and gathered her things. Jackson was too far ahead for Sandra to catch up with. She locked her purse in her trunk then ran after him in five-inch heels. "Jackson!" He kept walking. Cars were eagerly waiting to cross the four-lane intersection. "Jackson, please!" Jackson stopped and stood in the middle of the busy street. Drivers were blowing their horns for the jilted pedestrian to hurry and make his way to the sidewalk. Speeders slammed on their breaks to avoid running into Jackson and side swiping the cars in the neighboring lanes. "I need to talk to you."

Jackson finally turned around. "Talk to me about what, Sandy? You want to divorce me, why are you doing this?"

"Please, come out of the street."

Jackson walked to the curb where Sandra was standing. They stood toe to toe in the middle of the sidewalk as people abandoned their business to mind someone else's. Jackson's breath blew the few strands of hair that fell just before Sandra's ear. "Will you walk with me, please?" Jackson walked passed Sandra towards the direction of the diner. She followed just a few footsteps behind him, out of breath.

Jackson leaned against the trunk of his car with his hands inside his pants pockets. "What can I do to change your mind?"

Sandra shook her head. "Nothing. I just want us to be able to …"

"To what? Be friends?"

"Jackson … I'm pregnant."

Pregnant? Jackson shamelessly tried to convince Sandra that a divorce would only complicate things. This was their opportunity to start over. In his mind, he had just bought time. This was his absolution of any offense. Jackson reached for Sandra's hand; his emotions were assigned to motives. Jackson always got what he wanted. Sandra placed her hand in Jackson's hand; the handshake that tied a lifelong deal to the devil. He hugged her and assured her that he would be any and everything she needs. Sandra assured Jackson that she would keep him in the know regarding doctor's appointments. Jackson watched Sandra get inside of her car. He grinned, *Pregnant. You think it's over, but it's far from over.*

Jacob called Sandra as he promised once he left the house. Sandra felt so at peace with Jacob. He was her gentle bulldog. She feared that it would be easier for Jacob to walk away from her than to deal with a woman who was carrying someone else's baby. Jackson's baby. But it was her responsibility to inform him and digest whatever he dished.

"Are you coming over when you're done?"

"Of course. Do you need anything? I can pick it up on my way."

"No, I'm fine. Thanks."

"Sandra?"

"Yes?"

"I don't know what it is, but I get the feeling that something is bothering you."

"I do have a lot on my mind."

"Do you wish you hadn't told me you love me?"

"No. I don't regret that, but ..."

"There's a, but?"

"You may."

"Sandra, I need you to talk to me and I don't want to hear bits and pieces. Just spit it out."

"I told Jackson that I wasn't in love with him anymore."

"Did he do something to you?"

"And I asked him for a divorce."

"I know this is a lot to deal with. I know your emotions are all over the place."

"Jacob, please. I just need you to listen because what I'm about to say, may make you want to leave me."

Jacob could not imagine wanting to leave after Sandra had just opened her heart to him and she had received his heart in return.

Since the first day he laid eyes on her at Jackson's barbershop, he knew he loved her. It did not matter that she was coupled with a man who could ruin his life. Jacob could smell their rotting marriage. Women kissed Jackson's face while hugging him and snapping pictures of him never addressing the woman who stood proudly by his side. He was glorified in his fanfare and she still kept a smile on her face. Now, Jacob had the chance to show her what real love felt like. He had a chance to reintroduce her to falling asleep on the phone after hours of talking about nothing and being treated with respect and kindness. Jacob turned the radio down to a whisper and gave Sandra his undivided attention.

"I'm listening."

CHAPTER EIGHTEEN

Omar leaned back in his chair with the palms of his hands supporting the back of his head. He stared as Todd busily moved about the office. Todd was fashionably dressed in tan slacks and a pin striped dress shirt. No baggy jeans, no boots, no team Jerseys. He pulled a few criminal arrest files from the file cabinet before taking a seat at his desk.

"What?"

"You got an interview or something?"

"A man can't wear slacks without having an interview or going to church?"

"Well, you don't go to church so... no."

"I feel like I should take myself a little more seriously, that's all."

"You sure it ain't got nothing to do with your new lady friend?"

"What lady friend?"

"The leggy, red head I saw you with the other day."

"Let's talk about you and *your* new lady friend."

"What about her? She's just a friend."

"I don't kiss my friends like that ... All in my business."

"I hadn't seen the top of your desk since they moved it in this office. You got little baskets for your pens and stuff; papers filed neatly. Is that a coffee mug with your name on it?"

"It was a gift."

"That desk calendar was too, huh?"

"I may have been slightly encouraged by a certain red head."

"Seriously, I'm happy for you. I haven't seen you this together … ever."

"Let's go, sting operation 101 is in progress."

Todd needed this bust to go down smoothly. It had already been put on ice twice. Informants were in place, wired and scripted. The men in motion as Todd eclectically calls them were ready to make drops to all three locations. Vehicle Surveillance was ready for observation. The police were looking for three men who fit the distinct description of Brock Kilmore, Junior Tyson, also known as Pee Wee and Anthony Gordy. The officers had learned the names of their mamas, baby mamas, their code words and knew those boys were not smart enough to pull off an operation as diplomatic as the Thomas boys. District 14 wanted the kingpin, so, Loren gift wrapped one and sent him first class to Todd. Omar tapped Todd on the shoulder with his ink pen.

"When did Jackson take over Cobra?"

Cobra is what the locals nicknamed the South West side because of a street called Serpent Road. Serpent Road was six, rundown houses long occupied by Haitians. No grass, no trees, no sunshine. Serpent Road offered drugs, sex, fake IDs, prescription drugs, abortions, you could even go there to put a hit out on someone. Jackson was not crazy about the geographics, but he was exempt from having to scuff his Berluti's to bring home the lajan. Todd sat his legal pad on the gray folding table next to a coffee ring stain.

"We're following all leads."

"Someone called in with a tip on Jackson covering Cobra?"

"I thought it was you."

Omar was taken by surprise. "Me?"

"You know, the wife thing."

Omar sat back in his chair, forced to turn a blind eye. Sergeant Toney was long winded. He had lost his audience twenty minutes ago. After eight more minutes of wrap up, Omar gathered his things and followed the crowd. Todd had a missed call from Jacob. He waited until everyone was formally dismissed before he rushed out. "This is Todd."

"Diablo isn't running anything."

"So, who are his contacts?"

"Kendo, he's the owner of a shopping mall in Africa and three shopping plazas in the US. He pulls the strings. Diablo may give up a little more info, if we talk fast enough, but he's disposable."

"Damn. This is gonna be interesting. I'll get with Loren in the morning."

"You're welcome."

"Hey, what are you doing later? I need some good beer and I need to see what you did to that hole in the wall."

"Rain check. I have a couple promises to keep."

"You got girlfriend duties; I get it. Oh, everyone is on their marks, we're just waiting on the word, go."

"I hope when all the dots are connected, you get the picture you want. He's like a cat, nine fuckin' lives."

"The picture I want? You should want this more than me."

"You don't know how much more."

***

Sandra braced her hands on the kitchen counter then leaned forward afraid to move away from the sink because everything she had eaten suddenly disagreed with her. She rambled through her storage closet and found the box labeled, do not throw away. Inside was a folder given to her by June Orton from Iredrove Technologies. There was a chart and a few sheets of paper with questions outlined to help thoroughly document everything she ate or drank during her pregnancy. There were three little test tubes with black twist on caps for liquids, Sandra put them in her purse and documented the Coconut Shrimp and Orzo pasta as item numbers one and two. She could not stop crying. How could something so precious and innocent as an unborn child engender so much regret?

Sandra stood up slowly and ran towards the guest bathroom, she barely made it to the toilet before everything came up. Her makeshift robe and bathroom floor were covered in vomit. Sandra quickly brushed her teeth then grabbed a roll of toilet paper and tried to clean most of the mess before inviting her visitor inside. She grabbed a roll of paper towels from the kitchen and yelled to her guest who was impatiently waiting on the other side of the door.

"Give me just a second!"

"Open the door."

"Just … give me ten minutes."

"Ten minutes?! Sandra, open the door."

Sandra grudgingly opened the door. "I didn't want you to see me like this."

"What happened?"

Sandra began to cry. "I got sick; I need to clean my bathroom. I'm a mess, look at me."

"Come here."

"No."

Jacob took Sandra by the hand. "Show me."

Sandra pointed to the bathroom and stood nervously in the background while Jacob assessed the damage. Jacob walked Sandra upstairs to her master bathroom. He felt like he had entered Barbie's dreamhouse bathroom. Sandra had a furry toilet seat lid cover, a furry ottoman that sat under her makeup vanity, a furry rug; there was a wicker cabinet full of bath salts and essential oils. *How can you take a shit in here?* Jacob ran a hot bath with almond honey and goat's milk scrub. "Stop crying." He took a garbage bag from under the bathroom sink and stuffed Jackson's shirt in it. He unsnapped Sandra's bra and sat it on the toilet seat then pulled her panties down, just above her ankles then told her to step out of them. A yellow scrunchie was sitting on the back of the toilet, Jacob did the best he could and pulled Sandra's hair back into a ponytail. He helped her into the tub and told her that he would be right back. Jacob found a few small bottles of cleaning supplies under the kitchen sink and tidied the guest bathroom.

When Sandra told Jacob that she is having Jackson's baby, he was numb. He barely spoke to her for four days. He would have raised the child as his own, had Jackson not been informed. Jacob called Sandra at five in the morning, asking for forgiveness. Hoping his actions had not cost him a love.

Jacob patted his front pants pocket, looking for his cell phone when he heard a ringtone. He had left it on the hamper in the guest bathroom. No incoming call. He looked around the big, open space to see where the sound was coming from. Sandra's phone was sitting on the kitchen island next to a container of seafood and pasta. *Jax cell*. Jacob detested Jackson. *Your wife is in love with me. She doesn't love your, bitch ass anymore.* Jacob swiped Sandra's screen to ignore his call. Sandra had cried herself into exhaustion. She was asleep in the tub when Jacob returned.

"Hey beautiful."

Sandra sat up causing the foam from the bath scrub to separate. "What did I do to deserve you?"

Jacob smiled and kissed Sandra on the lips. "How are you feeling?"

"Kiss me again." Jacob kneeled by the tub and kissed Sandra with purpose. "Much better."

"I'm not going to keep you up too long."

Jacob briefly turned his attention to a message that he had been waiting on. Yandy purposely made all his stops an hour late, he wanted to lay low in case there was a mouse trap. Undercovers were parked around the corner from his pickups. Now he was on his way to drop the money off.

"Do you have to leave?"

Jacob stretched. "My bedroom furniture is being delivered in the morning and I have to let the contractors in the house."

"Can't you stay a little while longer?"

Jacob took an oversized bath towel from the linen closet and held it open. Sandra walked into Jacob's arms soaking wet. She nestled her face in the crook of his neck. "Please." Jacob helped Sandra get dressed for bed then tucked her under her furry comforter. He placed her cell phone on the nightstand then kissed her nose. Sandra grabbed Jacob's hand. "Don't leave. Lie down with me for a little while."

"How long is a little while?"

"Until I fall asleep."

Sandra was fighting sleep like black people fought for justice.

"Why are you fighting it? Take your butt to sleep."

"I'm not fighting, I'm not sleepy."

Sandra yawned in Jacob's face and positioned herself on top of him. He slid his hand down to her butt and raised her silk nightie just enough to reveal her bare bottom. Jackson was calling. Jacob peeked at Sandra, who had fallen back asleep. He slowly leaned towards the nightstand, careful not to disturb her then ignored Jackson's call. Jackson called back to back, Jacob ignored his calls again and again. *Damn! What the fuck do you want? Need to take your ass to sleep too.* Sandra stirred in her sleep, now her legs were wrapped around Jacob's legs. She mumbled, "I'm not sleep."

"You are sleep. I'm going to get ready to go, ok?"

"No."

"I know you're tired. It's been a long day."

"I'm not tired."

"You can barely keep your eyes open."

"If I wanted you to make love to me, would you still leave?"

"What is that some kind of trick question or something?"

"It's an honest question."

Sandra's phone rang. She looked over at the screen and rolled her eyes. Jacob threw his hands up, clearly irritated. "Are you going to answer that?"

"Do you answer your phone when you're about to make love?"

Sandra got out of bed and took Jacob's shoes off. She unbuttoned his pants. "Take them off …and your shirt." Jacob pulled his plaid shirt over his head without unbuttoning it. Sandra kissed his chest, tracing his tattoos with her tongue. She pulled Jacob's briefs down just above his ankles. He stepped out of them as he was instructed. Sandra was impressed with Jacob's size; she had never made love to a white man before. She kissed his head then kissed the length of him. He grabbed himself by the shaft, watching her lips form around his girth. Sandra moved Jacob's hand and took him in as far as he could go. The only sounds were of them breathing heavily. Her phone rang as she tasted herself from Jacob's tongue. He sucked her breasts while she held the thick of him in her hand. "I want to feel you."

Jacob and Sandra made a connection. He laid her on her stomach and kissed her from the nape of her neck to the heels of her feet. She withheld herself from him, he begged for her indulgence. Jacob deep stroked her until her body submitted to him, reality now mirrored fantasy. Sandra grabbed the pillow and bit down on it, muffling her moans; he was about to explode. Sandra wrapped her legs around Jacob so that he could not pull out. When he tried to move her legs, she tightened her grip. They were out of breath, collapsed on the damp sheets.

Jackson began sending angry text messages, back to back. Sandra crawled under the covers and invited her lover to lay beside her.

"Have you told me; you love me today?"

Jacob positioned himself behind Sandra and slid his arms around her waist; pressing himself against her body.

"I love you."

"I love you more."

CHAPTER NINETEEN

The city of Chicago always had a way of letting you know when it was time to leave. Jackson always had a way of overstaying his welcome. The drink waitress placed a square napkin on the table in front of Jackson then sat a bottle of Stella Artois on it. She sat a cinnamon toast crunch shot and a strawberry kiwi white wine slushy on a napkin on the other side of the table. Two young ladies wearing prom dresses and cheap makeup, laughing and conversing sauntered over to Jackson's table and sat down. Jackson looked up from his phone. The young lady wearing a spaghetti strap tank dress waved then snickered.

"I think you ladies have the wrong table."

Spaghetti straps reached into her purse and pulled out a compact mirror and a broken lipstick tube and reapplied lipstick to her full lips. The other young lady was dancing to a song that she hummed loudly causing a few patrons to disturbingly look over their shoulders. Gerald joined the party carrying two pink panty martinis.

"I see you've met our guests. Martinis for the ladies."

"Where did you find these street walkers in training?"

"Ladies, this is my audacious friend and senior co-anchor, Jackson Powerhouse Perry. Jackson this is Sylvia."

"Selene."

"And her friend Andrea."

"Amanda."

"They didn't have anyone to dine with. So, I invited them to join us."

Jackson sipped his beer, shaking his head at these two pitiful little girls who were failing miserably at playing grown up. The drink waitress returned and placed a folded piece of paper under a bottle of beer next to Jackson's key fob then asked the guests at the table if she could suggest anything on the menu. *Your dinner waitress will be with you shortly.* Jackson lifted the frosted bottle of beer revealing the note sent from someone who had been watching him in the dining area. Gerald was busy trying to get names straight to notice the exchange. Jackson unfolded the note.

I noticed your glass was empty ... and your ring finger. I'm hosting a party at the Paladium Center Hotel tonight at 8:00 in the Newark meeting room, I'd love for you to come. I'll be wearing yellow. 312-555-0011

"So, where are you ladies from?"

"Here."

"What do you do ... here?"

"I work at the buy and bag right now, but I'm supposed to get this office job."

"Oh, really? What building?"

"Umm, the furniture rental place on Johnson Street."

"That's what I thought."

Gerald chimed in, "Look at you, getting promoted to an office job. Congratulations!"

Jackson gave Gerald the side eye. He did not have to prep the pussy; they had already offered to let him see it by accepting a round of drinks. Jackson waved a twenty dollar bill at the drink waitress and told her to keep the change. Jackson discretely tugged on the bottom of her apron.

"Hey, who gave you this note to give to me?"

"A very flashy lady. She wanted me to wait until she left before I gave you the note."

"Flashy? What did she look like?"

"Very beautiful, not like Mona Lisa, but like Whitney Houston."

"I see. Thanks."

Jackson had a plane to catch tomorrow afternoon. It had been a very long two weeks. There were four shows remaining in the season. The producers were working on a panel show, with basketball greats, Henry Dugal and Rodney Fortress for the finale. Jackson was on top of the world. He had a successful cable sports show, a wife who was carrying his child, money and power. Jackson stood, preparing to excuse himself from the table. He pointed to the two girls who were now, taking pictures of themselves and sharing them on social media. "Don't forget to clean up your mess before you head back to Bennett in the morning."

The wind made it feel twenty degrees cooler than forecasted. Jackson waited on the valet to bring his rental car around. He briefly reconsidered being the fourth wheel in Gerald's romper room calamity but opted to go back to his hotel room and sleep it off.

Burgden Avenue turned its streets into a red carpet event on the weekends. Pedestrians were groupies and cars were celebrities wearing the latest fashions by Bugatti Veyron, Lamborghini and Aston Martin. A group of people dressed in formal attire moved out of the cold and into the Caprice Mansion for a wedding reception. The streetlights were bright and appeared to be flashing as natives poured in and out of luxury retailers and upscale restaurants; swiping credit cards, spending borrowed money and time on Mr. and Mrs. Right now. The air was flirty, Jackson initiated the Navigation System and searched for the address to the Paladium Center Hotel. *There are nine miles remaining until you've reached your destination.*

Jackson walked into the hotel without any expectations. He was curious to see who had paid close enough attention to know what kind of beer he was drinking. The gentleman behind the front desk directed Jackson to the second floor when he asked how to get to the Newark Meeting room. There were meeting rooms on both sides of the hall. Jackson entered through the double doors, to his surprise there was no one there. He noticed another set of double doors but did not attempt to go inside.

"Excuse me."

"Yes sir?"

"Can you tell me if there's a party in the Newark room?"

"There is."

"You know that for sure without checking?"

"Well, we're booked for the night on floor two. Was there something wrong?"

"No. Well, I went into the room and there was no one there. Am I supposed to go through the other set of doors?"

"It all depends. Did your guest invite you into their room?"

"What?"

"The Paladium Center is a place where you can rent spaces for parties, small receptions and other events. We have hotel rooms and suites attached to every reception area for the convenience of the host or hostess."

"So, this is not a regular hotel?"

"Not entirely."

"Can you tell me who booked the Newark room?"

"Not without proof that your bank or credit card was used to reserve it."

"Thanks."

Jackson took the elevator back to the second floor and re-entered the Newark room. He heard music coming from the other side of the double doors. He knocked, before trying the door. It was open. He quickly closed the door and waited. A feminine voice seeped from the door clearance.

"Just a minute."

Jackson leaned against the wall just beside the door and looked around. The space was nicely decorated equipped with a wet bar and plenty of counterspace. The hostess opened the door and Jackson walked in. Suddenly, his face demonstrated an array of emotional disorder. He could not tell if his heart was beating. Emmanuelle was wearing a yellow

Victoria's Secret Teddy with a matching robe, the same one that Sandra wore in a picture that she had taken for Jackson.

"What is this?! Have you completely lost your fucking mind?!"

"Here you are meeting strange people in hotel rooms." Emmanuelle placed his hands upon his chest. "And I've lost *my* fucking mind?"

"There's supposed to be a room full of people, partying. Not one lonely oddball trying to force someone to love him."

"I didn't have to force you to fuck me."

"You know what? Fuck it, here we are, face to face." Jackson threw his hands up. "Why won't you leave me alone?"

"Darling, isn't it obvious? I'm a woman scorned."

"You blackmailing me won't keep me, so what is the point in all this?"

Emmanuelle sashayed from the door to the couch and sat down. "Fair enough. However, it's not about you, beloved."

"Then what is it about?"

"You can't be this dense. Because if you are then you're just another pretty face with a hard body and an amazing piece of ass."

"Have a nice life."

When Jackson attempted to make his exit, Emmanuelle leaped from the couch and stood in front of the doors.

"Let's make love before you leave."

"Move."

Emmanuelle grabbed Jackson by the crouch and tried to unbutton his pants. "You're passing up the chance to mess up my lip gloss? You know how mommy feels about her lip gloss."

Jackson pushed Emmanuelle to the floor then stood over his disillusioned ex-lover. Emmanuelle tried to escape, using his hands and feet to scoot backwards. His robe slid off of his arms. Jackson unbuttoned his pants. He grabbed Emmanuelle by the throat and forced himself into his mouth. He gripped the back of Emmanuelle's head the way you would a newborn baby. Emmanuelle gagged, unable to breathe. Jackson forced himself even further causing Emmanuelle's eyes to water. Jackson face fucked Emmanuelle until he came. Emmanuelle spit Jackson's sperm onto the carpet. He quickly crawled to the corner and sat cowardly against the wall, chest heaving rapidly up and down, and lip gloss smeared across his cheek.

"The next time I tell you to fuckin' move, fuckin' move!"

Jackson buttoned his pants and noticed Emmanuelle's phone was sitting on the coffee table. He grabbed it and put it in his pants pocket. "I don't want to have this conversation again. Leave me and my wife the fuck alone!"

Jackson left the room and found his way to the parking garage leaving Emmanuelle in the corner disheveled and manic. Emmanuelle unlocked the safe where his cell phone, wallet and room keys were safeguarded. He ripped the seventy eight dollar nightie off and put it in the trash. *Fuck you, Jackson! Fuck you!* He threw the lamp against the wall, breaking the porcelain base. He began to cry dramatically; hurt left such nasty stains.

Jackson stripped down to his bare caramel skin and began packing in preparation for his flight back to Brigance. He ordered a burger and the soup of the day from the restaurant downstairs then took a shower. Sandra had been on Jackson's mind a lot lately. She seemed comfortable with him leaving for days at a time and secure in her decision for a divorce. Jackson thought to himself, *she's fuckin' somebody.* He checked the time; she did not answer Jackson's calls or messages after nine o'clock. It was 8:44 PM on the hotel clock, 8:47 PM on his cell phone. Sandra did not answer Jackson's call, but surprisingly she called him back several minutes later. Room service knocked just as he answered the phone.

"Sorry about that, I ordered a bite to eat."

"Enjoy your meal. We can talk tomorrow."

"I want to talk to you, now. We don't talk, we don't see each other. I miss you; you don't miss me?"

"I had a doctor's appointment today. I would have rescheduled so you could've been there, but it would have pushed me out another couple of weeks and that would've put us in the same situation with you having to be in Chicago."

"Everything good?"

"Yeah, everything's fine."

"Can I see you when I get back?"

"I need to get a few of my things from the house so, …"

"So, that's the only circumstance under which I can see you?"

"Jackson, let's not complicate things."

"I forgot; you don't love me anymore."

"I'm going to get ready for bed. I have a Yoga class early in the morning. I'll see you tomorrow, ok?"

"Yeah, ok."

It was 8:58 PM. *What the fuck? You can't miss one curfew to talk to your husband?* Jackson took a bite of his chili cheeseburger. It was disgusting. Emmanuelle's phone rang. Jackson took it hoping to recover his stolen information and pictures. A shortcut of the folder with Sandra's pictures in it was saved on the home screen. All of Jackson's contacts had been transferred to Emmanuelle's address book. Jackson answered the phone, knowing that this silly rabbit was far from being out of tricks.

"Hello."

"You taste different, has there been a change in your diet?"

"Yeah, I don't eat you anymore."

"Touché. I just want to assure you that there are no hard feelings."

"Where is all this coming from?"

"It's coming from the heart darling."

Jackson looked at the phone like it was a bomb ready to explode in his hands. He deleted the folder with Sandra's pictures in it and erased all the contact entries. Jackson's phone buzzed with one message notification after the other. Emmanuelle sent Jackson pictures of Sandra on a swing at Krome Park and one of Sandra waving at the camera outside of a movie theater in Vegas. Jackson snarled. "Daddy, did you actually think I'd let you walk out of my life with my only connection to you? Did you even call yourself from it to confirm my number? Oh, honeybee, I swear," Emmanuelle ridiculed.

"I'm not playing games with you anymore. Enough is enough!"

Emmanuelle had ditched the gay elocution and delivered his words with bass in his voice, "If you don't tell her, these pictures will. You have three weeks, unless something you say or do, pisses me off before then."

Jackson hung up the phone. He took the heel of his dress shoe and destroyed the apparent burner phone on the bathroom floor. Another message came through on Jackson's phone. It was a picture of a clock with a message attached.

[Tick tock.]

The city of Chicago always had a way of letting you know when it was time to leave. And Jackson Powerhouse Perry always had a way of overstaying his welcome.

CHAPTER TWENTY

Lance was educating a new employee on the culture at Smitty's. The atmosphere was like grandma's house, the staff was so warm hearted, and the guests were like favorite cousins. Jacob had an old picture of Smitty restored and hung it behind the bar. Customers were delighted with the refreshed atmosphere eating delicious food and enjoying themselves. Sandra promised Jacob she would stop by before going to Brigance since she fell asleep on him last night.

"Hey Miss Sandra! What can I get for you?"

"Hi sweetie. Nothing for me, thank you."

"Boss man is in his office. Oh, this is Hilary, she's one of our new hostesses. Hilary this is J R's girlfriend, Miss Sandra."

Hilary spoke with a smile. Sandra did not bother correcting Lance; girlfriend had a nice ring to it. She knocked on Jacob's office door.

"It's open."

Sandra peeked inside. Jacob was negotiating supplier contracts and reviewing job applications for the back of the house. He met Sandra on the other side of his desk and kissed her. "Hey baby."

"Do you know what you're doing?"

"With my lips or these contracts?"

"Well, I know you know what you're doing with your lips."

The two hopefuls shared a devilish grin and a lingering kiss. Jacob offered Sandra a seat at his desk to rest her feet. "I'm not going to be long. I met Hilary, she's a cutie."

"I stole her from the dive around the corner. Lance has a thing for her."

"Speaking of Lance, he introduced me as your girlfriend."

"Well, that's cause I have a thing for you."

"You've never asked me to be your girlfriend."

Jacob spoke confidently, "It's evident."

Sandra folded her arms. "Oh, really?"

"I spend all my time with you, and you spend all of yours with me. You've seen me pee, I've seen you without makeup, we're in love."

"Yet, you've never asked me to be your girlfriend."

Lance knocked on Jacob's office door. He was invited to come inside. "Hey, sorry to interrupt. Brianna is here to see you."

"I'll be there in a minute. Wanna meet Smitty's daughter?"

"Maybe another time, I'm going to head across town before it gets too late."

As Sandra reached for the office doorknob, Jacob grabbed her hand. "Where's my good-bye kiss?"

Sandra kissed her fingertips then placed them on Jacob's cheek. "Talk to you later."

***

Sandra had not used her house key in almost two months. Jackson insisted she use it today since there was a conflict with his schedule causing him to run a little behind. She sat an oversized travel bag on the closet floor and began putting clothes inside of it. Three trips to the car and Jackson still had not arrived. Sandra contemplated leaving but wanted to be fair, considering the last time they saw one another was the lesser of their better days. Sandra texted Jackson to see if he was on his way. He was just leaving the airport. It would be another thirty five minutes before he arrived. Jacob sent Sandra a message with a sad face and a broken heart emoji. She rolled her eyes.

[Why the sad face?]

[I didn't get a kiss before you left.]

[But you got plenty of kisses while I was there.]

[Not the point. Have you left yet?]

[No, still packing.]

[He's trying to get you to stay, isn't he?]

[He's not here yet.]

Jacob called and immediately apologized. Sandra walked to the front of the house so that she could hear Jackson when he pulled up. She peered at the house where the man of her dreams had been all along and frowned at how atypical of Jackson to go through these lengths to keep secrets from her. Sandra forgot to grab her overnight bag that was filled with her good panties and bras. *Shit.* Just as she raised her foot to step on the first stair, Jackson pulled into the driveway.

"I was trying to think of ways to ask you to be my girlfriend."

"It's just a question, Jacob."

"I know. I didn't want it to be awkward."

"Awkward, how?"

Jackson came in from the garage entrance. He followed the lights and found Sandra in the living room. They spoke to one another like two strangers in passing. Sandra tuned her back and lowered her voice. "He's here now."

"Tell him I said, fuck you."

"Jay…"

"Tell him."

Sandra looked over her shoulder and waved at Jackson then pointed to her phone. Jackson waved back, curious about who was on the other end of the line.

"He says, hey."

"Baby …"

"Yes?"

"This is not what I had in mind, but …"

Jackson was paying close attention to Sandra's responses trying to determine if she was talking to a male or female. He took his luggage into the laundry room then went into the bathroom and closed the door. "Will you be my girlfriend?"

Sandra had spent plenty of daydreams practicing, answering that question.

"You know I will."

"I promise you won't regret it."

"I know I won't."

Sandra heard the toilet flush. "Jay, we'll celebrate later, ok? ... I love you too."

Jackson walked out of the bathroom, drying his hands on his pants. Sandra dropped her cell phone in her purse. "Rough flight?"

"It seems to be commonplace now. My luggage is always an hour behind."

"I'm sorry."

"It's not your fault. Did you see the door?"

"No, I hadn't paid it any attention."

Jackson took Sandra's hand and led her to the front door. It was a beautifully crafted red double door. Sandra ran her fingers across the grooves. "It's gorgeous."

"You were right. The door changes everything. I was thinking, this place could use some fresh ideas. Maybe we can redo some stuff."

"Jackson ..."

"Or we can do some shopping for our baby."

"I forgot a bag upstairs."

Sandra walked towards the staircase, dreading having to climb up and then back down twenty stairs. Jackson recovered his luggage from the laundry room and followed behind her. When Sandra bent down to pick up her bag, she felt dizzy. She sat in her rocking chair to regain her composure. Jackson appeared from behind the closet entrance and asked if everything was Ok. "Just a little lightheaded. I should be fine."

Jackson opened the nightstand drawer and pulled out the tennis bracelet that he had gotten her. He squatted in front of her rocking chair and opened the box. The diamonds sparkled like they had blinking lights inside of them. "Wow!"

"It's for you."

"I can't accept this."

"Sandy, I'm still your husband. I can't give you gifts now?"

Sandra stood slowly to ensure she did not shake up whatever she had eaten earlier. Jackson slid his arms around Sandra's waist. "I miss you. I'm so miserable without you. I don't want you to leave. Please, be my wife. What else do I need to say to get you to stay?"

Sandra's voice softened. "Those things were all I needed to hear. I'm worth so much more than this."

"I agree. Baby, I love you."

"Jackson, I'm tired of being hurt by you."

"I won't hurt you anymore, I promise."

Jackson kissed Sandra on the forehead. "Just one more chance." He kissed her on the cheek. "Please, I fucked up, but let me make it up to you." He tried to kiss her lips, Sandra placed her hand on Jackson's chest, creating distance between them.

"You know, that's always been part of the problem, you don't listen to me. A part of me will always be your friend, but I can't be your wife anymore."

Sandra took Jackson's hands and removed them from her waist. She ran into the bathroom and closed the door. Jackson knocked on the door and asked if there was anything he needed to do. Of all Sandra's pregnancies, this was the first time he had seen her with morning sickness. Jackson put his ear to the door, he could hear her gagging.

"I'll go and make you a cup of green tea."

Her voice was muffled, "Thank you."

Jackson sprinted down the stairs. He stopped just before reaching the kitchen to listen for any movement outside of the upstairs bathroom. Jackson put a teacup of water into the microwave and set it for two minutes and thirty seconds. He opened the cabinet door beneath the sink and removed a piece of the cabinet bottom which was close to four inches in length and three inches wide. Underneath it revealed a section of the unfinished kitchen floor. Jackson grabbed a white pill bottle with a red and white label and took from it one pill. After sealing the bottle, he took two pills from a separate prescription pill bottle then returned them both to their hiding place. He quickly grabbed the pill grinder and crushed the three pills then waited for the microwave to stop. Jackson called up the stairs for Sandra from the kitchen. She did not respond. Jackson took two green tea bags from the cupboard and sat them on the countertop. Once the microwave stopped, he released the white powder into the steaming cup of water causing the powder to foam. Jackson stirred the contents in the cup until the water was clear. He put one tea bag inside the water until the color changed to light green. He dropped the used tea bag into the trash can then put a fresh tea bag inside the cup and stirred. Jackson replaced the makeshift lid, covering the opening inside the cabinet. He washed his hands then gripped the teacup by its handle. Light footsteps were casually approaching the bottom of the staircase. Jackson met Sandra in the living room, he could barely look her in her eyes.

"Here you go, I hope this makes you feel better."

"Thanks."

Sandra smelled the green tea. It smelled like heaven, but she was not confident that her bundle of joy would allow her to enjoy it. Sandra placed the teacup back into Jackson's hands. "I'm going to have to pass, I think I just need to lie down and get some rest."

"Go upstairs and lie down, I'll save this for you."

"That's really sweet of you, but I'd rather be at home."

"Sandy, we still have what it takes to make this work. You keep saying shit like, you'd rather be at home. This is your home."

"Jackson, I had what it took to make this work. You had every chance to meet me halfway, but you always came up short."

Sandra got in her car and drove around the city overwhelmed by her thoughts. She was someone's girlfriend. Her man is a sexy, tattooed, rough around the edges, six feet one inch, Italian hustler who made her feel like she was more than enough for him. She thought about how goofy she used to feel at the mention of Jackson's name. And how nervous he was the first time they made love. Sandra inquired, *Am I your first? No,* he said, *but if you play your cards right, you'll be my last.* All he had to do was be a good man and treat her like she meant something to him, and the reward would have been astrophysical. Catered to, loved, revered.

"He could've had it all."

Jackson stood stone faced. He was surely losing the crutch that kept firm hands against his back so that he could do anything but fall. He peeked under the kitchen sink to make sure he secured the piece of fiberboard properly. He poured the contents from the teacup into the drain then rinsed behind it to eliminate remnants. Jackson thought about how beautiful Sandra looked on their wedding day and how the media captured her as an American princess. She was the perfect accessory for his image. The house, the cars, jewelry, money.

"She could've had it all."

TWENTY ONE

The sound of cubed ice falling from the thin plastic bag into the small, thick, plastic cooler made Susan's skin crawl. Jacob ordered a case of his favorite African wine, The Chocolate Block Red Blend and promised Todd that he would gift him a couple bottles. Every household needs a bottle of Boekenhoutskloof kept on ice, Jacob bragged. Susan grabbed a bottle from the wooden crate for herself and stuck it inside her purse.

Jacob adjusted the wine bottles so that both were completely covered in ice.

"Would you stop that shit! I can't stand that noise."

"Then take your ass home."

"I want to see the fanny pack that sex kitten keeps your balls in. When is she coming?"

"As soon as you leave."

"Jackie, don't be like that. Scared she'll want to go home with me, instead?"

The doorbell rang, deferring Jacob's retort. Susan sat her purse on the counter and straightened her blouse. "Go on, get the door."

Todd was standing outside the front door, looking like a live ad for JC Penny. Jacob stepped aside and invited him in. Susan pretended to be concerned with a barcode sticker that was stuck to the bottom of Jacob's pepper grinder. Todd looked around, thoroughly impressed.

"Damn, this is nice, Italiano."

Susan and Todd exchanged glances failing to mask their grins. "What you doin' over here?"

Jacob interjected, "Waiting on you."

"Is that right?" Todd inquired.

"I don't *wait* on anyone. I'm here being nosey."

Jacob and Todd conversed briefly about wine, disagreed over sports and bantered about women then made their way towards the front door.

Susan stared at the back of Todd's head. "I know you aren't leaving without saying anything to me."

Todd put the cooler on the back seat of his Porsche and wrapped up his conversation with Jacob. He had a few cuts of Flank Steak bathing in his Chicago sweet heat marinade back at his place, they were just about ready for the grill. Susan grabbed her purse then high stepped it outside where Jacob and Todd were staged in the driveway. Todd purposely kept his focus on Jacob while Susan waited to be addressed.

Sandra pulled into the driveway and parked next to Susan's car. Todd waved his hello to Sandra then told Susan to meet him at his house.

Jacob hugged Sandra from behind, playfully pressing himself against her butt. He rested his chin on her shoulder and introduced her to Susan. Sandra recollected the frazzled, frumpy woman who came to her door that day, but the woman standing before her was beautiful and her makeup was picture-perfect. Sandra spoke first.

"Hi, it's nice to finally meet you."

"You are stinking gorgeous!"

Sandra smiled. "Thank you, so are you."

Jacob waved goodbye to Susan then told her to beat it. Sandra looked over her shoulder. "Jay, that's so rude."

"Yeah, dick weed."

Jacob stuck his middle finger up at Susan and mouthed the words, suck my dick weed. Susan retorted, "Do you kiss this beautiful lady with that filthy mouth?"

Sandra excused herself from the battling duo showdown, her bladder had a running faucet attached to it. They both paused and watched Sandra's strides in her red bottom high heels. Susan playfully punched Jacob in the chest. "She's giving me a woody. Good job, Jackie." Susan got in her car and started the engine. She checked her makeup in the rear-view mirror then rolled her window down as she backed out of the driveway. "Tell beautiful, I had to run. By the way, the house is phenomenal."

Jacob had completed renovation at 7731 Canston Circle. No filthy walls, no trash on the floor, no hanging banister but most importantly, he had someone to share it with. The neighbors were less than creative in trying to get their feet in the door to see what miraculous changes had been made, offering desserts and gossip.

Sandra was drying her hands on a paper towel from the kitchen when Jacob walked in.

"Did you eat some fruit today?"

"Yes, I ate fruit."

"The doctor said, you should include apples and bananas in your diet."

"Jay, I ate fruit."

"Cranberry sauce doesn't count, you know."

Jacob lifted Sandra off of her feet and carried her up the stairs. He led her down the hall to a closed door. Not another baby room, she thought. "I have a surprise for you. I hope I didn't overstep my bounds."

It's a damn baby room. Jacob opened the door and yelled, surprise! Sandra stepped into validation; Jacob truly loves her. There was a day bed that modeled an antique couch with furry throw pillows, a television mounted over a buffet style television stand, a bookshelf full of books, a furry rug and by the window, a Hosier and Decker rocking chair. Sandra looked Jacob in the eyes, searching for that one ambiguous thing she had missed when she had fallen in love with Jackson. But Jacob was not Jackson and Jackson was not capable of loving anyone half as much as he loved himself. "Say something. Do you like it?"

"I love it."

Jacob carried Sandra downstairs. They held one another in the middle of the family room floor while making plans for the weekend. Jacob growled, pretending to be a vicious dog, biting at Sandra's ear. Sandra popped Jacob on the butt. "Baby, stop it. Is that my phone or yours?"

"It's not mine."

Sandra had two missed calls. Audrey never left messages, but it was unlike her to call back to back. Sandra feared that something could be wrong. Jacob stored the rest of the bottles of wine in the cellar while Sandra checked on her friend.

"Would you be upset if I went to see about Audrey?"

"No, baby not at all. Everything ok?"

Sandra shrugged her shoulders. "I'm not sure."

Audrey peeked through the blinds as an army green Jeep Wrangler pulled into her narrow driveway. Jacob helped Sandra out of the Jeep and stood by until Audrey opened the front door. Audrey stepped onto the porch and gave Sandra a big hug.

"Is that *the* Jacob?"

Sandra looked back and smiled at Jacob who was begging her with his eyes to dismiss him.

"The one and only."

Audrey waved for Jacob to join them on the porch. He hesitantly walked towards the steps. "Jay, this is Audrey. Audrey, Jay." Jacob extended his hand to Audrey.

"Well, hello delicious." Audrey slapped Jacob's hand. "Put your hand down unless you're planning on copping a feel. We do hugs around here."

Jacob gave Audrey a hug then kissed Sandra on the lips, excusing himself. Audrey puckered her lips. "Where's mine?" She chuckled and warned Jacob that this is her being on her best behavior.

Sandra waved goodbye. "I'll call you when I'm ready."

Sandra had not been to Audrey's home in what seemed like forever. She always made her guests feel especially welcomed. And she always sent you home with something. She had more stuff than she had space, but today was different. Sandra sat on an orange bean bag and propped her purse on a shoe box. Pictures had been taken from the walls and boxes were taped up and staged against the closet door.

"What's going on?"

"Sandra, you know I love you. You have been such a dear friend to me, don't ever, *ever* change."

"Are we breaking up?"

Audrey smiled nervously. She removed her slouchy beanie hat from her head. Her hair was growing back from a buzz cut.

Sandra gasped. "Audrey …"

"I'm fighting breast cancer."

Sandra tried to hold back tears so that she could be strong for her bigger than life, friend who seemed so small in that moment. But she could not.

"When did you … you didn't bother to call me or anything."

Audrey wiped Sandra's tears. "You have your own life to live. And you know me, I never back down from a fight. Not even when my bully is cancer."

"Is there anything you need? What can I do for you? Anything at all, just name it and it's done."

"You're doing it now. I called; you came."

"Are you moving?"

Audrey walked into the dining room and picked up an orange folder from the table. She placed it in Sandra's hands. Sandra opened the folder and read over the lease agreement. "You're moving to Amsterdam?!"

"You know how I feel about the Netherlands. I'm just here doing whatever it takes to make it to the next day. I don't want to just live; I want to be alive! I want to do daring things. Cancer is trying to take my life. Well, I can't let that happen."

"What? Just up and move to Amsterdam?"

"My favorite cousin, you remember me talking about Sylvie, she's been there for fifteen years now. She helped me find a place, two blocks from where she lives. And …"

Sandra closed the folder then looked up. "And, what?"

Audrey blushed. "I met a man. He's everything I'm not and it's wonderful!"

"In Amsterdam?"

"On Cancer survivor singles dot com. But yes he lives there."

Sandra massaged her temples. "There's a dating site for … ok, so do you plan on meeting him in person before you move?"

"We've met."

"When?! He came here?"

"Can you believe he has two sons who live here. They run and own a motorcycle shop right in Renfro City."

"He came here, the two of you met and now you're moving there to be with him?"

"It doesn't sound as romantic when you say it."

"How long has it been?"

"Since we've had sex or since we've been together?"

"You had sex?"

"Yeah, I gave him a little bit. The Netherlands is a long way to travel without incentive."

"Audrey, I love you."

"Well, how could you not?"

Audrey asked Sandra to follow her into the bedroom so that she could finish separating her belongings into keep and toss piles. Sandra took her shoes off then sat Indian style on the bed and flipped through Audrey's photo albums. "So …" Audrey picked up a pile of clothes that were still on the hangers and dumped them on the bed. "what's up?"

"Where do I begin?"

"Right in the middle, that's where the juicy stuff is."

"Ariel accepted the job offer. She'll be here next month."

"Great, send my congratulations. And Jackson?"

"Jackson has been served. He got the divorce papers over a week ago. I don't want anything from him, so this should be painless."

"You think he'll contest it?"

"He signed and returned the papers when they informed him that I could still divorce him without his signature."

"God, I finally get to say this, I cannot stand that man! Your smile has never been this bright with Jackson."

"Thanks. If it weren't for you, I probably never would have said anything to Jacob."

"Speaking of Mr. Delicious, how's that going?"

"We're sickening, but I love it. He's in the process of buying another bar, his dream is to own as many as he can wrap his hands around."

"What about your dreams?"

Audrey threw an arm full of dresses in the toss pile. Sandra sat the photo album aside and grabbed a pillow for emotional security.

"What do you mean?"

"Everyone who knows you, knows that your dream is to own a bookstore. Remind me to get toilet paper."

"I guess I hadn't thought much about it." Sandra texted Audrey while she was sitting on her bed.

[Don't forget the toilet paper.]

"Liar, do you remember our two hour conversation about you and your very own bookstore? It's what makes you explode on the inside, aside from Mr. Delicious. Listen, you owe it to yourself to do this. Jackson has his own thing and now Jacob has his. What does Sandra have?"

"There's this little coffee shop on 23rd and Lucas, you know the one I'm talking about?"

Audrey snapped her fingers. "Yeah, the one with the faded, rustic looking door and the wooden awnings. I used to get my morning coffee from there when I worked on Banton Street. Oh, my God they sell the best freshly baked cookies!"

"Well, the owner wants to sell it. She's a little Spanish woman who wants to travel."

"Really? I didn't realize it was for sale. That would be the perfect little nook for your bookstore. I can see it now. Young hipsters piling in, researching their history through storytellers and people like myself who just wants to be a part of a beautiful movement."

"Audrey, I don't even know where to begin. I don't know what to do or how to do it."

"Buy the damn building, take a class and you'll figure it out."

"Just … go and buy the building. Hop in the car and … just go."

"Exactly!"

Audrey slid on her sensible shoes and grabbed a blue jean jacket out of the keep pile. "Put your shoes on and let's go."

"Where are we going?"

"To pick up toilet paper, cookies … and a bookstore."

CHAPTER TWENTY TWO

Jackson sat in the corner of the cold bathroom floor naked, dripping wet, arms gripped around the front of his legs, head resting against the wall. The shower was still running. The only light in the house came from a blinking message indicator on Jackson's cell phone. Reality had left him with no room for error and error had left him with no room for forgiveness. Despite the success of Jackson's sports show, the network called an urgent meeting and announced that they would not be bringing the show back for a third season. Jackson would be allowed to fulfill his current contract and tape the remaining shows. Any subsequent contracts would be paid to term to avoid a breach. Gerald still had his syndicated radio show, which had received widespread recognition due to his appearances as co-anchor on Jackson's sports show. Jackson stared into the darkness and wondered where it all went wrong. Where did he get lost, what road could he take to get back to a familiar place?

Jackson tried to listen for his grandmother's voice. But he could not hear it. She was too far away. He closed his eyes and tried to focus, but still the distance was too great.

"Hey lil' cuz, come here."

"I can't grandma is calling me."

"She don't want nothin' come here."

"Grandma! I'm coming!"

"Shut up! Get your ass over here."

Jackson tried to listen for his grandmother's voice. But he could not hear it. She was too far away. He called her name, but she did not answer. "Close that door."

"Why?"

"You a hardheaded lil' nigga ain't you?"

"I'm going to see where grandma went."

Dank Jr. put his foot against the bedroom door. Jackson ran to the window to peek out. Grandma's car was not in the driveway. "What you want, Dank?"

"I just want to talk to you lil' cuz. You're a man, now. I need to talk to you about man thangs. You ever kiss a girl?"

"No."

"You ain't never kiss a girl? Look when you kiss a girl, take her in your arms like this."

Dank Jr. grabbed Jackson and held him the way you would a distant lover, reunited. Jackson felt uncomfortable. "Then you lean in and kiss her like this." Dank Jr. kissed Jackson on the lips and tried to stick his tongue in Jackson's mouth. He kicked Dank in the shin, burst through the bedroom door and ran down the hall as fast as he could. Dank Jr. ran after him and grabbed him by the back of the shirt. "Where you goin' lil' nigga? See, I was trying to make you a man, but you acting like a little boy."

"Grandma!"

"Get in there and shut up!"

Dank shoved Jackson into the bedroom, pushed him to the floor then locked the door. Jackson got up and ran to the window. He banged relentlessly on it while yelling for help. "Ain't nobody gone help you. Ain't nobody here. Stop banging before you break the fuckin' window!" Dank ordered Jackson to stand against the closet door. He slapped Jackson and told him that if he ever told anyone they would make fun of him and call him little faggot boy. "You wanna be called a lil' faggot boy? Huh?"

Jackson began to cry. "No."

Dank unbuttoned Jackson's pants and pulled them down to his ankles. He grabbed Jackson's crouch and squeezed.

"Girls gone love you cause you pretty. They love them some lil' curly haired, pretty boys."

Dank told Jackson to take his underwear off. Jackson stood silent, powerless. "Take them off!" Jackson did as he was told. He stood there half naked and confused, shaking. Dank grabbed Jackson by the penis and stroked him. "You like that?" Jackson shook his head, no. "No? Then why is your dick hard?" Dank Jr. robbed Jackson of his innocence in the light of day. He stood there, leaned against the closet door, erect while his older cousin performed oral sex on him in the bedroom where he and his sister slept. "Damn, you working with a lil' something too." Dank unzipped his pants and began stroking himself.

"Can I go now?"

Dank began sucking faster, getting closer to his agenda. Jackson had never felt this feeling before. It was beyond what his twelve years of inexperience could process. His breathing was heavy, his heart was beating fast. He peered at Dank Jr. who was covered in his sperm. "Can I go now?" Daniel Kenneth Jr. stood up and wiped his mouth.

"Yeah. Clean yourself up and go play."

Jackson crawled to the toilet on his hands and knees and threw up. He reached for the toilet handle and flushed putrefied remnants of his demons. He got back in the shower and stood under the cold water trying to wash away his past. But it was engraved in time and forever the worst part of him. Jackson Powerhouse Perry, he had become bigger than what his soul could accommodate; he stood on the heads of the people who loved him to stay eye to eye with the monster he, himself had created.

Jackson tried to pull himself together. He was afraid to fall asleep. If he fell asleep, he would have to face tomorrow. Jackson sat in Sandra's rocking chair, he rocked slowly; back then forth then back again. She had the strongest shoulders of all his worshippers, she carried her husband's weight proudly. It was her privilege and his petition. Jackson began to fall asleep, when the chair rocked backwards, he would regain consciousness. He was fatigued. The bed was made, all he had to do was lie in it and close his eyes. He began rocking; back, forth, back and forth, then back.

Granma, grandma where you at? Grandma, I don't wanna go to no church.

The rain fell in sheets. It was blinding, the lines that coordinated street lanes were obscured. Cars pulled off the road to keep from causing wrecks. Justine was on her way to her mother's house from working overtime. It was the weekend and she was ready to pick her babies up and love on them.

Justine sat in the parking lot for thirty minutes until the rain let up. She decided to stop at a convenient store to get junk food for a movie night at home with the kids. A red Ford pickup truck turned onto 33rd street, swerving in and out of his lane. Justine pulled out of the tight parking lot onto Becker Drive, stopped by a red traffic light. She considered making a right onto 33rd street to avoid all of the traffic lights ahead but decided against it when she saw the light turn yellow for ongoing traffic. The Ford pickup truck saw the yellow light too and decided to gun it to catch the light before it turned red. When Justine's light turned green, she proceeded into the intersection when out of nowhere at seventy five miles per hour the red Ford truck slammed into the passenger's side of Justine's Camaro. The impact hurled her body against the car door causing her head to slam against the window, cracking the glass just before making contact with another car in the left lane. Her body was pinned to the driver's seat; neck broken, head trauma. The seat belt had ripped the flesh from her neck, chest and shoulder. Justine never made it to her mother's house where her three year old twins, Jackson and Jaqueline were waiting.

"Jackson, Jackson wake up. Jackson! Come on now, you and your sister go on and get ready for church."

"Grandma, I don't wanna go to no church. I don't believe in no, God."

"Boy, don't make me cut your butt! Where that foolish talk come from?"

"We ain't got no mama cause, he took her away."

"Baby, you and your sister got me. Grandma, loves the both of you with all my heart. Your mama loved the ground you and your sister walked on till the day she left from here and don't you ever forget that."

"Yes, mam."

"Jaqueline, get up baby. Ya'll hurry up, it's first Sunday."

Wake up, wake up Jackson. Jackson!

Jackson jumped out of his sleep and looked around for the voice that was calling his name.

"Grandma … where you at?"

Jackson picked up his phone that had fallen from his lap onto the floor. There was one missed call. He quickly checked the voice message that was left for him.

I know it's late, I was taken to the emergency room because my body overheated … I fainted. They treated me for dehydration. Three hours later, I'm back at home. I just wanted to keep you informed. Talk to you soon.

Jackson had not given one authentic paternal thought to his unborn child since the day Sandra told him they were expecting. He was obsessed with a woman who had fallen out of love with him. Life was sending Jackson a message that he refused to acknowledge. Time runs out even on the dearest of things. He responded to Sandra with a rehearsed concession, letting her know that he was sorry he missed her call and thank God she is feeling better.

Jackson sat on the edge of the bed and glowered at the paperwork that brazenly stared at him from the nightstand. The divorce decree. Jackson's phone buzzed.

[Rise and shine Mr. Perry. Less than two weeks till game day. I woke up plagued with curiosity. Are you going to tell Barbie over dinner or after making love? I was thinking something more dramatic, like a singing telegram or maybe 8x10s in glossy print, framed of course.]

It was 5:56 AM. Jackson put on his boxers and a sweatshirt then finally rested his head on the pillow. Another alert confirmed an incoming message. He wished it was Sandra's name highlighted in his inbox telling him that she was still in love and wanted her husband back, but he knew better.

[Tick Tock.]

Life-2, Jackson-1.

CHAPTER TWENTY THREE

The more things change the more they stay the same. Jacob parked his Jeep in front of Jackson's barbershop. The other four free parking spaces were occupied. He walked into the Broken Bottle and could not believe his eyes. It was a dump, no wonder Dre wanted out. The area was slowly being rehabilitated with businesses relocating to the empty lots of land and bringing prominent revenue. Office buildings with beautification awards and hotels were beginning to line the Avenues; the Broken Bottle would be a nice touch for night life after a long meeting or for a nightcap. A bartender who looked like he was barely the legal drinking age asked Jacob what his pleasure would be.

"Is Dre around? He told me he'd be free around two o'clock."

"Yeah, he should be in the back."

"Can you go in the back and get him?"

"I kind of can't leave the bar."

Jacob waved the waitress over, who was surfing the latest social outlet. "Go in the back and tell Dre, Jacob is here, please."

Jacob envisioned the changes he would implement at the Broken Bottle and the look he wanted to go for. It would be just as warm as

Smitty's with a few perks to target the suits and ties that worked for fortune 500 companies just blocks away. The waitress returned from the back and pointed in the direction from where she had just come.

"He said, come on back."

Jacob walked to the back of the bar and held his nose. He looked around to see if he could locate where the smell was coming from. Everything was a mess. The floor was wet, a broom was leaned against the wall, bristles wet from a small, dirty puddle near the storage area and the restroom door was wide open, exposing pieces of toilet paper and trash on the floor. Dre was sitting on a broken computer chair that should have been on the curb for trash pickup. His makeshift desk, comprised of two small file cabinets pushed together, the top drawer on one of them would not close completely due to a dented edge. Dre mugged Jacob, looking him from head to toe.

"Look at this vanilla nigga. You always thought you was fancy, bartending in slacks and shit. Why you all dressed up? You dressed up for this business deal?"

"There's nothing wrong with taking care of yourself. And, yes when I do business, I like to look the part."

"So, let's get right down to business. Hundred fifty and it's yours."

"The deal was Seventy."

"Well, Skeeter the deal has changed."

Jacob straightened his suit jacket. "So has my mind."

Jacob walked out of Dre's office, trying to hurry and escape the awful stench that seemed to follow the sound of his footsteps up the hall. Dre wobbled behind Jacob trying to keep up with his pace. Jacob gasped for fresh air when he made it to the sidewalk. Dre held the bar door open. Jacob waved Dre off.

"Skeeter, I apologize. A good businessman never shows his hand. Come on back in."

"And who the fuck is Skeeter?"

Dre threw his hands up. "Forgive me, Mr. Rossi. Can we go talk dollars?"

Jacob walked back inside and followed Dre down the short hall to his office. Dre plopped down in his chair and scooted back to give Jacob room to come inside and close the door. "Seventy is a little low, don't you think?"

"Dre, we already agreed on seventy. That's why I'm here. My realtor said, it's worth sixty six, max."

"The area is booming, and you want me to give it away."

"The building is run down. And what is that smell?"

"Pipes."

"If you want more, I'll have to get my inspector to come out and you'll have to fix whatever she finds then we can talk numbers."

Jacob turned to make his exit. Dre pleaded with Jacob to have a seat.

Giving in, Jacob moved a stack of papers and sat on the file cabinet. "It's your call."

"This is seventy in cash, right?"

"If that's how you want it."

Jacob stood and locked Dre's office door. Dre observed and sat up in his chair, alert. "Look, I need to talk to you. I don't need you going ape shit, just hear me out."

"What are you talking about, Jacob?"

"Remember when your bar got robbed?"

Dre stood up. "Yeah, I heard Stix did it. That motherfucka' got what he deserved too; somebody took his drunk ass out. They didn't find him till he was damn near liquid."

Jacob braced himself. "It was Stix … and me."

Dre tried to grab Jacob by the collar, Jacob head butted Dre and grabbed his hands and bent them backwards at the wrists. "This ain't what you want big boy. One move and you can say goodbye to your spoon and fork. I told you to be cool, just listen to me." Jacob held Dre's hands until he agreed to calm down. Dre was out of breath. He sat back down in his chair and waited for Jacob to enlighten him. "Man, I was flat broke, and you were on that bullshit cutting my pay and treating me like shit. I didn't deserve that, Dre."

"So, you rob me with a drunken crackhead, and I deserved that?"

"You didn't, but it was the only option I had at the time. I'm doing better now and ..."

"I can see that. But you gone have to trade in that nice blue suit for an orange jump suit."

"If you call the police make sure you tell them about the product you run on Fifteenth Street, the girls you have in the back selling ass at night and let's not forget your little credit card scam."

"Ok, Jacob. So, why you telling me all this if you got insurance?"

Jacob reached in his suit jacket and pulled out a stack. He sat it on the file cabinet. "Ten grand, double for your trouble."

"Fifteen."

Jacob put the money back in his jacket pocket. "This is non-negotiable."

"Hold on now. Ten grand does have a nice ring to it."

Jacob took the money and an envelope from his pocket. He opened the envelope and handed Dre a piece of paper to sign. "What's this?"

"It's a document saying that you know I took money from your property and my debt to you has been paid with interest in the amount of ten thousand dollars. It also says, that by signing this you are prohibited to take any legal action against me regarding this theft. And you are not to discuss this with anyone. Do we have a deal?"

Dre looked at the short stack of one hundred dollar bills and agreed.

The money had not touched his hands and was already spent. Jacob pointed to the blank lines. "I need you to sign there and there. One of my business contacts will notarize it, I'll send a copy to you." The businessmen shook hands. "Nice doing business with you Andre."

"Congratulations."

Jacob folded the document and slid it back inside of the envelope then secured it inside his jacket pocket. He handed Dre the stack of new bills.

"I'll be in touch, so we can set up a time for my inspector to come out and take a look around. I need to know what I just got myself into."

"Jacob, I need you to put me on man. This money ain't gone last long. This bar ain't made me no real money. I heard you bought Smitty's. I came through one night. It's real nice."

"Thanks. I need you to take care of yourself though. Drop some weight and dress the part."

"You gone have me selling bean pies or some shit?"

"Hardly, get yourself together then call me."

Jacob took his jacket off before climbing into his Jeep. The cost of freedom was ten thousand American dollars, he felt unrivaled. There was nothing Jackson could do to him. The woman of his dreams rested her head on his chest at night, he had a successful business and a place to call home.

Susan texted Jacob, 911 with an exclamation point. She had not used

911 since she had run out of feminine pads and needed Jacob to stop by the drug store on his way home. Jacob tuned in to his favorite old school radio station then peeled off.

Stand up now and face the sun, won't hide my tail or turn and run. It's time to do what must be done, be a king when kingdom comes ...

Jackson stormed across the street, wearing cotton sweatpants and a football jersey. He had kicked in his own front door. Susan was sitting on the couch watching television when she heard a series of loud thuds. She had better things to do than house sit, but she was there to be seen since Jackson would be in Brigance for the next six days.

Susan ran into the kitchen to grab a butcher's knife to ward Jackson off. He grabbed Susan by her sweater; her purse fell to the floor. He kicked her purse and told her to get the fuck out of his house. Susan pleaded with Jackson to let her grab her keys that had slid under the barstool then she would gladly leave his prison. Jackson began cursing and yelling at her. When he muscled his way into the living room, turning over chairs and punching walls, Susan texted Jacob, 911! then stuck her phone inside her bra.

Jacob noticed the front door was wide open. He pulled into the driveway, jumped out of his Jeep and ran inside, leaving his car door open and the engine running. Jackson had returned to the kitchen to confront Susan, yelling and man handling her. Jacob wedged himself in between the two of them and pushed Jackson out of his face. Jacob ordered Susan to go home. She dropped to the floor and quickly gathered her belongings.

"Susan, go home, now!"

Susan stalled. "Beat his ass, Jackie!"

"Go home!"

Jackson swung a tight fist at Jacob and missed. Jacob punched Jackson in the nose followed by a punch to his left jaw. Stunned, Jackson rushed Jacob causing the both of them to fall to the floor. Jackson quickly took the advantage of being on top and gripped both hands around Jacob's neck and squeezed, the look on his face was gratifying. Jackson lodged his knee into Jacob's stomach, shifting his weight for added pressure. Jacob could not loosen his grasp. Jackson squeezed tighter and asked Jacob if he was working for Diablo.

"I know you're working for Diablo, admit it! Is Diablo moving Loren's weight? Talk! You trying to cut me out of my own money? Huh?!"

Jacob was fighting to stay conscious. He managed to gain enough strength to strike Jackson in the throat with his knuckles. In the split moment that Jackson's grasp was relaxed, Jacob flipped him on his back and punched him in the face repeatedly. Jacob covered Jackson's throat up to his chin with both hands and squeezed. Jackson struggled to get Jacob off of him. Jacob squeezed tighter as Jackson began wheezing, gasping for air. He lodged his knee in Jackson's groin.

"Do us all a favor and die!"

Jacob stood to his feet then stood over Jackson who was trying to stand. He kicked Jackson in the back of the head twice then in his mouth. Jackson tried to grab Jacob by the leg and pull him down, but Jacob Stomped him in the stomach with the heel of his dress shoe. Jackson coughed as air filled his lungs, he began to spit blood from a busted lip. Jacob kicked Jackson in the back. "Get your sorry ass up! I've been wanting a piece of your bitch ass!" Jacob grabbed Jackson by his Jersey and yanked him up on his knees. He kneed Jackson in the chin twice then yanked him to his feet. Jackson could barely stand up straight, reaching for the kitchen chair for support.

"Fuck you! You think you're runnin' shit by gettin' in bed with Diablo, I don't give a fuck! Ya'll can have each other, fuck you and fuck Loren's short fat ass!"

"I ain't got shit to do with you and Loren, I don't work for Diablo and I don't work for you."

"Bullshit! I own you, white boy. You will always work for me!"

Jacob punched Jackson in the eye, grabbed him from behind and put him in a choke hold. "Dre and I had a little conversation today, man to man and we've come to a mutual agreement. You don't own shit!"

Jackson tried to strike Jacob in the face. "Get the fuck off me!"

Jackson tried to break Jacob's grip, but he squeezed tighter. Jackson's voice was strained and paltry. "I want you out of my fucking house now!

Get your shit and get the fuck out!"

"Jackson, take a look around. No one lives here, but your ego. Oh, and if you're thinking about fucking with Susan just remember, if she goes down ... you go down and that's a promise, Mr. Accessory to a murder. Yeah, we were afraid at first for obvious reasons, but you fucked up, just like we can always count on you to do."

Jacob slung Jackson to the floor. Jackson was bleeding badly from a cut on the side of his eye, his mouth and head. He held eye contact with Jacob, both ready to react if the other should make a sudden move. Jackson propped himself up on his knees, he pointed towards the front door. Jacob grabbed a barstool and hurled it across the kitchen, knocking the pots down from the pot rack onto the counter.

"Get the fuck out!"

Jacob patted his back pocket to ensure that his wallet had not fallen out of it. He had lost three buttons from his shirt. Jacob took his right arm and cleared the kitchen island, four Bordeaux wine glasses, a bottle of wine, four dinner plates and four soup bowls; glass shattered everywhere, sounding like fifty wind chimes swaying at the same time in different directions. Wine began to bleed through the broken pieces of glass causing red trails on the floor.

"It is with great pleasure. Good day, Mr. Perry."

Well you can tell everybody, yeah you can tell everybody, go ahead and tell everybody. I'm the man, I'm the man, I'm the man ... yes, I am, yes, I am, yes, I am.

CHAPTER TWENTY FOUR

Sandra wrapped the sheets around her body like a bath towel then got out of bed. Jacob winced from the pain as he sat up. Jacob had bruises around his neck, back and stomach, scratches on his face and busted knuckles. Sandra sat on the tufted blue leather chaise and crossed her legs.

"Are you ready to talk about what happened?"

"I got into a fight."

"You told me that. Why did you get into a fight and with who?"

"Babe, can you just get back in bed, please?"

"Jay, you came home in the middle of the night, beaten up ..."

Jacob snapped, "He didn't beat me up."

"Who is *he*?"

"It's no big deal."

"Jacob, you literally have someone's fingerprints around your neck! What do you mean, it's no big deal? We made love in the dark, that was no big deal, but were we supposed to shower and eat breakfast in the dark too?"

"Sandra ..."

"Did you think that I wouldn't notice?"

"I was hoping, yeah."

Sandra walked into the bathroom and came out in her bra and panties. She laid the flat sheet at the foot of the bed. "Where are you going?"

"Jacob, I love you. I'm so in love with you. I feel like I've been getting it wrong for all these years and then came you, my beautiful surprise. But I can't pretend that the obvious doesn't exist. I won't make that mistake ever again."

Jacob eased out of bed, naked and bruised all over his body. It hurt when he stood up too fast. He was sore and weak. Sandra's eyes began to water as she took in the discoloration the bruises had left.

"You're right. I'm sorry."

Sandra put her clothes on then marched out of the bedroom. Jacob could not move as fast. He put on a pair of gym shorts and hobbled down the hall after her. "Sandra!" Sandra had made her way to the foyer, carrying her heels in her hand. "Sandra. Damn, you win, ok! Come here, please." Sandra stood before the front door but did not turn around to face Jacob. She was afraid that his lies would sound familiar. The rambling, lack of eye contact and the *I'm sorry*. She wanted to forget what the pain felt like. Jacob kept his distance. "Will you at least look at me, please?" Sandra took a deep breath. She turned around and looked at Jacob who was on his knees. She approached him, lightly touching the scratches that marked his handsome face. He looked into her eyes as they sought understanding from him.

"Baby, what happened yesterday?"

"I got into a fight … with Jackson."

***

Sandra woke up feeling melancholy. She could not get her eyes to focus. She splashed cold water on her face from the bathroom sink, her eyes were red as if she had been crying in her sleep. Sandra sat on the toilet and rubbed her belly with both hands.

"Good morning, baby. I tossed and turned all night, I'm sorry. Mommy kept you up this time, huh?"

Sandra took a small load of clothes out of the dryer, she blushed at Jacob's boxers being mixed in with her laundry. Sandra had given Jacob a gift that had been intended for Jackson. Trust. She gave Jacob her trust. He treated her with such care and respect, like she was carrying his unborn child. Sandra began to cry, but she did not have any substance to assign her tears to. She called Annie Pearl. The phone rang until it connected to her voicemail. She called Aunt Tootie, *I'm sorry, but the person you called has a voice mailbox that has not been set up.*

Sandra showered and dressed, hoping this unsettling feeling would dissipate. She changed from jeans and Converse to gaucho pants and thigh high boots hoping to make herself feel pretty. A Federal Express commercial reminded her that she agreed to wait on a certified letter for Jackson. He was flying out to Chicago this afternoon to film one of the last few shows remaining until cancellation and would not be able to sign for it. Sandra seized the opportunity to pack the rest of her this and thats.

Sandra rambled in her purse, trying to grab her cell phone and keep her eyes on the road at the same time. Aunt Tootie was returning her call.

"Hey Auntie."

"Hey, I missed your call cause your mama over here playing dress up. Got me judging outfits and all kinds of carrying on."

"Dress up? Where is she going?"

"Mr. Willie taking her to dinner. Got her all giggly over here."

Annie Pearl could be heard in the background, *hey baby, don't listen to your auntie. It's just a pastor's anniversary dinner, but I still need to be cute.* Aunt Tootie entertained two conversations. "Annie Pearl, try that green dress back on, I like that one. You know it's funny you called. I had you heavy on my mind. Is everything ok?"

Sandra wanted to open her heart and tell her favorite aunt that she woke up with an eerie feeling that she just could not shake. "Yeah, everything is ok."

"You talking to Aunt Tootie. I have a sixth sense for liars and sinners. Now, is everything ok?"

"Aunt Tootie… sing to me, please."

Aunt Tootie sounded like a young Gladys Knight when she opened her mouth to sing. She was the Pied Piper for sinners and backsliders, bringing them to the alter in droves just by standing in front of the microphone. She would sing to Sandra when life was unkind, all she had to do was ask. Tears welled in Sandra's eyes. She released whatever was sent to steal her peace when Aunt Tootie began to sing.

"I've had some good days; I've had some hills to climb. I've had some weary days and some sleepless nights. But ohhh, when I look around and think things over, all of my good days outweigh my bad days, babygirl, I won't, I won't complain."

Sandra knocked on Jackson's front door then rang the bell. He appeared at the door with no shirt on and his pants were unbuttoned. She frowned at the bruises and lacerations on Jackson's face. They were still very fresh and needed to be treated and bandaged. When Sandra walked inside the mood was so hardhearted that it gave her a chill, even though Jackson smiled when he saw her.

"No heels, no makeup? I'm shocked you even know how to dress down. You still look beautiful, though."

Sandra looked down at her blue and red Chucks and her favorite blue jeans. "Thanks. It's just one of those days, I guess."

As Jackson walked into the laundry room, Sandra noticed a gash in the back of his head. Damn. Did they try to kill one another? she thought. He reappeared wearing a dress shirt that Sandra had picked out for him years ago when she was in Cincinnati for her cousin's wedding. It was still a nice shirt. "Jackson, what happened to you?"

Jackson tucked his shirt inside of his dress pants. "What do you mean?"

"Really?"

"Got into a little disagreement."

Sandra conceded that Jacob got into a little disagreement, Jackson got into a street brawl. "Are you ok?"

"Yeah, I'm fine."

"Who did you get into a disagreement with?"

"A couple guys tried to rob me at a gas station. They recognized who I was and thought they could get me for some money and jewelry."

"Did you contact the police?"

"No need, they didn't get anything."

"Are you going to be able to go on the air?"

"Tyrel works miracles with makeup. I called and he's ready for whatever."

"I'm sorry that happened. You need to get those wounds looked at." Sandra pointed towards the stairs. "You don't mind if I grab the rest of my things, do you? I think it's just a box of old cards and a few pairs of shoes."

"Of course not, help yourself."

Sandra felt queasy. She made her way up the stairs and used the hall bathroom. *Please not now.* Jackson knocked on the door after Sandra had gone missing for several minutes. "Are you ok?"

"I'm just a little nauseous. It's been days since I've felt like this."

Jackson stood on the other side of the bathroom door and waited. Sandra threw up yesterday's lunch, realizing she had not eaten since then. Ariel had suggested that she start carrying a toothbrush, toothpaste and a washcloth in her purse for surprises like these. Sandra pulled herself together. "I'm sorry, give me just a minute."

Jackson shook his head; *babies, these things are more trouble than they're worth. But it's the nature of the beast, right?*

"No worries, hopefully it'll be over soon."

Sandra opened the bathroom door to Jackson leaning against the wall. He followed Sandra into the bedroom. "Hey, I have to get ready to get on this plane, why don't you get some rest?" He lovingly held Sandra's arm, helping her ease into her rocking chair. "I'll be right back." Sandra closed her eyes for a moment. Maybe taking a nap once Jackson left would help restore her energy. Sandra wrapped her arms around her belly and rocked in her chair. She whispered, as if she knew her baby was sleeping.

"I love you so much. I will do everything within my power to be the best mommy I can be. You're perfect already, I can't wait to meet you."

Jackson stood in the doorway with a hot cup of green tea. Sandra held back tears and forged a smile. Jackson leaned in and kissed Sandra's forehead.

"I love you."

He rubbed her belly, acknowledging for the first time that there was something greater than their failed marriage. He placed the teacup in her hands. "I'm out of here. You can leave the letter on the console in the vestibule with your key."

"Sure. Safe travels."

"Thanks."

Jackson walked down the hall refusing to look reality in the face, he wanted Sandra to need him and he needed her to want him. Sandra positioned herself so that she could look out of the window. Jackson was idle at the end of the driveway, waiting for a car to pass so that he could back out. Soon, he was out of sight. Sandra held the white ceramic teacup with the word, love on it in her hands. She was humming the words Aunt Tootie sang to her on the way over. The smell of the tea was like aromatherapy, it put her mind at ease, her breathing was relaxed. She crossed her legs at the ankles and rocked slowly. She lifted the cup to her lips and blew lightly. The steam rolled aimlessly in the air then disappeared. Sandra pursed her lips around the rim of the teacup and drank the hot, green tea.

CHAPTER TWENTY FIVE

Sandra had fallen asleep in the rocking chair. She woke up when her body had become uncomfortable in the position she was in. Sandra reached inside her bag and checked her phone. She had a missed call from Jacob. There had been a change in his plans, instead of Eloisa coming to Renfro City to celebrate her grandson's successes, Jacob drove to Midland to visit his grandmother since she had not been feeling well lately. Sandra had been asleep for almost two hours, hoping she had not missed the delivery man she collected her belongings and went downstairs. She viewed footage from the security cameras. No one had been on the property since Jackson left. Sandra chose to abandon her due diligence and leave. She removed Jackson's key from her Minnie Mouse keychain and laid it on the console. The wind was beginning to pick up and the sky was light gray, Sandra pulled her hood over her head and hurried to her car.

"Hey baby."

"Hey, just letting you know that I'm heading home."

"I'll be leaving soon. I want to beat the rain; it floods pretty bad out here. You want me to pick up something to eat?"

"I'm cramping, I just want to lie down."

"I'm leaving now."

"Jay, spend time with your grandmother, I'll be fine."

"She's finally resting, I don't want to disturb her."

Sandra felt a discharge as she tried to bare the pain of her cramps. She gripped the steering wheel and groaned. Jacob searched Eloisa's junk drawer for something to write with. "Sandra …"

"Oh my God, I can't …"

"Sandra, what's wrong?"

Jacob left a note on a piece of mail for Eloisa and wrapped it around ten, one hundred dollar bills. He kissed her cheek, *Ti amo* then let himself out. He was about thirty seven minutes from Sandra's loft. If traffic was merciful, they would arrive at the same time. The tone in her voice was distressing. "Baby, talk to me. What's wrong?"

"I'm aching, God, please…"

Sandra began to cry, irrepressibly. She just needed to make it to the highway so that she could get home. Pain traveled down her back and spread to her hips. She sat erect and pressed her back against the heated driver's seat, she felt the rush of a gushy discharge. Her panties were soaked. Jacob was floating down the two lane road, expecting the worst, but hoping that he was overreacting. *Tap. Tap. Tap. Tap, tap.* The rain was steadily falling, threatening the promise of a down pour. Sandra was approximately nine miles from her exit. She tried to calm herself down, but she was afraid. She had lived in the anguish of this very moment several times before. "Jay …" Sandra called out. Jacob had finally made it to the expressway, he was pushing ninety miles per hour. In and out of lanes, driving with altruistic intent.

"Yes, I'm here."

"I'm home."

"Good, I'll be there in a minute."

Sandra pulled into her designated parking space. She looked around the parking garage to make sure she was alone before getting out of her car. Blood stained her jeans and transferred onto her car seat. She grabbed a jacket from the trunk and tied it around her waist. Sandra lowered her shoulder bag just below her stomach and quickly stepped into the elevator.

Sandra stood in the bathtub and took her pants and panties off. The cramps had subsided. She rolled her panties inside her jeans and laid them on the bathroom floor. She took a shower in anticipation of Jacob showing up at any minute. The storm had arrived, lightening lit up the whole living room causing shadows to rain dance on the walls.

Sandra was holding for Dr. Tittleton when Jacob banged on the door. She opened the door for him, and he hugged her for the first time again.

"What's going on? Is everything ok?"

"Dr. Tittleton, yes… Cassandra McCall… No, this is the first day, but it's heavy... I don't think so, no. I have on an overnight pad now."

Sandra began experiencing abdominal pain. Jacob felt stranded. He hung on her every word trying to piece fractioned information together for his own understanding. "I'm cramping again, it's becoming increasingly painful." Sandra closed her eyes tightly, barely able to finish her sentence. Jacob took the phone from her.

"Hello? Uh, this is Jacob, I'm Sandra's boyfriend. Can we meet you somewhere or something? She's in a lotta pain." Jacob made the writing motion, Sandra assured him that she knew the location of the hospital. "Ok. Yes, thanks. Ok, thank you. We'll see you shortly."

There were so many people restlessly awaiting medical attention. Ailing people, young and old people, hypochondriacs, addicts and recoverees all associated by the concept that a hospital visit would turn their conditions around. A weather update interrupted the regularly scheduled broadcast. An elderly gentleman wearing suspenders and a belt, lifted himself up by the wooden arms of the waiting room chair and stood in front of the television.

"This storm ain't playin' is it? Already started flooding in some areas."

Sandra signed in and provided her insurance information to the receptionist. Jacob added, that they were waiting to see Dr. Tittleton. In less than a nine minute wait, a nurse standing behind a wheelchair, called for Cassandra McCall.

Dr. Tittleton closed the door to Sandra's hospital room. She found Jacob sitting in the small waiting area at the end of the hall, across from the restroom with the huge Handicap sign on the door. Jacob followed Dr. Tittleton a few feet past the drinking fountains to give themselves a little privacy. She hid her hands inside her coat pockets to keep from expressing herself with her hands. Patients found it distracting when listening for significant keywords regarding their health. They stood face to face in front of a breastfeeding campaign poster. Dr. Tittleton waited for an expecting mother to waddle past before she began to speak.

"You guys got here in record time. By the time I got to her, she had soaked through the pad she was wearing. Her body expelled the fetus, we did a pelvic exam and ultrasound. There's no fetal tissue so, she won't need any further treatment. She will have some bleeding for approximately five to six days. She can take a low dose pain reliever if she wants for cramping, like she would for a regular menstrual cycle. Do you have any questions for me?"

"So, wait… she lost the baby?"

"Yes, I'm so sorry. But with her history it was highly likely that it would repeat itself."

"Can … is it ok if I go …" Jacob pointed up the hall.

"Sure, she's waiting for you. Take all the time you need; I'll get her squared away with the front desk then you can take her home."

Jacob paced outside of the door for a few minutes before going inside. He did not want to say anything stupid, so he practiced being quiet. Sandra looked defeated and broken. Her skin was pale, and her eyes were swollen. Life had been sucked out of her and all she could do was go home. Jacob looked at the EKG and Diagnostic machines, equipment that doctors used to inform them on how you were feeling. Jacob hated hospitals. The colors were always so drab, and the air was always thick and stale in hospital rooms. The last time Jacob stood over a hospital bed was to say goodbye to his father two years ago. Jacob reached out to Sandra, but she did not move.

"Have you ever tried to resist something … anything?"

"I'm sure I have."

"But you can't help yourself. You give in and you indulge anyway."

Jacob sat next to Sandra. "We're human."

"You know what the outcome is going to be, but you don't care because It feels so good."

Jacob took Sandra's hand and squeezed. She finally looked up at him. He was a beautiful man, inside and out. Sandra wiped Jacob's tears. "I didn't mean to scare you." Jacob chose silence over empathy. This was his loss too.

Sandra wanted to be alone with her feelings tonight. Jacob held her in his arms for as long as she allowed then buried himself in office work at Smitty's. Sandra cleaned her bathroom and put her dirty clothes in the washing machine. She recalled the first time she and Jackson lost a baby. The experience was devastating for Sandra. She lost her appetite and could not eat for over a week. Jackson told her that starving herself would not reverse what happened. Let's move on, he said. We have a lot of life left to live, he said. Sandra sat on the floor and leaned against the front of the couch. She had not reached out to Jackson to tell him that they had lost another baby. Sandra called Ariel and told her that she had lost her Godchild. Annie Pearl and Aunt Tootie were not afforded the news for fear of having to have this conversation with them just three short months later. Ariel did what best friends sign up to do. She allowed Sandra to be pitiful without judgement and listened while she played the blame game. Once it was out of her system, Ariel stepped in to save Sandra from herself.

"Friend, nothing happens by chance. It's just too soon to see the blessing in this."

Sandra woke up in the middle of the night missing Jacob's body pressed against hers, his arms around her waist and him breathing heavily in her ear. She marveled at how he was in love with old school R&B and even knew all the words. She chuckled at how he turned into a five year old when he spoke to his grandmother on the phone. He brushed his teeth before he went to bed, he was well endowed and knew how to use it. They laughed out loud in public while holding hands. He paid attention to details and he could beat Jackson in a fist fight wearing a five-hundred-dollar suit.

Jacob grabbed the pair of jeans that he had tossed in the dirty clothes basket; stumbling using the wall for support, he was trying to get his foot inside the pant leg. He dragged his pants down the stairs and across the floor. He checked the cameras and opened the door immediately. Jacob embraced Sandra, lifting her off of her feet. She had lost a love and it hurt like hell, but love was standing right in front of her, with one leg inside his pants, kissing her all over her face.

"Why didn't you call me? I would've come to you."

"I woke up thinking about you and before I knew it, I was at your door."

Jacob gazed into Sandra's eyes; he gave her an Eskimo kiss. "You ok?"

"I am now."

CHAPTER TWENTY SIX

Jackson tapped his fingers on the dinner table, waiting for Mr. Justin G. Degadia to arrive. Jackson held his hand up when the waitress tried to refill his water glass for the second time. Justin walked in looking like Mr. Hollywood by way of New York, dressed in a Brioni suit. He patted Jackson on the back and sat at the other end of the table.

"Are we eating? Let's eat, where's the waitress?" Justin drummed the table.

"I'm not hungry."

"Come on, my treat. Order the Beef Wellington if you want to."

Justin bashfully replied to a message sent to him just as he took his seat. He was a new husband and his new wife sent him a newlywed message. Jackson took a look at the menu and decided to order something after all. If he could not finish it, he would eat it later once he was in for the night. Justin covered his face. "Melissa, she's my world … man, she's so sweet. She sends me this message and asks me what I'm doing. So, I say, I'm missing you and she says, not half as much as I'm missing you."

Jackson rolled his eyes. "I take it she's your first girlfriend, I mean marriage."

"Yeah, and we want babies, man. We're just practicing for now though." Justin let out a hearty laugh then drummed the table again.

"Order me the Chipotle Steak and Collard greens and a Salmon salad since you're paying. I'll be right back."

Jackson stood in the antechamber and placed a call to Sandra. He had not spoken to her since Thursday, just before he left for Chicago. Her phone rang twice then connected to voicemail as if she had ignored his call. He held the line momentarily, considering leaving a message before hanging up. He sent her a text message; *[Just checking on you. Hit me back.]* Jackson stalled before returning to the table anticipating a return call from Sandra.

Justin had ordered appetizers for the both of them. Honey Glazed chicken wings and an onion ring tower.

"Who's going to eat all this food?"

"Hey, that's what To Go boxes are for, my friend. I put your order in. That salad sounds good, I got me one too. So, how's that beautiful wife of yours? Cindy, right?"

"Sandy. She's good."

"Sorry about that. Good, tell her I said, hi. She probably doesn't remember me anymore. You gotta bring her around more often."

"I'll keep that in mind."

Justin leaned in and lowered his voice, "Jackson, I gotta ask ya, what happened to your face? You're walking around looking pummeled."

"I almost got robbed and uh, I had to fight a couple guys."

"Geez, Louise! You gotta be careful out here. Did they let you on the air like that?"

Jackson cleared his throat. "No, they issued a public statement, so ... I'll be back on in two weeks."

"Ok, now that we've caught up and we've ordered food ... wait, no drinks. We need drinks."

Justin held his finger up and caught the waitress's attention. He ordered a bottle of wine and two beers. Justin is the producer of Box Seats Sports and Locker Room News. Jackson was a guest on both of his shows a while back when he returned to the States to kickbox. Box Seats Sports was new, and Justin needed a popular face to jump start the show's success. In turn, he put in a good word for Jackson with his good friend, Gene at All in Sports where Jackson ultimately became the face of the show.

"What have you heard about my show?"

"What do you mean?"

"Come on Justin, what's the word on the street? They're pulling the plug, but ain't nobody talkin' and nobody knows nothin'."

"I don't know, Gene's not over there anymore. So, I'm out of the inside scoop loop."

"I heard Gerald is coming to your network."

"Whittaker?"

"Yeah."

"He may be. But I don't own the network."

"Justin, look I need you to pull some strings for me."

"Jacks, you know I would, but there's no room for you, right now."

The food followed the drinks to the table. Everything looked and smelled delightful. Jackson cut a corner of his eight ounce steak. It was tender and juicy. Justin finished off the onion ring tower then dug into his salad. "I'll tell you this, if you're smart, you'll buy some businesses and retire early."

"I own a business."

"You're not talking about that barbershop, are you?"

"Yeah, the barbershop and I own a few properties, I can get a few million for easy."

Justin washed down a mouth full of ruffage with a sip of beer.

"Look, I produce two shows, but that's just bread, no butter. I own a string of restaurants, six to be precise. I got a couple of movie theaters over in Scottsburg and two in Williamsburg. Something I can leave to my kids and set them up for success. You're worth what, maybe sixty-five to seventy-five million, invest a little. But I'm Jewish, what do I know?"

Jackson sighed. He appreciated the pep talk, but what he needed was to see his name in lights. He did not want to be forgotten. He glanced at his phone. No calls, no messages. Justin got the waitress's attention then pointed to the half-eaten plates of food and held up two fingers. "Hey, the next time you're out here bring Sandy, I'll bring Melissa and we'll paint the town purple." The waitress brought the bill and two plastic To Go containers and placed them in the small free space on the tabletop.

"Sounds good. Maybe we can have dinner at one of your restaurants."

Justin drummed the table. "We just did."

Jackson sulked around the studio as Gerald covered his and Jackson's commentary. It was Gerald's show for the next two tapings. He sat confidently behind, what the production crew liked to call; the Sports station. Jackson was scheduled to interview American kickboxing great, Ali Lovette next week. He suggested they postpone the interview since kickboxing was his area of expertise. The director never said no to anyone, he always sent his excuses to do his grunt work.

"Due to scheduling and advertising, postponing the interview could hurt pocketbooks and ratings. You can understand that, right?"

Jackson trolled around Chicago's city limits until he found a pulse. He backed into a handicapped parking space and watched as a palette of brown, tan and black people swarmed the blocked off streets to indulge in the exhibitions of the vendors. Jackson rolled his window down to get a better look at the banner that was tied in between two portable light posts; the Ebony Arts Exposition.

Sandra had begged Jackson to take her there so that she could commune with the underground writers who sold their handwritten works and songstresses who would sing for you on the spot, meet the artisans and thespians who were celebrities amongst their city.

Sandra returned Jackson's call. He sat up in his seat and cleared his throat. He knew he had what it took to make Sandra a happy wife, he just needed a little more time.

"Hello."

"Hi."

"Hey, I was just calling to check on you, I hadn't heard from you. Are you feeling any better?"

"I am, actually. And I'm sorry I didn't reach out to you sooner. I wanted to, I just ... I don't know. I didn't want to tell you over the phone."

"Tell me what?"

"I went to the hospital Thursday evening."

"What did they say?"

"We lost the baby."

Jackson looked out the window and watched a young lady with big curly hair and big breasts to match her backside, hike up the stairs to the museum entrance in high heels. A young man wearing African attire caught up with her and slapped her on the butt, breaching Jackson's admiration. "You there?" Sandra asked.

"Yeah, I'm just shocked. Sandy, I'm sorry, I wasn't there. We'll get through this. Let's sit down and talk when I get back."

"Sit down and talk about what?"

"We lost our baby; you don't think we should talk about it?"

"Jackson, we've been here before. I don't want this to consume me."

"Sandy."

"What?"

"Is there any chance that we could work something out? Forget about the divorce, all those papers mean is we don't have a title, but we don't need a title. Remember when we said, no matter what we would always talk to each other before making rash decisions?"

"That was in reference to buying a time share. And you bought it anyway, without consulting me."

"I almost forgot, I ran into Justin today, remember him?"

"Jackson."

"Degadia. Justin Degadia. He wants to have dinner with us."

"Jackson, stop. Just stop it. We're not going to dinner with Justin and we're not going to work things out. The one thing that tied us together, we lost. And the one thing that would have tied us together, forever... we lost. All we can do now is cut our losses and move on."

"So, to hell with our marriage, you ain't even fighting for us no more?"

"We don't have a marriage and I don't have any fight left."

"Sandy, I know if we just sit and talk, I can make you see that ..."

"Jackson, we don't have anything left to talk about. What we had is over."

"That's how you feel?"

"Unfortunately, yes. That's how I feel."

Jackson hung up on Sandra. A failed marriage was the inevitable outcome of a degenerate lifestyle. Jackson was back in his hotel room, sitting on the edge of the bathtub. Piece by piece life subtracted the things that were damaged and could not be used anymore, leaving him a broken vessel. He did not need Sandra to be justified, he needed her to love him.

Jackson got inside of the tub, fully clothed and rested his head against the marble tile. He remembered his grandmother telling him as a young boy, *you can run, but you can't hide. Life will always find a way to catch up with you.* Jackson clenched his teeth, nostrils flared, and fists balled up tight, fighting to govern his emotions.

Her forehead was pressed firmly against Jackson's forehead, her breathing was heavy and incessant causing Jackson to feel suffocated. Her weary eyes were fixated on Jackson's eyelids. His deceit left a trail of destruction; hurt left him burdened. Her voice was drenched in the pain of every heartbreak he had ever felt and all the pain he had ever caused.

Look at me.

He rebelled, refusing to open his eyes.

Look at me!

Jackson slowly opened his eyes exposing his damaged soul; forced to look reality in the face.

CHAPTER TWENTY SEVEN

Sandra had worn Ariel out. They had been to five different apartment homes; including the loft that was for sale in Sandra's building, two shopping malls and lunch at Smitty's. Ariel was in town for a few days in preparation for her new beginnings. She had narrowed her dwelling options down to two definites and one maybe. Ariel, fat girl danced in the kitchen, enjoying her Bar-B-Que meatloaf and garlic mashed potatoes leftovers while Sandra rambled through her luggage for clothes to steal. Sandra held up a red sweater dress.

"No, you can't have that. I *just* bought it."

"But you have two and they don't sell them here."

"Yes, they do."

"Not this particular style."

"God, take it and close my bag."

"So ..."

"So, what?"

"What do you think?"

Ariel took a bite of her cornbread muffin then closed the container. "About what, Jacob?"

"Yes! You haven't said anything."

"I think he's a keeper. And he's cute for a white boy."

"But ..."

"But ... I just want you to be careful. You have a lot going on right now."

"He's one of the good guys. I didn't even require half the man that Jacob is from Jackson and that was my fault. Jackson isn't capable of being that kind of man, I know that now. Jacob is different, he has a soul."

"I'm team Jacob, but one wrong move and ..."

"I know, you'll whoop his ass."

Ariel joined Sandra in the living room. She nonchalantly mentioned that she had been sleeping with Gregory, her manager, but now that she was being promoted, they would be colleagues and could go on dates without Human Resources having a fit. Gregory was also transferring with the company. He would be moving in late Spring with the last leg of the transferees. Sandra solicited a full description including his zodiac sign and bad habits and Ariel delivered. Ariel had not planned on bringing rain to the parade, but she needed to make certain that her best friend was not masking tears behind her pretty smile.

"So, are you ok?"

"Ugh, if one more person asks me that. Yes, I'm ok."

"Just making sure."

Sandra sat Indian style on the sofa and cuddled the throw pillow, digressing. Jackson always made her feel like it was her loss and not theirs. Ariel was right, Sandra was beginning to see the blessing in this heartbreaking lesson.

Ariel noticed the edge of a folder sticking from underneath the couch.

"What's this?"

Ariel opened the folder and read the items that Sandra had listed on the document sheet, "Coconut Shrimp, Red beans and Rice, Mustard … what's this?"

Sandra began explaining why she documented the things that made her ill. They were to help determine any contributors that may have led to the termination of her pregnancy. Ariel read the small print and told Sandra that her documentation was useless. "Writing down what you ate was for your personal records. She needed you to bring the samples of food to her so that she could test them. And it's sixty dollars per test."

Sandra took the piece of paper from Ariel and read the fine print. "It doesn't matter anyway."

"What did you eat, Thursday?"

"I didn't eat anything. The day before, Jay bought me Chinese food for lunch."

"Why didn't you eat, Thursday?"

"Can we change the subject, please?"

"So, what's this good news that you can't wait to tell me about?"

Sandra's face lit up. "I was going to take you to see it tomorrow, but …"

Sandra brought a folder down from upstairs and put it in Ariel's hands. Ariel's facial expression confirmed her gladness. Sandra scooted closer to Ariel, reading along with her. "I still can't believe it."

Ariel stretched her arms out to Sandra. "I am so, so, so proud of you! So, what's the next step? Oh my God! I am so proud of you!"

"The owner can either accept or reject my offer. If she accepts then I'm on my way to owning a café! … slash, bookstore."

Sandra put a contract on the little coffee shop on 23rd and Lucas thanks to Audrey, who promised to be there with bells on, on opening day. Ariel was excited for her childhood friend. She had finally taken steps to peruse her lifelong dream. Ariel sprung from the sofa and put her shoes on.

"Come on, take me to see it!"

***

Sandra pulled the covers over her head then stuck her leg out from under her comforter. She turned over on her back and threw her pillow onto the floor. She heard Doctor Tittleton's voice, *we need to schedule an evaluation for genetic and hormonal abnormalities.* Sandra turned on her side. She heard Jackson's voice; *I love you.* She curled her toes when she felt his kiss upon her forehead. He rubbed her belly, *I love you.* Sandra curled into the fetal position and moaned. The picture was crystal clear. Jackson kissed her forehead and rubbed her belly, *I love you*, he said. Sandra gripped the edge of the bed and began to cry. He kissed her forehead and rubbed her belly, *I love you*, he said then placed the cup of tea in her hands.

Sandra cried out, "No … no. No!"

Sandra pulled the covers from her face, jolted from her sleep, out of breath. Ariel ran up the stairs. Sandra's face and hair were damp. "I have to go!"

"Sandy, where are you going?"

Sandra bolted down the stairs and grabbed her car keys. Ariel ran after her, trying to keep from stepping on her night gown and falling. "Sandy!" Sandra opened the front door. Ariel grabbed her by the waist then kicked the front door closed. "What the hell is wrong with you?!"

Sandra reached for the door handle. "I have to go!"

"Where do you think you're going? You're in panties and a bra! Sandy, it was a bad dream. Honey, look at me. You were dreaming."

Sandra ran upstairs and put the clothes she had worn from the day before back on. Ariel did not know what was going on, but she put her clothes back on from the day before and prepared for a ride. "What are you looking for?"

"Damnit! I left my key on the console in the foyer. I took the key off my keychain, shit!"

"Tell me what you're looking for, so I can help you!"

"I have a spare key! Thank you, God! Now, where is it?"

Ariel began looking through boxes from Sandra's storage closet for a spare key. Sandra ran upstairs and grabbed an old wooden jewelry box from the top shelf of her closet. She closed her eyes, hoping to find what she was looking for. She opened the jewelry box with the broken latch and lifted the small compartment that she used for earring backs. She grabbed the spare key and stuck it in the front pocket of her jeans. "Ariel, I got it!"

Sandra drove through the streets like a mad woman. Ariel did not ask questions, she held on tight and was ready to fight if she had to. Sandra entered Brigance and felt lightheaded. She parked in front of the mailbox and stared vulnerably at the house across the street with the big, pretty, red double doors. Ariel followed Sandra inside of Jackson's house through the side door.

"Wow, this is beautiful!"

Sandra entered the passcode to the security system and viewed footage from Thursday and Friday. No one ever came to deliver a certified letter. She viewed footage from the night Jacob and Jackson had gotten into a fight. She saw Jackson storm across the street and kick the front door several times. Ariel stood behind Sandra and watched her disable all the cameras for the maximum duration of fifty nine minutes. She then deleted the surveillance footage from eight minutes ago of them parking in front of the house and walking onto the property. Sandra ran upstairs to the master bedroom and turned the sitting area light on. Ariel pointed to the rocking chair. "Were you here before you went to the hospital?"

There was dried blood on the seat of the rocking chair. Sandra took the washcloth from the plastic bag that she kept in her purse along with her toothbrush and toothpaste. Ariel took the cloth and ran warm water over it in the bathroom sink. Sandra took the test tube from her purse and untwisted the cap. Ariel cleaned the chair then folded the washcloth so that Sandra could put it back inside of the baggie.

"I came over because he said he was waiting on a certified letter and he wouldn't be able to sign for it. He was leaving for Chicago and I needed to get the rest of my things. I didn't feel well. I ... I hadn't slept and ..."

"Sandy, slow down. Why are we here?"

"He always kissed my forehead and rubbed my belly and he would tell me, he loved me. Then he would give me a hot cup of green tea."

"Ok, what does that mean?"

"With each pregnancy, each one, he would kiss my forehead and rub my belly. Then ... then he would tell me ... he would say, I love you. Then he ..."

"Then he what?"

"He would give me a hot cup of green tea. I didn't eat anything Thursday, but I did have a hot cup of green tea."

Sandra picked up the teacup that she had sat on the windowsill, it was cold; there was a thin film on top of the liquid. She took the cup into the bathroom and poured the tea into the test tube over the sink then tightened the cap around the rim. Sandra poured the rest of the green liquid into the sink then sat the cup on the counter. Ariel grabbed the teacup then tailed Sandra down the winding staircase.

"Let's get the fuck outta here."

CHAPTER TWENTY EIGHT

Jacob stood in the mirror and straightened his tie. He took the lint brush and rolled the white, sticky paper down each pant leg then each arm. He had a fresh haircut and was finally able to find a suit worthy enough to wear with his Tom Ford alligator shoes. He sprayed cologne in the air then stood under the mist. His Jaguar had been washed and detailed. And he had condoms if he were to be so lucky.

Sandra slipped into her Geraldise Avi; nightlife collection, otherwise known as the little black dress. Her makeup was done by Anton Dubose, a local makeup artist who was nicknamed, magic hands. She sprayed her hands with perfume then massaged the scent into her neck and chest. She clamped her silver bracelet cuff around her wrist then slid her pedicured toes into her Louboutin, glittered dragonfly pumps. Sandra sprayed the sheets with Hawaiian Ginger linen spray; if she were to be so lucky.

Sandra opened the door, unable to take her eyes off of the man who stood confidently in front of her holding two dozen red roses. Jacob kissed Sandra on the cheek to avoid smearing her lipstick. He extended the roses to her.

"Wow! You look absolutely, stunning!"

Sandra blushed. "Thank you. These are beautiful."

Sandra did not have a vase big enough for twenty four, long stemmed roses. She sat them in the kitchen sink in the meantime. Jacob wanted to celebrate Sandra for sealing the deal on her very own bookstore.

Menus with no prices, four courses before the entrée, a view of the city from every window and live music. Sandra grabbed her silver clutch and took Jacob's hand. "I've always found you attractive, but you are so sexy tonight."

Jacob turned red, he kissed Sandra's hand. "Thank you. Ready?"

Sandra fixed Jacob's collar then kissed him on the lips. "Yes."

The mayor was having dinner with his mistress. Community leaders were staged to blur her identity from the public's watchful eye. The music was spellbinding; melodies from the fingertips of two young black men, one playing the violin the other the piano. The waiter served southern comfort with their dinner choices, being certain to secure a generous tip.

Dessert for the beautiful lady?

"No, thank you. May I have a glass of water, please?"

Most certainly. And for you, sir?

"Nothing for me, thanks."

Jacob talked about executing his plans for the Broken Bottle. He presented a few name suggestions to see how Sandra felt about them. They laughed and shared heartwarming stories about their deceased fathers. Jacob opened up about his relationship with his mother. They brought their pasts to the present, reminiscing about a time when they were familiar strangers. They talked about Jackson and Jacob's ex-girlfriend, who was now divorced from the man she had left him for. Loving glances, naughty remarks and one hundred sixty two dollars later their dinner at La'Bosco had concluded.

"I had a really nice time. Dinner, the horse and carriage ride, everything was perfect."

"Maybe we can do this again real soon."

"I'd like that. Would you like to come inside?"

Jacob peeked inside Sandra's loft. "Are you sure your parents aren't home?"

"They won't be home until Monday night. It'd just be me and you."

"In that case …"

Jacob stood in the doorway and kissed Sandra. She pulled Jacob inside by his necktie. He looked around the living room. "This is a nice place; your parents must be rich."

"Maybe, but they always tell me they don't have any money. Wanna see my room?"

Sandra took Jacob by the hand and led him upstairs to her bedroom. She stepped out of her pumps and positioned Jacob's arms around her waist. "Do you like it?"

"Yeah, it smells like pretty girls in here. I like pretty girls."

They kissed softly and intimately. Sandra lowered her dress straps until her arms were free. Her dress trickled down her body, uncovering her bare breasts and black panties. Jacob cupped Sandra's breasts with his hands, kissing them, playfully biting her nipples.

"What else do you like?"

Jacob looked up at Sandra. "Your face."

Jacob laid Sandra on her stomach. He rubbed her back and massaged her shoulders. Sandra turned over and questioned Jacob with her eyes.

"I don't want a massage. It's been almost a month. Why is that?"

"Well, we ... you had to have time... to heal."

"Baby, I had a miscarriage, not back surgery."

"Sandra, this is all new to me. The pain you were in ... I just didn't want to; you know mess something up."

Sandra unbuttoned Jacob's shirt. "I'm not in any pain now."

Jacob took his time making love to his girlfriend like he had snuck into her parent's house while they were away for the weekend. "I've missed you." Jacob buried his face in between Sandra's legs in search of something sweet. Sandra let him know when he was getting close. She was his cheerleader. "You feel so good." She dug her nails into Jacob's back when his strokes became deep and steady. She moaned, biting him on the ear. "Keep it right there."

"I don't wanna cum yet," he muttered.

Sandra wanted all of him, she felt his body tighten.

"Don't hold back on me."

Sandra watched Jacob's body sink into hers from her full length mirror. Muscles flexed from his shoulders to his calves with each thrust. Jacob held on for as long as he could. *Fuck!* He nestled his face in the bow of Sandra's neck and shoulder then released. She felt his heartbeat against her chest. Sandra grinned. "Next time don't stay away for so long."

Jacob's body was heavy on top of Sandra's. She pulled her leg from under Jacob's leg and wiggled her foot that had fallen asleep.

"Jay." Sandra caressed his face.

Jacob lifted his head then laid back down. "Jay, you do realize you're *still* inside of me." Jacob lifted himself until they were disconnected; they had fallen into a coma after round two and a half. Sandra got out of bed and slid into Jacobs shirt.

"Where you goin'?"

"To the kitchen for something to drink. Want anything?"

"No, I'm good. Hurry back."

Sandra stood at the top of the stairs in a live daydream, watching Jacob who had stolen her pillow and taken up most of the bed hoping that what they have in this moment never fades.

She sat her bottle of apple juice on the nightstand and got back into bed. Jacob wrapped his arms around his everything and pressed his body against hers, breathing heavily in her ear. "I love you."

Sandra thought to herself, the perfect ending to the perfect night.

***

It was 3:26 AM. Emmanuelle wrapped himself in his silk pink robe with the fur around the collar. He checked his phone to see if Jackson had replied to any of his seven text messages. The message delivery notification confirmed that the messages were sent successfully but had not been read. He phoned Jackson but was immediately directed to voicemail. Emmanuelle tied his robe at the waist and retrieved his prepaid phone from an old Nike shoebox that he kept on a shelf in the corner of his Armoire. He called Jackson from the burner phone and was able to transmit the call, but Jackson did not answer.

"Beloved, are you playing cat and mouse with me?"

Emmanuelle drafted a message containing six pictures.

[Have you ever wondered why your husband rarely answered your calls while he was in Chicago, always having to call you back?]

Emmanuelle removed his princess cut diamond ring and stored it in its ring box.

"Mr. Perry, you know I have a way of getting your attention."

He drafted another message, attaching six more incriminating pictures of Jackson.

[We both knew what we had, and we stayed anyway. Will us girls ever learn?]

He drafted a final message, attaching half naked pictures of Sandra.

[By the way, you are fucking gorgeous!]

Emmanuelle placed several calls to Jackson but failed to make a connection. He gasped, insulted, "Shame on you. You know I don't like to get my nails dirty, but what choice have you left me with?"

Emmanuelle prepared himself to leave a voice message. He checked his smile in the hand-held mirror that he kept by his bed, cleared his throat and fluffed the fur on his robe collar. He opened a jar of facial moisturizer cream and placed dots under his eyes and around his cheek bones. He massaged the white cream into his skin then he placed a call to Jackson.

Please leave your message after the tone ... Beep.

"Jackson, I must say, you're a courageous man. Most adulterers aren't fans of Russian Roulette."

Emmanuelle sat with his legs wide open, elbow propped on his thigh with the phone up to his ear. His tone was organic, "Time's up."

Emmanuelle entered Sandra's number as the receiver of his drafted messages. His left hand covered his chest while he held his phone in the palm of his right hand. He fired one shot, then another then the last. The delivery notification had confirmed that the messages were sent successfully. The adrenaline felt like a strong orgasm from Jackson's penetration. Emmanuelle crossed his legs and reloaded, fiending for the sensation of another climax. He fired twelve more rounds before finally emptying the clip, sending the pictures to all of the contacts that were saved in Jackson's phone.

Emmanuelle fanned himself. He tossed his phone on the round ottoman that posed at the foot of his canopy bed. He blew out the Chanel N° 5 scented candles that were lit on a silver serving tray on his dresser then took his robe off and crawled onto the bed. He positioned his Aloe sleeping mask over his eyes.

"My darling Jackson, take note. Now, that's how you fuck somebody."

CHAPTER TWENTY NINE

Sandra's hair covered her face. She was asleep, curled up in the middle of the bed wearing Jacob's shirt. He massaged her back until she finally woke up.

"Good morning, beautiful."

Sandra smiled. "It is, isn't it? Why are you dressed, you have to leave?"

Todd needed to meet with Jacob at his earliest convenience about the chain of command before meeting with Loren. The sooner everyone knew their positions the better. They had paid good money for Diablo's information and was gradually tunneling a path to Kendo.

"Yeah, I have a meeting. Me and Lance need to start putting in work at the Broken Bottle. I gotta go home first and get cleaned up."

Sandra sat up. She noticed Jacob had on his suit jacket with no shirt. "Do you need this back?"

"No, it looks better on you. Don't get up, I'll let myself out."

Sandra heard Jacob walk halfway down the stairs then turn around. She waited for Jacob to speak, before assuming something was wrong. His eyes were saying a million things, but only one word came out of his mouth, "Sandra."

"Yes, baby?"

"Let's get married."

"What?"

Jacob sat on the bed and looked Sandra in the eyes, it was the sincerest gesture he could find. "Let's get married."

"Jay ... "

"I don't want to live without you. We can go to the courthouse. No one has to know until you're ready to tell them. If you want a big wedding, that's cool too."

"Baby, marriage is ... I mean, it takes ...You want to marry me?"

"Yes. We can go pick out rings, you can get whatever you want."

"Jay ..."

"Sandra, I may disappoint you, but it'll never be intentionally. I may do things backwards and get on your nerves, but I'm willing to learn. You'll never have to question how I feel about you." Jacob crawled onto the bed and faced Sandra. "I love you. Will you marry me?"

"Jacob, I love you too."

Whether it be in his favor or not, Jacob was not leaving without an answer. Life will sometimes offer grand opportunities, but only once. The greater the risk the greater the reward. Just as Jacob was foolish enough to ask Sandra to be his wife. She was foolish enough to say, "Yes."

The temperature had dropped again and was to continue to fall throughout the weekend. Sandra hated the cold, but she needed to clear out the last few items in her storage unit so that she could return the key. Sandra brushed her hair, thinking about last night. The way Jacob took care of her to the way he made love to her; she was so in love with the very thought of him. *Mrs. Rossi, wow.* Her phone rang disturbing her euphoria. Sandra grimaced at the series of messages that had been sent to her phone. When she realized the nature of the incoming call, she quickly deterred her attention from what was probably Jackson going on a ranting rampage. *I should change my number.*

"Hello?"

"Hi, this is Violet, from Iredrove Technologies. I'm calling on behalf of June Orton. May I speak with Cassandra Perry, please?"

"Yes, it's McCall now, Sandra McCall."

"My apologies, we'll get that updated in our system. Mrs. Orton has the results of your lab work. We know this is short notice, but if you're available to come in today, that would be great. If not, we can get you rescheduled for next Friday."

Next Friday would be another seven days of dreaded anticipation. Sandra agreed to an appointment with June Orton at 1:15 PM. "Thanks, we'll see you soon."

Sandra finished dressing in the bathroom. If she left now, she could clean the storage unit, close her storage account and still make it to her appointment in time. Sandra grabbed her purse and checked to make sure her keys were inside. She checked the messages that had been awaiting her attention all morning.

Sandra's shoulders slumped; she was incapacitated. Her eyes were in denial, but the truth was vivid, provoking her. Her heartbeat could be heard beating outside of her chest. She scrolled through the pictures; attacked by revolting emotions that each picture portrayed. She was strangled by callous intentions and was unable to catch her breath. Her breathing was abnormal. Her breaths were short and quick, growing faster until she began to hyperventilate. *Oh my God!* With every blink, the room became dimmer. She was dizzy. Sandra held her breath, trying to slow down her heart rate. She tried drinking the apple juice that she had left on her nightstand. She ran into the bathroom and fell to her knees, gripping the seat of the toilet, she threw up. *Jackson, what the fuck?! Oh my God!* Sandra ran cold water from the bathtub faucet then held her head under the running water. She did not realize she was crying until she tasted the salt on her lips. Everything that she believed to be true about Jackson, his words and what he claimed he felt for her was a gross fabrication of the truth. Bold and abhorrent lies. The hurt turned to rage, and her rage almost caused her to black out on the bathroom floor.

"I don't even know who the fuck you are! My God!"

Sandra was tested for Hepatitis B, sexually transmitted diseases and HIV on her first prenatal visit, her results were negative. She set a reminder on her cell phone to make an appointment for next week to have herself retested and she was taking her fiancé with her.

Sandra had packed her heart and took her love away from Jackson, but he always had to have the last word.

***

Sandra signed her name on the visitor's log in sheet and pinned the guest badge on her jacket just above where her zipper stopped. She walked down the hall until she reached the blue floor then took the blue elevators to floor four. She sat on the clear plastic chair and waited on instructions from the floor receptionist.

"Ms. McCall, please follow this gentleman, he's going to take you down to one of the consultation rooms and Mrs. Orton will meet you there, momentarily."

"Thank you."

Sandra followed the young man who wore a lab coat and a man bun to a small room that looked like a scientist's playroom. There were two chairs pushed under a table that was covered in Metabolic pathway maps and Molecular Biology leaflets and silver foil packages that looked like oversized pop tarts. He smiled at Sandra and closed the door on his way out. June Orton walked in the room shortly after, like the receptionist had advised with a big smile, holding a short stack of folders.

"Hey, how's it going?"

"Good, how about you?"

"Gosh, we have been so swamped these past few weeks, but I'll live. I'm sorry it took so long to get back to you. I ordered another set of tests on your sample." June sat two folders in front of Sandra. "These are your copies of everything I'll go over with you, today. That includes test results, what they mean and what methods we used to get those results. Sound good?"

Sandra nodded. "Sure."

June began by opening the folder with the case number written across the front. There were red lines under certain words and asterisks marked in front of the numbers two and four. Though, Sandra did not provide food samples, June still provided feedback on the bacteria and nutritional value that are found in the foods listed on Sandra's documentation sheet. June moved the top sheet to the other side of the folder. Sandra opened the folder in front of her and attempted to follow along.

"We started with a basic testing called, Column chromatography. We needed to verify that the components which make up green tea were present. Next, we did a chemical test. This allowed us to separate the components of the tea during purification. We eliminated Amino acids, vitamins, caffeine; the common things that are always invited to the party. Catechins is the host of the party. It's a type of polyphenol, which is like a super food and are the main components in green tea. Michael, my assistant saw a conflicting element. Meaning, there was an imposter, pretending to be the host. We took the teensy, weeny dot that he found and tested it. Every component has a chemical signature and we were able to prove the existence of a chemical compound *not* found in green tea."

Sandra's heart dropped. She closed her folder and waited for June to make sense of all this. June closed the folder with the testing analysis and opened the folder with the test results. "We found Mifepristone in the green tea sample. We also found a tiny particle of Misoprostol attached to it."

"Misoprostol? What is that?"

"Generally, it helps reduce complications with ulcers, but more commonly associated with promoting premature labor or ending a pregnancy when used with Mifepristone. Mifepristone blocks progesterone which is needed to maintain a pregnancy."

Sandra thought she was going to be sick. She began to shake. June reached out to her. "Are you ok? I know this is tough to hear."

Sandra could barely form the words. "Are you telling me that … that someone put an abortion pill in my tea?"

"Yes."

"But I've been tested so many times, I'm sure it would have shown up somewhere."

"Misoprostol can be undetectable in the bloodstream. It's undetectable in urine as well. The only reason we were able to catch it was because the component that was left behind was not grounded completely. It was a very, tiny small crumb that the naked eye would've overlooked."

"I can't take anymore." Sandra stood up and wrapped her arms around herself. "How much am I supposed to take?"

June closed the folder and told Sandra that there was no charge for the chemical testing, or the documented information provided. She asked that Sandra give her a few minutes before she left. Sandra took the folders and held them to her chest. *This son of a bitch is psychotic! Who the fuck did I marry?!* June returned to the consultation room and stuck an envelope in Sandra's folder.

"If you need anything at all, please don't hesitate to call me."

Sandra had never been so broken and so emotionally bankrupt. She wanted to drive to Brigance and dump everything inside of her on top of Jackson. Her rage, her disappointment, her hurt, distress, hate, everything. She looked through the folders, trying to gain her bearings. *Had me thinking that I was less than a woman, that something was wrong with me! Miscarriage, after fucking miscarriage! I fucking hate you, Jackson! Fucking murderer!* Sandra stared at an incoming call from Jacob, tears flowing, nose running. She could not answer because the sound of her voice would alarm him. She needed someone to help her understand how Jackson could do something so horrific, so vile. His grave intentions came from the same heart that he told her he loved her with. Sandra went through crying fits and bouts of anger, regret and anxiety. She opened the envelope that June slid inside of her folder. There was a business card and a piece of paper that looked like an official document of some kind. Sandra pulled the card from the envelope.

Simmons County

Criminal Prosecutor

Timothy Orton

1685 Bedrod Circle, 2nd Floor

Simmons County Office Building

Renfro City, IN 46249

812-216-2560

Sandra stuck the card back inside of the envelope then removed the document. It declared that, the documents provided are original documents and can be used in a court of law. Sandra fastened her seat belt and stuck the envelope back in the folder. She unfastened her seatbelt, knowing that if she pulled out of the parking lot, she was more than capable of hurting herself or someone else. *God, how much am I supposed to take?* She called Audrey.

"Hey buttercup!"

"I need you. Are you home?"

"Yeah, just got back in, actually... Sandra, is there something wrong?"

Audrey heard the pain in Sandra's voice. It was heavy and dense. Audrey still had her keys in her hand. She hurried outside and got in her car. "Sweetie?"

"I can't take anymore."

"Sweetheart, where are you?"

"I just ... this is too much. I'm not built for this shit."

"Sandra, where are you?"

Sandra mumbled, "June's office."

"Don't move."

CHAPTER THIRTY

Jacob had to close Marie's, better known to the public as the Broken Bottle for a few months to bring everything up to code, get licenses in place and a train a new squad with what he coined, the Smitty culture. Lance and his boys had done it again, refinishing the hardwood floors making them look like a million bucks and helping with most of the redevelopment.

Lance signed for liquor deliveries and staged the boxes against the wall in the storage room. Watchdog Security Systems had wrapped up their installation and was educating Lance and Jacob on how to operate the key features from their cell phones before heading over to 23rd and Lucas. Lance had been promoted to manager of both bars. He was Jacob's right hand and third eye.

"Unc, where's your better half? She hadn't been by in a while."

"She hadn't been feeling well, but she's much better now." Jacob checked his watch. "I'm supposed to meet her at the bookstore in a few."

Jacob moved Sandra in with him so that he could keep a close watch on her after receiving devastating news. He drove to Brigance every day for weeks and waited for hours for Jackson to come home or come out of his house. When Aunt Tootie and Annie Pearl received word on the disorder that Jackson had single handedly constructed, they were on the road the next morning to tend to their babygirl. When they left a month later, Ariel took over.

Todd created a parking space at the corner of the street. He and Jacob had become buddies, since his and Susan's relationship had become more apparent.

"Todd, you remember Lance."

"Young man, how's it going?"

Lance spoke and shook Todd's hand. He excused himself and found busy work to do in the stock room. Todd motioned for Jacob to follow him outside. "The setup is in motion; the drop will go down this weekend and we're in place to make the bust."

"Been a long time coming, huh?"

"Yeah. But listen, I gotta make this quick. Congratulations, you and I are partners now. Yandy is the new, old you. Now you need to give him someone to boss around. Be careful who you let in this circle, loyalty ..."

"Ain't cheap."

"Work all that out then get with me later. Oh, and you can scratch another notch in your headboard, we got Kendo."

Todd hopped in his Porsche, made an illegal U-turn and was gone just as fast as he appeared. Jacob sent Yandy a message and told him, they needed to meet sometime after four o'clock today. Jacob walked back inside and called for Lance.

"Nephew, I'm headed to the bookstore, you got it from here?"

"Yeah, I'll lock up in about thirty minutes then head back over to Smitty's."

"I appreciate you, you know that, right?"

"Yeah, I know. Tell Auntie, I said, hey. Glad she's feeling better."

"Will do."

Jacob heard footsteps approach him as he reached for his car door handle. He looked over his shoulder and could not believe his eyes. He squinted.

"Dre?"

Dre held his arms out and turned himself around, showing off his khakis and stark white, button down shirt. Jacob told Dre that he needed to clean himself up before he could use him. Dre held up his end of the deal and was back to ensure that Jacob made good on his promise. "Oh, shit! You look like new money!" Dre had dropped thirty-five pounds and got rid of his cornrows. He was clean shaven and dressed like he had some business.

"You got this place lookin' like new money. I came by yesterday. Young blood said, you were gone for the day."

"What can I do for you?"

"You said, you'd put me on. The question is, what can I do for you?"

"I have to run, but hit me up around 5 o'clock, I have something in mind I think you'll like."

***

Two police cars pulled up, flashing red and blue lights against the windows of the Brigance residents, no sirens. A third police car arrived moments later and parked across the street. The officers stood shoulder to shoulder in front of their black and whites, looking like soldiers in rank. One of the officers pounded on the door with the side of his fist and announced himself as a member of the Renfro Police Department while his partner covered him. Mr. Dartwell who was walking his Great Dane slowed down, observing the dramatized scenery. The officer banged on the door again, the space between the brick and the outside foyer captured the sound, causing a loud echo. Officer Bailey analyzed the entrance then kicked the middle of the door with the force of a mule, cracking the mull post. The door swiftly swung open running from the pressure of the second kick. The officers moved in quickly, tossing couch cushions, dumping drawers and turning over furniture. Two officers took on the upstairs and searched the rooms that looked the most lived in.

A very meticulous and conscientious officer stopped in the middle of the mayhem and asked his partner to join him in the kitchen.

"If he made a drink then drugged the drink, we need to look in wet places. Bathrooms, kitchen, the wet bar. Let's not waste our time and do a disservice to the reason we're here."

Officer Meticulous searched all the cabinets in the kitchen and in the butler's pantry. He felt under the countertops to see if they were loose. He ran his hands across the shelves of the cabinets that hung over the counters. He removed a box of green tea bags and handed them to Officer Washington. "Put this into evidence." He emptied cabinet drawers, leaving its contents on the floor. Before he cleared the kitchen, he opened the cabinet doors underneath the kitchen sink and began moving household items from one side of the cabinet to the other.

It was notably uncommon to have everything stored on one side of a cabinet under a kitchen sink. "Washington, come look at this."

Officer Washington bent down to get a better look. He took his flashlight and noticed a piece of the cabinet floor had been cut. He used his pocketknife to help lift the piece of plywood.

"Ain't that some shit."

Officer Washington reached into the small opening with his gloved hand and pulled from it two small, white, prescription bottles. One labeled Korlym and the other Misoprostol. The other officers joined their fellow force men in the kitchen after coming up short. Officer Meticulous secured their findings in a clear plastic evidence bag.

"There's something else in there."

Washington felt inside the hole and recovered a pill crusher and a prescription pad. "Damn, he thought this would be easier than just saying, I don't want kids?"

When the officers filed out of the house there was a small crowd, standing around watching in awe. People who had never spoke to one another were in the streets communing, wondering what was going on in their crème de la crème haven, blaming themselves for not seeing the misfit in one of their neighbors when walking their dogs or checking their mail. The officers stood around and compared notes briefly before returning to their assigned cars and finally leaving the scene.

He sat on the arm of the accent chair, peeking from the corner of the loft window watching the police break into his home with the rest of the neighborhood.

Jackson read the four month old text messages that were beginning to rot in his inbox. Family members inquiring and reaching out for confirmation, business contacts distancing themselves and questioning his integrity. Emmanuelle gloating, scorned no more. Jackson took a shot to the chest every time he read Jacob's text messages; he responded to Jacob, unable to sever the shackles from his narcissistic DNA. Drowning in the pit of his turmoil, he still could not let go of his college sweetheart.

[Don't ever contact Sandra again.]

[Who the hell are you to tell me what to do with my wife?]

[You really are demented, aren't you? Your EX wife is the love of my life. You hurt her like you wouldn't believe and I intend to protect her like you wouldn't believe.]

[Love of your life? What the fuck are you talking about? White boy, your dick ain't big enough to handle a woman like her.]

[I guess that's why she left you.]

[You'll never be able to see that pussy. You ain't her type.]

Jacob sent two pictures of him and Sandra to Jackson. One of Sandra sitting on Jacob's lap on a park bench, feeding him strawberry ice cream from her waffle cone. The other, of the two of them engaged in a kiss, showing off their ring fingers.

[I'm her type like a motherfucker.]

Jackson stared at the loaded, Walther; P99 resting on the seat of the accent chair. He remembered his grandmother telling him as a young boy, *you can run, but you can't hide. Life will always find a way to catch up with you.* Jackson walked into the hall bathroom and turned the light out.

"Grandma, sometimes life ain't fast enough."

Jackson put the gun to his temple and pulled the trigger.

CHAPTER THIRTY ONE

It was just after three o'clock in the afternoon. Unmarked vehicles were positioned on two street corners. Two officers wearing plain clothes conversed on the sidewalk to elude the appearance of a set up. Traffic was steady as a result of a dance recital at the Hiram Center off highway exit 9. An officer sitting in an unmarked surveillance van called for his men to get into position. They had been waiting on activity for three hours.

Fellas head back to your vehicle and circle the block. Joggers move in.

The officer raised his trail seeker binoculars to his eyes and waved for his colleague, who was behind the wheel to pull up slowly. *We got movement!* A male and female officer, dressed in fitness apparel jogged steadily up the street.

He peeked out of the window for several minutes then peeked from behind the door, carefully observing his surroundings, looking in both directions before walking down the stairs. He stepped off the curb and into the street. *Move in! Go! Go! Go!* The joggers turned around abruptly and sprinted towards their subject.

"Don't move! Get on the ground!"

He slowly raised his hands in the air and got down on both knees. Both officers had their weapons drawn. "On the ground, now!"

He laid flat, stomach pressed against the cold, damp ground. His arms were pulled behind his back and cuffs were tightened around his wrists. The female officer patted him down and retrieved a gun from his waist. *That's a 10-95 folks, good job.* The suspect was lifted to his feet, wearing a dirty shirt and baggy blue jeans, socks and no shoes. The female officer handed the gun that she had retrieved to the arresting officer. Two police cars flashing lights and blazing sirens pulled up to the scene and blocked through traffic.

"Jackson Perry, you are being arrested for the non-consensual termination of a pregnancy otherwise known as fetal homicide. You have the right to remain silent. Anything you say can and will be used against you in a court of law. You have the right to speak to an attorney and have one present during questioning. If you can't afford an attorney one will be appointed for you. Do you understand these rights?"

Jackson nodded and mumbled, *yes* then was seated in the back of the Renfro City police car.

"Why did you take that boy's ball?"

"Cause I wanted one just like it."

"It wasn't yours to take. That's why you out there fightin' cause he came back to get what was his. Son, your actions have to be accounted for."

"What does that mean, grandma?"

"You can't just do whatever you wanna do. Life don't work like that. You can run, but you can't hide. Life will always find a way to catch up with you."

***

Jacob danced through the front door of the house carrying two plastic bags, singing. He sat the bags on the kitchen island and drummed the beat of the song on the countertop. Sandra came downstairs and stood in the open entryway to the kitchen, watching in admiration as Jacob sang and danced to Earth Wind and Fire's Love's Holiday.

"Hi handsome."

Jacob turned around and smiled. *"Ohh, love has found a way in my heart tonight…* Hey!" He danced over to Sandra and stole kisses from her lips. "We're putting some healthier options on the menu and I brought samples of everything."

Sandra took the food containers from the bags and opened their lids. Salmon sliders, Greek stuffed chicken, cauliflower baked ziti; what should have smelled like a delicious medley of entrées came across as a putrid odor. Sandra's mouth began to water, and nausea kicked in. She excused herself before Jacob took notice. When she rejoined Jacob downstairs, he was munching on a salmon slider.

"Jay, don't eat too much, we have dinner with Ariel and Gregory this evening."

"I thought we were going to a movie tonight."

"No, the one we want to see doesn't come out until next weekend."

"Where are we going? Do I have to change?"

"No, it's nothing fancy, we're going to Sunset Bistro."

"What time?"

"In an hour. I didn't have this conversation by myself. We talked about this a couple days ago."

Jacob stuffed the rest of the slider in his mouth, dripping oil on his sleeve. "I'll change my shirt."

Gregory is tall, bald and handsome, he had dimples that pierced his cheeks every time he smiled. He stroked his beard when he was intrigued, like Ariel had foretold. He is a lefty who did not like bananas but loved banana nut bread. He doted on Ariel as he told the story of how they first met. Occasionally, peeking over at her and smiling with his big, pretty, white teeth; that looked extra white against his dark brown skin. Ariel ate it up, squeezing in her two cents every so often.

Sandra finished her steak strips and fries and considered having the sweet potato soufflé with pecans for dessert. Ariel glanced at Sandra as she scooted her chair from under the table.

"Gentlemen, will you excuse us?"

Sandra got up from the table and followed Ariel into the restroom. Ariel checked under the stalls then leaned against the sink. "Something you wanna tell me?"

Sandra looked confused. "Like what?"

"Like why you just ate a dinner sized portion of steak strips and fries then eyeballed dessert."

"I had an appetite, so what."

"You ate more than Jacob!"

"He ate earlier, kind of."

"Yesterday you ate a Philly steak sub and the other half of my chicken melt."

"I hadn't eaten all day."

"You're craving steak. You don't even like steak like that."

"What do you want me to say?"

"You sure you aren't …"

"Yes, I'm pretty sure… I don't know."

"We're stopping by the drugstore on the way home."

Dinner was a success. Jacob and Gregory both shared a love for classic cars, weightlifting and old school music. Sandra and Ariel had already set up a play date for them in two weeks while they were on their girl's trip.

The weather was nice enough to leave the jackets on their hangers. Jacob sat barefoot on the patio and talked to his grandmother about bringing her sisters from Italy to Midland for a family reunion. Eloisa had not been well enough to travel lately.

Sandra kissed Jacob on the forehead. "Tell grandma, I said hey. I'm going upstairs."

Sandra dressed for bed then called Ariel. Gregory was staying with her until he found a place of his own. So, Ariel went into the bathroom to have girl talk. Sandra closed the bedroom door and grabbed the small box that she had wrapped inside of a plastic bag from her purse. She hid it inside of her Tampon box in the bathroom closet. "I don't want Jay looking over my shoulder when I take the test. I don't want him to be disappointed if I'm not and I don't want him to get too excited if I am. He's going to wake up, I know it. He doesn't sleep hard unless … you know."

"Well, looks like he's gettin' some tonight."

"I don't feel like putting on a production. I'm not even sure I feel like laying there and taking it."

"Girl, put some lipstick on and meet Mr. Winkie under the covers."

"That could work, but I'm sleepy."

"I'm on my period, my appointment with Mr. Winkie is in approximately one hour."

Sandra was half asleep when Jacob finally came to bed. He took his pants off then proceeded to tell her about his conversation with Eloisa. She could not wait to cook authentic Italian dishes for Sandra and Sandra could not wait to try her Beef Brasato. After the twenty three minute dissertation, he began talking about how excited he is about the new menu items. He wanted to trial them at Marie's first, but was confident the colorful dishes would go over well on both ends. He wanted Sandra to try the sliders; fresh salmon and Teriyaki ginger on Brioche. He offered to go back downstairs and heat one up for her.

Oh my God, will you shut up and go to sleep!

Jacob went into the bathroom to brush his teeth.

"Did I tell you, nephew's Greyhound had puppies? Purebred, he said we can pick one out if we want."

"Greyhounds are big, I'm not a fan of big dogs."

"That's what I told him, but I still had to ask." Jacob wiped the toothpaste from around his mouth and took his shirt off. "Lance and Hilary are doing good; he's thinking about asking her to move in with him. She graduates next summer. Babe, I was at the dealership getting my oil changed, I saw this Jeep that was so hot. It's like the girl version of my Jeep, same color and everything. I'm going to get it for you."

"Baby, I don't need another car. If you want to do something for me …" *You can shut the fuck up and go to sleep!* "you can help me start a garden. I've always wanted one."

"A garden, huh? That sounds cool, when do you want to get started?"

Sandra sat up in the bed and put her hair in a bun. She pulled the covers back. "Come here."

Jacob got under the covers and slid over to Sandra's side of the bed. She sat on top of him and kissed him until she felt Mr. Winkie swell beneath her. She massaged his body, leaving kisses everywhere her hands left a touch. Sandra disappeared under the covers and pacified the both of them.

Like every morning at five in the morning, Sandra had to pee. She looked at Jacob who was sleeping like a baby, one leg hanging from under the covers, his lips slightly parted. She eased from under the comforter then tip toed into the bathroom, closing the door gently. She opened the box and read the instructions from the small booklet. She began to dance from the intensity of having to pee. Sandra sat the test strip inside the shot of urine for ten seconds. She removed the strip then slid it inside the applicator. Five minutes had come and gone. The applicator sat on the sink, bearing test results. Sandra poured the unused urine into the toilet then put the opened box back inside the plastic bag.

"Ok, here we go. Just walk up to it and look."

Sandra reached for the applicator and knocked it on the floor. She looked over her shoulder, listening for Jacob on the other side of the door. She stood over her results, peeking through her fingers.

Positive.

THIRTY TWO

Gerald removed the black, plastic makeup bib from around his neck. He was the new face of Inside the Huddle at IJJ Network. A lady wearing a headset straightened his tie and checked his microphone. He took his seat behind the big, glass desk and prepared for production. Sound, *set*. Camera, *set*. The producer counted down with his fingers. *4... 3...2... Roll!*

"Good afternoon, I'm Gerald Whittaker with a special report. Today is bittersweet for me because someone that I've had the pleasure of working alongside and learning from is awaiting sentencing today. Jackson Powerhouse Perry was convicted of drugging his wife with an abortion pill without her consent. And from what we understand, he's done this a total of four times. Wow. I have joining me today, two-time WNBA champ, Tanesha Yahafat of the Chicago Tarheels. Tanesha, this is pretty disturbing news. Being someone who can relate to complications with childbirth, explain to those of us who'll never know how devastating this must have been."

"Look, dude done went off the deep end! All he had to do was say, baby, ya man don't want kids. He did this four times, ya'll! Now, they got new allegations against him, saying he was into drugs or sold drugs. But wait, there's more! They're saying, you know ... he had a boyfriend.

Jackson is a big dude; I can't even imagine. Have you seen his wife, I'm sorry ex-wife? If she was mine, I would carry, and breast feed the kids. Chicago, I wanna hear from you. Drop me a line, 312-815-3210. But first let me pay some bills, this is ya boy, Mike the Money Maker, 103 dot 5 FM QWQY.

"Good afternoon everyone, I'm Sinclair Roberts reporting to you live from Barker Studios in Baine, Ohio. As Jackson Powerhouse Perry faces his fate today, he also faces attacks on his sexuality. Perry has been convicted of using illegally obtained drugs to terminate his wife's pregnancy without her knowledge. Sources say that allegations of Perry being involved in a drug cartel have not been confirmed, but police are following all leads. We'll have those stories and live coverage from Simmons County Courthouse, following these messages."

News reporters surrounded the courthouse steps, staring into the lenses of cameras, reporting spoon fed news. Fans and haters of Jackson Powerhouse Perry stood behind police barricades taking pictures and streaming live feed for social media gratification. Family members and friends of Cassandra Marie McCall sat in anticipation, waiting to toss their fists full of dirt onto Jackson's casket. Annie Pearl and Aunt Tootie were sandwiched in between Skip and Ariel. When Jackson entered the courtroom, Ariel grabbed Jacob's sweaty hand and squeezed. June Orton slid inside the courtroom and stood against the back wall beside Audrey who was standing behind Jaqueline Perry-Anderson, toe to heel along with the others who were not afforded a seat.

Jackson had lost a substantial amount of weight. There was a time when he naturally absorbed everyone's attention when he walked into a room. On this day, he stood inconsequential, looking like someone they may have known in the past. His wavy tresses had been cut very low, almost bald. He had grown a full beard and was wearing prescription glasses. Life had caught up with him. He turned his head to the side several times as if he wanted to look over his shoulder. Jackson could feel the daggers from the eyes of the scorned breaking his skin and drawing blood.

The Bailiff was wearing a black bullet proof vest over his uniform dress shirt. He looked like a young James Evans. He stood on the left side of the bench and spoke with reverence.

"The Court of Simmons County is now in session, the Honorable Judge Eartha Sampson presiding. Please remain standing until the judge is seated."

The judge; a salt and pepper haired black woman, who looked like she had birthed the law sat down and put her glasses on. Annie Pearl rocked from side to side as tears began to fall. She was glad her husband could not be a witness to this. Aunt Tootie closed her eyes and prayed. The courtroom fell in dead silence as the judge made herself comfortable in her seat, preparing to hand down Jackson's judgement. She flipped through a few pages of her embroidered notebook before addressing Jackson, who stood before the judge, vacant and emotionally disconnected.

"Mr. Perry, the officers recovered a gun from you. Is that correct?"

"Yeah."

Judge Sampson peered over her glasses, reprimanding Jackson. "Yes, your honor."

"Yes, your honor."

"What were your intentions, sir?"

"To kill myself... Ma'am."

Judge Sampson threw her hands up. "Well, what happened? You could have saved us all a lot of time and money."

"The safety was on."

"Mr. Perry, I don't think you realize the cruelty and nastiness of your actions. Nonconsensual, termination of a pregnancy. We're all adults here, let's call it what it really is... murder. You murdered your own children, because you didn't want to be a father. You had the opportunity to communicate your feelings and you deliberately chose not to. Instead, you made a gross mockery of the very thing that constitutes a woman."

Judge Sampson leaned forward, staring Jackson in the eyes. She clasped her hands together then cleared her throat. The audience could be heard expressing themselves. The judge held her hand up to silence the room. "I would sentence you to hell, if I could, Mr. Perry. You're not fit to function outside of these courtroom doors. I pray that God has mercy on your soul. Because the day you leave here, will be the day you meet him."

Jackson stared at the judge as if he were reading from the lines in her forehead. Her smirk formed a wave of curves around the corner of her mouth. "Today, I've been on the bench for twenty years. Twenty years, today. Today is the 20th of May. I'm feeling like twenty is my lucky number."

Sandra sat in her rocking chair, sipping a cup of hot green tea. How ironic, she thought. The cameras zoomed in on Jackson's face. Sandra shook her head in disbelief, she barely recognized him. The judge had ordered Jackson to submit to mental health treatments and waive any rights to have those documents sealed from the courts and undergo group counseling once a week for the next twenty-four months. Sandra turned the television volume up. The judge was moments away from sentencing Jackson.

"It is my absolute honor and a privilege to sentence you today. So, without further ado, Mr. Perry, I am sentencing you to twenty years. Twenty years for each abortive pregnancy. Since it's my anniversary, I'm going to tack on twenty more years. That's an additional five years for each failed pregnancy, totaling twenty five years for each baby boy … or baby girl."

The courtroom burst into applause and cheers. Judge Sampson, held her hand up. "This is still a court of law, don't find yourselves in contempt. There are no winners here, just damaged people. Mr. Perry, let's talk about Cassandra McCall, you remember her, right? She's the mother of your slain children. I am rewarding her twenty million dollars in restitution. I'm going to leave that restitution open for any medical attention she may need in respect to her mental well-being. Only God knows what kind of toll this took on her. I understand that you own properties in the Brigance Hills and a few barbershops." Judge Sampson looked over her glasses at Jackson. "It says here, you own four houses, three barbershops and three vehicles; a Ferrari, Mercedes Benz G class, my grandson calls it the G-wagon and a BMW all paid in full. Do these things sound familiar?"

Jackson nodded and mumbled. "Yes, ma'am."

"These four properties, three businesses and three vehicles are to be signed over to Cassandra McCall as the sole owner, immediately. Mr. Perry, If I had three wishes, I'd waste one on you. Praying that if you had another chance, you'd do the right thing. But in my heart, I know better."

Reporters were trickling down information like a production line. The crowd grew bigger outside of the courthouse and inside the courthouse halls.

Jackson was escorted by two armed officers. He dropped his head, forfeiting the chance to say, I'm sorry. He refused to look at the audience, cheating them of the opportunity to look into his eyes. Everyone gawked, capturing an image that they will never forget as the courtroom door closed on the back of Jackson Powerhouse Perry.

"Jackson Powerhouse Perry has been sentenced to one hundred years in prison. The judge stating that if she could, she would sentence him to hell. We're live at Simmons County Courthouse. I'm Reba Armstrong for TYT News, channel 12."

"What's up Chi? I am, Mike the Money Maker, the judge wasn't playin'! She laid down the law on her twentieth anniversary. I know he's glad it wasn't her fiftieth! Check it out, wifey got the houses, the cars, the

businesses and she got twenty mill. Do you think she should have gotten
all that, or should she have gotten even more? We're all the way live at
103 dot 5, QWQY. Chicago, I wanna hear from you, 312-815-3210.

"Welcome back to, Inside the Huddle. I'm Gerald Whittaker, we have
just witnessed the sentencing for kickboxing great, Jackson Powerhouse
Perry. Judge Sampson gave him twenty five years for each offense,
restitution totaling twenty million, excluding the properties and other
assets that were rewarded. I have special guest, Defense Attorney,
Milton Orton with me; his brother Timothy Orton was the prosecuting
attorney in this case. Being that your specialty is getting people out of
trouble, was there anything that Jackson's attorney missed?"

"First, let me say, thanks for having me. It's an honor. Uh, I don't
think he stood a fighting chance. The evidence was solid, and he
admitted to putting a substance in his wife's tea. Those factors didn't
leave much wiggle room for his attorney."

"Some would say that, it was an abortion and people have abortions
all the time. What made this so different, explain to our viewers why this
act was punishable by law."

"Well, Gerald, most people who have abortions choose to do so. In
this case, the carrier, which was his wife at the time did not consent to an
abortion. So, what he did was, he committed homicide. But because the
victims were in the pre-birth stage, meaning not yet living outside of the
womb, it's called feticide. Indiana law, Code 35-42-1-6 states that if you
intentionally terminate a human pregnancy with the intent other than to

produce a live birth or remove a dead fetus, you have committed feticide."

"Attorney Milton Orton, joining us today, with some powerful feedback. Milton, thank you for coming. We'll be right back."

Sandra laid Jacob Jr. in his crib and kissed his forehead; he had finally stopped fighting sleep. The reporter was standing in front of the Simmons County Courthouse steps recapping today's events. Sandra turned the television off. Her life with Jackson had come to a close. Sandra was safe in her husband's loving arms, resting her head against his chest. Jacob peeked over Sandra's shoulder and star gazed at their son. Life was finally kind.

The halls of the courthouse were solemn. People were returning home from a long day's work. The streets were no longer congested with onlookers and traffic, the camera lights were turned off. Time had its way and was now moving quickly to the next object that validated it, be it a vacation, doctor's appointment, a birth or even a death.

The things we love the most are the things we most take for granted.

Time.

We do not recognize time as something we take for granted, because it does not belong to us. We cannot control it and we cannot hold it.

Jackson stooped in the corner of his six by eight jail cell, facing the concrete wall questioning time. At one time, he had it all. Now, time was all he had. He had recurrently and blatantly defied time by disrespecting the objects that were assigned to it. Now, one hundred years was assigned to his transgressions leaving him with the task of identifying with this simple truth; if you fail to give time meaning by not acknowledging its importance, time will eventually run out on you.

61254293R10195

Made in the USA
Columbia, SC
24 June 2019